CW01020237

PATRICIA
THE DOWER HOUSE MYSTERY

PATRICIA WENTWORTH was born Dora Amy Elles in India in 1877 (not 1878 as has sometimes been stated). She was first educated privately in India, and later at Blackheath School for Girls. Her first husband was George Dillon, with whom she had her only child, a daughter. She also had two stepsons from her first marriage, one of whom died in the Somme during World War I.

Her first novel was published in 1910, but it wasn't until the 1920's that she embarked on her long career as a writer of mysteries. Her most famous creation was Miss Maud Silver, who appeared in 32 novels, though there were a further 33 full-length mysteries not featuring Miss Silver—the entire run of these is now reissued by Dean Street Press.

Patricia Wentworth died in 1961. She is recognized today as one of the pre-eminent exponents of the classic British golden age mystery novel.

By Patricia Wentworth

PATRICIA WENTWORTH

THE DOWER
HOUSE MYSTERY

With an introduction by
Curtis Evans

DEAN STREET PRESS

Introduction

BRITISH AUTHOR Patricia Wentworth published her first novel, a gripping tale of desperate love during the French Revolution entitled *A Marriage under the Terror*, a little over a century ago, in 1910. The book won first prize in the Melrose Novel Competition and was a popular success in both the United States and the United Kingdom. Over the next five years Wentworth published five additional novels, the majority of them historical fiction, the best-known of which today is *The Devil's Wind* (1912), another sweeping period romance, this one set during the Sepoy Mutiny (1857-58) in India, a region with which the author, as we shall see, had extensive familiarity. Like *A Marriage under the Terror*, *The Devil's Wind* received much praise from reviewers for its sheer storytelling élan. One notice, for example, pronounced the novel "an achievement of some magnitude" on account of "the extraordinary vividness...the reality of the atmosphere...the scenes that shift and move with the swiftness of a moving picture...." (*The Bookman*, August 1912) With her knack for spinning a yarn, it perhaps should come as no surprise that Patricia Wentworth during the early years of the Golden Age of mystery fiction (roughly from 1920 into the 1940s) launched upon her own mystery-writing career, a course charted most successfully for nearly four decades by the prolific author, right up to the year of her death in 1961.

Considering that Patricia Wentworth belongs to the select company of Golden Age mystery writers with books which have remained in print in every decade for nearly a century now (the centenary of Agatha Christie's first mystery, *The Mysterious Affair at Styles*, is in 2020; the centenary of Wentworth's first mystery, *The Astonishing Adventure of Jane Smith*, follows merely three years later, in 2023), relatively little is known about the author herself. It appears, for example, that even the widely given year of Wentworth's birth, 1878, is incorrect. Yet it is sufficiently clear that Wentworth lived a varied and intriguing life that provided her ample inspiration for a writing career devoted to imaginative fiction.

It is usually stated that Patricia Wentworth was born Dora Amy Elles on 10 November 1878 in Mussoorie, India, during the heyday of the British Raj; however, her Indian birth and baptismal record states that she in fact was born on 15 October 1877 and was baptized on 26 November of that same year in Gwalior. Whatever doubts surround her actual birth year, however, unquestionably the future author came from a prominent Anglo-Indian military family. Her father, Edmond Roche Elles, a son of Malcolm Jamieson Elles, a Porto, Portugal wine merchant originally from Ardrossan, Scotland, entered the British Royal Artillery in 1867, a decade before Wentworth's birth, and first saw service in India during the Lushai Expedition of 1871-72. The next year Elles in India wed Clara Gertrude Rothney, daughter of Brigadier-General Octavius Edward Rothney, commander of the Gwalior District, and Maria (Dempster) Rothney, daughter of a surgeon in the Bengal Medical Service. Four children were born of the union of Edmond and Clara Elles, Wentworth being the only daughter.

Before his retirement from the army in 1908, Edmond Elles rose to the rank of lieutenant-general and was awarded the KCB (Knight Commander of the Order of Bath), as was the case with his elder brother, Wentworth's uncle, Lieutenant-General Sir William Kidston Elles, of the Bengal Command. Edmond Elles also served as Military Member to the Council of the Governor-General of India from 1901 to 1905. Two of Wentworth's brothers, Malcolm Rothney Elles and Edmond Claude Elles, served in the Indian Army as well, though both of them died young (Malcolm in 1906 drowned in the Ganges Canal while attempting to rescue his orderly, who had fallen into the water), while her youngest brother, Hugh Jamieson Elles, achieved great distinction in the British Army. During the First World War he catapulted, at the relatively youthful age of 37, to the rank of brigadier-general and the command of the British Tank Corps, at the Battle of Cambrai personally leading the advance of more than 350 tanks against the German line. Years later Hugh Elles also played a major role in British civil defense during the Second World War. In the event of a German invasion of Great Britain, something which seemed all too possible in 1940, he was tasked with leading the defense of southwestern England. Like Sir Edmond and Sir William, Hugh Elles attained the rank of lieutenant-general and was awarded the KCB.

Although she was born in India, Patricia Wentworth spent much of her childhood in England. In 1881 she with her mother and two younger brothers was at Tunbridge Wells, Kent, on what appears to have been a rather extended visit in her ancestral country; while a decade later the same family group resided at Blackheath, London at Lennox House, domicile of Wentworth's widowed maternal grandmother, Maria Rothney. (Her eldest brother, Malcolm, was in Bristol attending Clifton College.) During her years at Lennox House, Wentworth attended Blackheath High School for Girls, then only recently founded as "one of the first schools in the country to give girls a proper education" (*The London Encyclopaedia*, 3rd ed., p. 74). Lennox House was an ample Victorian villa with a great glassed-in conservatory running all along the back and a substantial garden--most happily, one presumes, for Wentworth, who resided there not only with her grandmother, mother and two brothers, but also five aunts (Maria Rothney's unmarried daughters, aged 26 to 42), one adult first cousin once removed and nine first cousins, adolescents like Wentworth herself, from no less than three different families (one Barrow, three Masons and five Dempsters); their parents, like Wentworth's father, presumably were living many miles away in various far-flung British dominions. Three servants--a cook, parlourmaid and housemaid--were tasked with serving this full score of individuals.

Sometime after graduating from Blackheath High School in the mid-1890s, Wentworth returned to India, where in a local British newspaper she is said to have published her first fiction. In 1901 the 23-year-old Wentworth married widower George Fredrick Horace Dillon, a 41-year-old lieutenant-colonel in the Indian Army with three sons from his prior marriage. Two years later Wentworth gave birth to her only child, a daughter named Clare Roche Dillon. (In some sources it is erroneously stated that Clare was the offspring of Wentworth's second marriage.) However in 1906, after just five years of marriage, George Dillon died suddenly on a sea voyage, leaving Wentworth with sole responsibly for her three teenaged stepsons and baby daughter. A very short span of years, 1904 to 1907, saw the deaths of Wentworth's husband, mother, grandmother and brothers Malcolm and Edmond, removing much of her support network. In 1908, however, her father, who was now sixty years old, retired from the army and returned to England, settling at Guildford, Surrey with an older unmarried sister named Dora (for whom his daughter presumably had been named). Wentworth joined this household as well, along with her daughter and her youngest stepson. Here in Surrey Wentworth, presumably with the goal of making herself financially independent for the first time in her life (she was now in her early thirties), wrote the novel that changed the course of her life, *A Marriage under the Terror*, for the first time we know of utilizing her famous *nom de plume*.

The burst of creative energy that resulted in Wentworth's publication of six novels in six years suddenly halted after the appearance of *Queen Anne Is Dead* in 1915. It seems not unlikely that the Great War impinged in various ways on her writing. One tragic episode was the death on the western front of one of her stepsons, George Charles Tracey Dillon. Mining in Colorado when war was declared, young Dillon worked his passage from Galveston, Texas to Bristol, England as a shipboard muleteer (mule-tender) and joined the Gloucestershire Regiment. In 1916 he died at the Somme at the age of 29 (about the age of Wentworth's two brothers when they had passed away in India).

A couple of years after the conflict's cessation in 1918, a happy event occurred in Wentworth's life when at Frimley, Surrey she wed George Oliver Turnbull, up to this time a lifelong bachelor who like the author's first husband was a lieutenant-colonel in the Indian Army. Like his bride now forty-two years old, George Turnbull as a younger man had distinguished himself for his athletic prowess, playing forward for eight years for the Scottish rugby team and while a student at the Royal Military Academy winning the medal awarded the best athlete of his term. It seems not unlikely that Turnbull played a role in his wife's turn toward writing mystery fiction, for he is said to have strongly supported Wentworth's career, even assisting her in preparing manuscripts for publication. In 1936 the couple in Camberley, Surrey built Heatherglade House, a large two-story structure on substantial grounds, where they resided until Wentworth's death a quarter of a century later. (George Turnbull survived his wife by nearly a decade, passing away in 1970 at the age of 92.) This highly successful middle-aged companionate marriage contrasts sharply with the more youthful yet rocky union of Agatha and Archie Christie, which was three years away from sundering when Wentworth published *The Astonishing Adventure of Jane Smith* (1923), the first of her sixty-five mystery novels.

Although Patricia Wentworth became best-known for her cozy tales of the criminal investigations of consulting detective Miss Maud Silver, one of the mystery genre's most prominent spinster sleuths, in truth the Miss Silver tales account for just under half of Wentworth's 65 mystery novels. Miss Silver did not make her debut until 1928 and she did not come to predominate in Wentworth's fictional criminous output until the 1940s. Between 1923 and 1945 Wentworth published 33 mystery novels without Miss Silver, a handsome and substantial legacy in and of itself to vintage crime fiction fans. Many of these books are standalone tales of mystery, but nine of them have series characters. Debuting in the novel *Fool Errant* in 1929, a year after Miss Silver first appeared in print, was the enigmatic, nautically-named *eminence grise* Benbow Collingwood Horatio Smith, owner of a most expressively opinionated parrot named Ananias (and quite a colorful character in his own right). Benbow Smith went on to appear in three additional Wentworth mysteries: *Danger Calling* (1931), *Walk with Care* (1933) and *Down Under* (1937). Working in tandem with Smith in the investigation of sinister affairs threatening the security of Great Britain in *Danger*

Calling and *Walk with Care* is Frank Garrett, Head of Intelligence for the Foreign Office, who also appears solo in *Dead or Alive* (1936) and *Rolling Stone* (1940) and collaborates with additional series characters, Scotland Yard's Inspector Ernest Lamb and Sergeant Frank Abbott, in *Pursuit of a Parcel* (1942). Inspector Lamb and Sergeant Abbott headlined a further pair of mysteries, *The Blind Side* (1939) and *Who Pays the Piper?* (1940), before they became absorbed, beginning with *Miss Silver Deals with Death* (1943), into the burgeoning Miss Silver canon. Lamb would make his farewell appearance in 1955 in *The Listening Eye*, while Abbott would take his final bow in mystery fiction with Wentworth's last published novel, *The Girl in the Cellar* (1961), which went into print the year of the author's death at the age of 83.

The remaining two dozen Wentworth mysteries, from the fantastical *The Astonishing Adventure of Jane Smith* in 1923 to the intense legal drama *Silence in Court* in 1945, are, like the author's series novels, highly imaginative and entertaining tales of mystery and adventure, told by a writer gifted with a consummate flair for storytelling. As one confirmed Patricia Wentworth mystery fiction addict, American Golden Age mystery writer Todd Downing, admiringly declared in the 1930s, "There's something about Miss Wentworth's yarns that is contagious." This attractive new series of Patricia Wentworth reissues by Dean Street Press provides modern fans of vintage mystery a splendid opportunity to catch the Wentworth fever.

Curtis Evans

Chapter One

AMABEL GREY was hemming the new curtains for Daphne's room. She sat on a low chair, and the bright orange-coloured stuff lay across her knees and was heaped upon the floor beside her. Daphne had chosen the stuff, but she was not helping to make the curtains.

"I suppose I ought to make her help," was the thought that slipped into Amabel's mind, only to be pushed out again. "You can't *make* people take an interest in things; but if only Daffy would—"

A little foolish blur of tears came between Amabel and her sewing. It cleared in a moment, but after a few more stitches she let her needle rest, and looked across at Daphne sitting idle in the window seat. Outside the rain was coming down gently, unremittingly. There was an open book on Daphne's knee, but it was at least half an hour since she had turned a page. The rain came down, and Daphne stared at it.

"She ought to interest herself in things—she ought, but I can't make her." The same thought, the same distress which it always brought. "After all, she's more Agatha's child than mine—it's Agatha's world that interests her, and Agatha's friends. I suppose it's natural enough—and of course Little Middlebury *is* dull, and the weather's been too dreadful."

Amabel took another stitch or two. Then she said, speaking rather quickly:

"Daffy dear, do come and help with this hem. It would be done in no time if you would."

"There's no hurry," said Daphne. She spoke without turning her head. Her voice, as clear and pretty as Amabel's, was a half tone deeper.

"But, Daffy, don't you want to see what they look like up?"

Daphne made a restless movement. Her book fell on the floor.

"I know what they'll look dike. The stuff was too cheap. It was stupid to get it, really. It ought to have been linen. Amber's curtains were linen." She spoke rather jerkily.

A wave of unhappiness swept over Amabel. Daphne was her only child, and such a pretty child. She looked at her and thought, for the thousandth time, how pretty Daphne was in spite of the shingled hair which she hated. Daphne had had such lovely hair— the silky, black hair which goes with blue eyes and a very white skin. Agatha had encouraged Daphne to have her hair shingled; but then Agatha was nothing if not modern.

Amabel wondered whether she would have let her sister Agatha have Daphne to educate if she had known what would come of it. Well, what had come of it? There was Daphne at nineteen, as pretty and charming as any mother's heart could desire.

"You can't say I haven't turned her out well, Amabel." That was Agatha's comment; and she had added, "You must move with the times, my dear. You're absolutely mid-Victorian. I always expect to find you in a crinoline, and your room full of antimacassars, and crochet mats, and daguerreotypes, and Family Bibles."

There were no antimacassars in the little brown room. It was a shabby room, but very comfortable. Some of the things in it were really old. The row of brightly coloured birds on the mantelpiece, for instance, and the miniatures of Professor Grey's great, great grand-parents which hung on the wall above. A little wood fire burned upon the deep, old-fashioned hearth. There was a great bowl of bronze chrysanthemums on the rather battered oak table at Amabel's elbow.

Agatha was certainly without justification. Agatha, when told so, had merely laughed:

"My blessed Amy, I'm not talking about *outsides*. In your true inwardness you are simply clothed in antimacassars."

Amabel was half laughing as she remembered this conversation.

"Daffy—" she began. But Daphne had sprung up, and was flying to the door. The postman's knock sounded, and she came back with two letters in her hand.

"Yours is from Agatha," she said, and tossed it lightly on to the orange folds that covered Amabel's lap. Then, sinking down upon the window seat, she tore impatiently at the tough linen envelope of her own letter.

Amabel heard a smothered "Damn!" She moved to get a better light on Agatha's illegible scrawl, and was in the middle of disentangling a long sentence in which the words Amber Studland and Jimmy Malleson occurred, when a sudden cry from Daphne made her drop the sheet and look up.

"Mummy, they want me to go to Egypt with them—to Egypt—just think of it!"

"Daffy, who?"

"Amber—Amber Studland. It's a party of eight. She says I *must* come." Daphne laughed. It was a laugh of pure, tremulous excitement. "I know what that means jolly well. Jimmy won't go unless I do—that's what it means. Amber would have seen me at Jericho otherwise; but—'I *must* come.'" She laughed again. "Oh, my dear Amber, I'm not such a fool as not to see through you!"

Amabel pushed the orange stuff away, and stood up.

"Daffy!"

"Egypt! Just think of it, Mummy—oceans, and oceans, and oceans of sunlight, and—and a frightfully jolly party."

"But, Daphne—"

"There isn't any 'but.' It's simply the best thing that ever happened."

"It hasn't happened yet." There was a shade of dryness in Amabel's voice. "Is Mrs. Studland asking you to go to Egypt as her guest? Even so—Daphne dear, *don't* count on it; it's bound to cost a lot, and I don't see—"

"I must go." The words came quick and hard. "You're always thinking about what things cost. Why, it's simply the chance of my life, and she says—"

"Who's the letter from? You haven't told me—you really haven't told me anything yet, Daffy."

"It's from Amber of course, and she says—here's the place—she says it'll be quite a cheap trip. So you see—"

"Daffy, quite a cheap trip might mean almost anything. Does she say how much?"

"I expect she does. Amber's quite businesslike, that's one comfort."

She turned the page; and Amabel, watching, saw her face change. "She says"—the defiant note went out of Daphne's voice; it shook and fell to a whisper—"two hundred pounds—two hundred pounds—oh!"

There was a moment of dead silence; Amabel, distressed, seeking for words; Daphne, rigid, the letter in her hand.

"I was afraid," Amabel began.

Daphne turned on her like a wild thing.

"You always are. It's always 'No' to everything I want to do—no, look here, I was a beast to say that, I know it's the money. There must, there simply must be some way of getting it—there simply must."

Amabel put her hand on the girl's shoulder. She got an impression of something tense, of an excitement beyond her comprehension.

"My dear, let's sit down and talk about it quietly. You really don't think that I can find two hundred pounds! Why, it's a whole year's income—you know that, don't you?" She sat down on the window seat as she spoke, and tried to draw Daphne down beside her; but with a jerk the girl drew back.

"You could borrow it."

"Daffy darling!"

"You could."

"And how should I ever pay it back? Ducky, do be reasonable."

Daphne retreated a step.

"I am being reasonable. I was excited at first, and I thought you'd understand." She paused, drew a long breath, and went on in a low, carefully controlled voice. "You didn't, so I suppose I must explain. It's not an ordinary visit. It's my chance—my one chance."

"I don't understand."

"No, I know you don't. It's—it's Jimmy," said Daphne defiantly.

"Yes, Daffy?"

"Jimmy Malleson, He's Malleson's Mustard, you know. The old man died last year, and Jimmy simply doesn't know how much money he's got."

"Yes, Daffy?"

There was a pause. Daphne tapped with her foot.

"He's flirted with lots of girls, so I wasn't sure. He's—he's frightfully run after, of course. I tell you, he simply doesn't know how much money he's got; and I thought he was just flirting till I got Amber's letter."

"Yes?"

"Well, then I knew there must be something more in it, because Amber would give her eyes to catch Jimmy herself—I know that well enough—she's got a jolly soft corner for him. So when she says that Jimmy is going to Egypt with them, and that I *must* come too"—she laughed and tossed her head—"I know that Amber must think that Jimmy won't go if I don't. If she saw half a chance of getting him to herself, you bet she'd be on to it. I know Amber."

Amabel straightened herself.

"I dislike Mrs. Studland very much," she said. "Why on earth do you want to be friends with a woman like that?"

"Oh, Amber's not too bad. You can't blame her for playing her own hand. She's not a bad sort really. Why don't you like her? You only saw her once."

Amabel laughed—she had a pretty laugh. A whimsical expression came into her grey eyes.

"It's odd of me, I know," she said, "frightfully odd."

"But you must have a reason."

"Must I? Well, I expect it was her magenta lips. You know, Daphne, I don't think you need really worry about Mrs. Studland's attractions. I can't imagine any young man falling in love with a woman who makes up magenta,"

Daphne looked pityingly at her mother.

"But you don't know very much about men, do you?" she said. She spoke quite simply, from the heights of superior knowledge.

"Of course Jimmy's rather old-fashioned; but men do admire what's smart and up-to-date—and Amber's simply nothing if she's not smart. Why, she told me we were going to wear things like drain-pipes *at least* a month before anyone else had the slightest inkling. Of course Jimmy's not in the least in love with her; but she's an awfully fascinating woman, and if he goes to Egypt and I don't—" The words came slower. Daphne took a step forward and went down on her knees at Amabel's side. "Mummy, I must go, I *must*. Manage it somehow!" The last word quivered.

Amabel felt Daphne's slight figure shake.

"Why, Daffy dear, how can I?"

"There must be a way, there *must*. Can't we sell something?"

"Darling, what?"

"Oh, I don't know." She turned, leaning against Amabel, and looked about the room. "The miniatures—aren't miniatures worth quite a lot?"

"It depends who painted them. These are not valuable—and, besides, Daffy, I couldn't sell things like that."

Daphne drew away, got up.

"Why couldn't you?"

"Well, I couldn't. But indeed, they're not valuable."

"In fact, we've got nothing that's worth twopence!" She laughed—a little hard laugh. "Twopence or two hundred pounds is all the same if you're a pauper, isn't it?" Then, with a sudden change of manner, "You could borrow it though—I'm sure you could borrow it."

"I won't borrow what I can't pay back. How can I? It isn't honest."

"But you don't understand. If I marry Jimmy, I shall be able to pay you back a hundred times over. Mummy, think what it means. Think! It's my one chance of getting out of all this. You know it is. If I was to live in Little Middlebury on two hundred a year, you should have kept me here and sent me to the village school. You didn't. You let Agatha have me. You let her send me to Paris and Lausanne. You let me see all the things that I want—and then you say, 'No, you can't have them. Come and live in Little Middlebury, and take an interest in the parish pump.'"

"Daffy!" said Amabel, very pale.

"It's true. You know quite well that it's true. I don't blame Agatha; I blame you. You shouldn't have let her have me. I suppose you'll say that you thought she'd provide for me. Well, so did I, and so did everyone. But, now she's married that little worm of a Moreland, he'll take jolly good care she doesn't provide for anyone but him. No, Agatha's no earthly—I knew that the moment she told me she was going to be married."

"Daphne, wait a minute. Give me Agatha's letter. I dropped it; and there was something—something about Mrs. Studland." She took the sheet, turning it until she found what she was looking for. "Agatha's writing—really! She says: 'Amber Studland wants Daphne to go to Egypt.'" Her voice died into silence as she read on: "'Jimmy Malleson is going too. If you can possibly raise the money, let her go. It's a good investment. I believe he's seriously attracted; and there's money to burn there. There's surely something you can sell. I'll give the child a frock or two, but I can't do more. Cyril is inclined to be jealous, and I must walk warily.'"

"What does she say? Here, let me see!" Daphne's tone was sharp. She pulled the letter out of her mother's hand, glanced at it, and dropped it on the floor with an "Oh, damn Cyril!"

"Daffy, please!"

"Well, I told you it was no earthly. Now it's up to you. I *must* go."

Amabel looked steadily at her daughter.

"Daphne, don't speak to me like that. You mustn't, you really mustn't."

Daphne flushed. How Victorian, this insistence on their relationship! Her anger rose at it. The soft, hurt look in Amabel's eyes hardened her. That everlasting appeal to sentiment!

"Oh, let's be reasonable," she said. "Listen to Agatha, if you won't listen to me. Spend two hundred pounds now, and give me my chance. In six months I can pay you back a dozen times over."

"Daphne, don't! No, no, I really can't bear to hear you talk like that. You say, let us talk reasonably, but you're not being reasonable, my dear. If Mr. Malleson cares for you, he can come and see you here. Why,"—Amabel's chin lifted a little—"everything else apart, Daphne, I don't think I care for the idea of my daughter running after this very rich young man."

If she hoped to sting Daphne, she failed.

"I'm not running after him. I'm only giving him his chance, and asking to have mine. If I don't go, Amber will play it as a trump card, and make him think it's because I want to avoid him."

Amabel bent down and picked up her sister Agatha's letter. When she had straightened it out and laid it on the window seat, she said:

"I don't want you to marry for money. Money isn't everything."

The brilliant scarlet flared in Daphne's cheeks. She caught at her self-control, but caught at it in vain. Springing back a pace, she faced her mother with her head up, and what Amber Studland had once called her black panther look.

"Who said I was going to marry for money?" she cried, speaking so quickly that the words tumbled one upon the other. "I want money—every reasonable person wants it—but if Jimmy hadn't a halfpenny—" Her voice broke. "Now will you let me go?" she said with a sob, and stood there panting.

Amabel got up, fairer than Daphne and a head taller.

"Daphne, do control yourself."

"Will you let me go, then?"

"My dear, I can't." There was a weary finality in the tone.

Scenes with Daphne were exhausting. They meant blow after blow upon the tender places of her heart—the pressure of a harder and more relentless nature than her own. She felt bruised, and very tired. But what could she do? This time Daphne was asking the impossible.

"You mean you won't," said Daphne on a low note that shook with pain and rage. "You won't do it. It's my one chance, and you won't give it to me. Can't you understand that I love Jimmy? Or doesn't it mean anything to you? After all, why should it? You simply don't understand. You gave up your own love affair pretty easily; didn't you? And I suppose you think that everyone's the same—but they're not—I'm not."

"Daphne, stop!" said Amabel in quite a new voice. But Daphne went on:

"You gave up the man you were in love with, and married my father. I suppose Grandpapa and Grandmamma told you to—he was Grandpapa's friend and about the same age, wasn't he? Well, you couldn't have cared much, that's all I can say."

Amabel stood rigid. The blows had never been so hard as this before.

"Daphne," she said with white lips that hardly moved, and in a voice which did not rise above a whisper. "Daphne, who told you all this nonsense?"

"Agatha told me—so I suppose it's true."

Daphne was a little frightened now, but still defiant. After all, she hadn't said anything very dreadful. It was absurd of Amabel to look like that. The anger, the buffeting emotion, ebbed slowly, imperceptibly; its place was taken by an odd embarrassment.

After a silence which seemed to last a long time, Amabel moved. Crossing the room, she began to fold up the orange curtains. She folded them very carefully, and put them away in the corner cupboard. Then she came back to the window seat and sat down. She did not look at Daphne, but said gently:

"Sit down, Daffy."

And, still in the grip of that odd embarrassment, Daphne obeyed. Amabel looked at her then. The scarlet colour was gone from her cheeks; her face was white, her mouth sulky, her eyes hard and very blue.

"You know, Daphne," said Amabel, "you don't think. If you thought, you wouldn't say things like that—at least, I hope you wouldn't." She saw the sulky look deepen, and tried again. "Daffy, you were talking nonsense just now; but it's the sort of nonsense that hurts. I don't know what Agatha said to you, but I want you to know the truth. It's not right that you should think—" She broke off and waited for a moment. Her hands held one another tightly. "I'm sorry Agatha said anything. She oughtn't to have said anything. It's—it's all very simple really. You don't remember your father; but other people remember him still, you know, Daffy. If he couldn't leave you money, he left you a very distinguished name. I used to think him the most wonderful person in the world. When he came in in the evenings and talked to my father, I used to listen and think how wonderful he was. Then, when I was seventeen, he stopped coming. I couldn't understand why—he'd always been there, and we all loved him so much. I fretted dreadfully. Then one day my mother told me that he didn't come because he felt it wiser to stay away for a time. She said he felt that he was getting too fond of me, and that I must be sensible, and make things easy for him and for them all. I don't know what I said, or what I did—I was too happy. It seemed too wonderful that a man like Ethan Grey should really care for me. They made me wait for six months, and then we were engaged. We were to be married when I was eighteen." Amabel paused.

Daphne was leaning forward now and listening eagerly.

It was difficult to go on. The past began to rise up vividly. The emotions, the hopes of twenty years before, stirred and came alive—the girl of seventeen in a rapture of hero worship; the parents, affectionate and delighted at the honour done their child; and Ethan Grey at the height of his fame, acclaimed by all Europe as the leading man of science of his day.

Amabel began to speak quickly and steadily:

"He had to go to Vienna to the big congress there. I went down into the country to pay a visit to a school friend. She was living with a brother and his wife. They were all very kind to me, and there was a lot going on. I had never met many young people, and I enjoyed it all tremendously. Everyone was so young and gay. It was all quite new to me. She paused for a moment, and took a hurried breath. "It was just that, you see, Daffy—they were all so young. And one of them fell in love with me, just in a headlong, young sort of way. It—it carried me off my feet. I can't think how I came to do it, but

I did say that I would break off my engagement; and I went home meaning to do it. We were both very young, Daffy, and it took us off our feet. But when I got home, I found I didn't have to break off my engagement because your father had broken it off. He—he had just found out that he was going blind—an oculist in Vienna had told him so,—and he went straight to my parents and broke it off."

"But—I don't understand." Daphne was puzzled, frowning, and certainly interested.

The colour had rushed into Amabel's face. Her eyes shone. She looked like a girl—like the girl who had given everything in her generous enthusiasm.

"Oh, Daffy, don't you see?" she cried.

"They persuaded you?" said Daphne.

"No, no—of course not. Just think what it meant to him. Oh, Daffy, I was only too thankful that I hadn't said anything first. It would have been too dreadful.

"I don't understand a bit," said Daphne. "Do you mean to say you just gave in?"

Amabel got up. Daphne's tone, with its hint of scorn—Daphne's obvious lack of comprehension—

She spoke very simply.

"Daffy dear, try and understand. If you remembered him it would be easier. When you love someone, and they are in frightful trouble, there's no room for anything except the wanting to help, and being so very thankful that one can."

Daphne got up too.

"Oh, well," she said, and stretched herself. "You're the self-sacrificing sort, Mummy: I'm not. It's a vice, really—all the best modern philosophers say so." She laughed lightly, and flung an arm about Amabel's shoulders. "Mummy, *let* me go to Egypt," she said.

Chapter Two

AMABEL SAT UP very late that night. She finished the orange-coloured curtains, and then sat quite still, her hands folded on the brilliant stuff, thinking.

Daphne was her only child—and Daphne was not hers at all. She could love her; but she couldn't reach her. Why were there such gulfs between people who loved one another? She simply could not reach Daphne at all. Yet the child loved her. Amabel always clung to that—Daphne did love her. When she was at her naughtiest; when she flared with rage, or looked at Amabel with the half-pitying contempt which was harder to bear, there was still that curious, unbroken strand of love linking the two together. Daphne chafed under it, resented it; but it was there.

Amabel sat very still, while the fire died and the lamplight began to fail. When at last she moved, it was to go to the window, open the shutter, and lean out.

The rain had ceased. There was a damp mist rising from the ground, thin, and white, and cold; a faint shaft of moonlight silvered it. The trees rose out of the mist like the cliffs of some black, unknown shore. The stillness and the silence were grateful.

Try as she would, Amabel could not still her thoughts or silence the echoes of those scenes with Daphne. "Self-sacrifice is your strong suit. Suppose you do a little sacrificing for me this time"—that was Daphne angry. "You gave him up pretty easily, didn't you? I don't wonder he was furious. Your affair of course; but I'd have stuck it out and had him in spite of everyone"—that was Daphne half casual, half contemptuous. Oh, it hurt, it *hurt*; after all these years it hurt most frightfully.

Twenty years were wiped out as Amabel looked into the mist. The urge of youth to youth had been very strong. The gold and the glamour of romance had not been easily renounced. One may stand in the fires of self-sacrifice and sing aloud there; and yet—and yet—Daphne couldn't understand that at all. Julian had not understood it either. The fire would not have been so hard to bear if Julian had understood. "We were both so dreadfully young." The echo of her own words to Daphne came back upon Amabel now. Just for a moment Julian might have been there before her; she had such a vivid impression of his blazing scorn, his furious resentment. The very ring of his "You're afraid to face up to it. You're afraid of what people will say," was in her ears.

With a quick movement she closed the shutter, fastened it, and, crossing to the hearth, began to rake out the last remnants of the fire. The log, as she stirred it, sent out a little shower of brilliant sparks. She looked at it with a touch of rather sad humour. You think a thing's dead; and then, all of a sudden, the sparks fly up— hot, burning sparks. Why, it was years and years since she had thought of Julian with pain like this. Curious how memory will stir. Julian's name in the paper this morning had not hurt at all; she had been interested, pleased to think that his work had been crowned with success after so many ups and downs. She picked up the *Times*, and read the paragraph again, the lamplight flaring and falling across the page:

"Mr. Julian Forsham is to be congratulated upon the results of his arduous labours in Chaldæa. Just how remarkable his discoveries will prove to be will only emerge upon the publication of his eagerly awaited book. Pending this publication, Mr. Forsham is declining to grant interviews or to make any statement to the Press. He is, we understand, remaining in Italy for the present."

Amabel laid the paper down again.

Agatha's indiscreet gossip had not included Julian's name, for the simple reason that Agatha had never known it. At least she was thankful for that. She could follow Julian's career, hear his discoveries talked of, and note the growing interest in them without being exposed to comment. She felt pleasure and pride in his achievement. Whence then this pain, this stirring of things long buried? It was Daphne that had stirred the past. It was what Daphne demanded of life that had called up a past in which, for a moment, she too had stood on the threshold of things and had stretched out her hands to take. It was Daphne's pain that had waked her own. The one was inextricably mixed with the other.

Amabel felt all that was passionate and vital rise up in her at Daphne's call. She had suffered; but why should Daphne suffer? Why should Daphne turn back from the threshold of life and take the shadowed way? Amabel stood there, her hands just touching the table. She felt a rush of emotion that changed slowly into something harder—something calm and determined. She put out the lamp with a steady hand. The flickering light leapt once, and died. As she stood there in the dark, her thoughts ordered themselves.

"I'll let the house—that'll help. And I'll find something to do. I could ask three guineas a week for the house. I'll do it. She shall have her chance. I'll manage it somehow. Mr. Berry might know of something for me. I could catch the ten-thirty, and go and see him. I'll do anything. But the child shall have her chance."

She lit her candle, and went upstairs. At the door of Daphne's room she paused for a moment, then turned the handle and went in, the candle shaded by her open hand.

Daphne was asleep, curled up like a kitten, with one hand under her cheek, her little head looking round and very black against the white pillow; her eyelashes were black too—black and wet.

"She's been crying!" The thought pricked like a sharp thorn.

Amabel set down the candle, using the huge, framed photograph of Amber Studland to screen it. She bent over Daphne, her heart soft against that pricking thought. And suddenly Daphne turned with a sob, and woke. The wet lashes showed blue eyes drenched with tears. Daphne's hands came out with a groping gesture, and clutched at her mother's wrist.

"Daffy! Daffy darling!" Amabel's arm went round her and felt the slight figure tremble violently.

"Mummy, oh, Mummy, if you could!"

"My Daffy dear."

"Mummy, I love him so—so dreadfully. I swear it isn't the money—I know you think it is, but it isn't—it's me and him." The words came in gasps. "It's everything—it's my whole life. I was a beast to you—but it's everything. Oh, Mummy!" Daphne's scalding tears were on Amabel's hand. There was a long, trembling pause. Then Daphne's clutch relaxed. With a violent movement she pushed the bed-clothes back and sat up. "Oh, Mummy, isn't there anything we can do?"

"I could go and see Mr. Berry—and I could let the house, perhaps," said Amabel.

"Yes, yes, of course you could." The words came headlong and without a thought. "And Mr. Berry—perhaps he'll offer to lend you the money."

Amabel laughed.

"Lawyers don't build up flourishing businesses on lending money to their poorer clients. If I let the house, I shall have to find something to do. Don't build on it, Daffy; but I'll go and see Mr. Berry, and find out whether anything can be managed."

Daphne caught at her mother's hands.

"Mummy, you angel!" she cried. "I knew—I knew you could manage something if you would only try."

Amabel lay awake till the dawn. How had she and Ethan managed to have a child so full of passionate impulses, so little disciplined? Was it all ingrain, or was her upbringing—Agatha's upbringing—to blame? Such a violence of feeling; so much self-pity; such a strength of wilful determination—these things terrified Amabel for the future. Everything in herself which she had locked away behind iron bars of self-control seemed to live in Daphne. She lay awake, and felt that the night was long, and dark, and cold.

Chapter Three

"JUST SO," said Mr. Berry, "just so." He said the words with that air of bland interest which had done so much to establish his reputation.

Mr. George Forsham, sitting opposite to him, finished signing his name to the document which lay before him, blotted the signature, and passed the paper to Mr. Berry, all in frowning silence. When he frowned his thin lips tightened—a tall man, stiffly built, with a long nose and a high forehead—the aristocratic type, with rather the effect of having faded, as an old photograph will fade.

Mr. Berry, with his thick white hair, black eyebrows and florid complexion, presented as complete a contrast as possible. He continued to smile whilst his client frowned.

Mr. Forsham put down his pen, looked across the table, and said in a tone of deep annoyance:

"It is, of course, a perfectly preposterous position."

"Oh, entirely," said Mr. Berry.

George Forsham's frown deepened. He did not wish to listen to Mr. Berry; he wished to speak.

"Unfortunately," he continued, "the fact that the position is preposterous does not—er, does not, in fact, help us to—er, well, in fact, to let the house."

"It has been unlet for so long?"

"Since my Aunt Georgina died there—in fact, for four years. I decided to let Forsham Old House and the Dower House at the same time. I had no difficulty in doing so. Mr. Bronson took the Old House, and has been, I must say, a most satisfactory tenant. Yes, I must say that I have no possible fault to find with Mr. Bronson as a tenant. He is, in fact,—er, most satisfactory."

If Mr. Berry felt that his valuable time was being wasted, he concealed that feeling with the aptitude born of very long practice.

"You are to be congratulated," he said.

"The Dower House," said Mr. Forsham, in a slightly repressive voice,—"the Dower House I—er, also let to two Miss Tulkinghorns—er, terrible name, Tulkinghorn—but admirable women, prepared to interest themselves in the parish, and—er, in point of fact, most desirable tenants—quiet, estimable ladies. Yet, one fortnight after moving into the house, they vacated it, declaring it to be haunted. The preposterous rumour dates from that time."

"Old ladies are sometimes nervous," said Mr. Berry.

Mr. George Forsham leaned forward and tapped upon the table. He desired Mr. Berry's full attention.

"They had taken the house for three months, furnished, it being understood that they would stay on if they liked the neighbourhood. Their hurried departure had a most deplorable effect. Technically speaking, the Dower House has been let twice since then. I—er, use the word technically quite advisedly, Mr. Berry, because, in point of fact, although the house was let on those two occasions, it was only occupied once for forty-eight hours, and once for a bare twenty-four—and each time the same perfectly preposterous tale as to the house being haunted. I never in my life heard such a—well, such a perfectly preposterous story. The house my grandmother occupied; the house my aunts, Georgina and Harriet, lived and died in—the most blameless women, absolutely devoted to good works! Why, it's preposterous beyond belief!"

"Exactly," said Mr. Berry. "Only you can't let the house? Ever tried living in it yourself?"

"My dear sir, I can't get a servant to go near the place. The village is full of—er, the most ridiculous tales, and not a soul would sleep in the house if you paid them a fortune. My brother Julian and I spent a couple of nights there last time he was at home. Naturally, we saw nothing; but that hasn't put a stop to the tales. I—er, believe that—er, in point of fact, the experiment merely made matters worse. The village—er, believes that any Forsham is immune. That, at least, is what I am informed. The ghosts, being—er, Forsham ghosts, won't, in point of fact, haunt us." George Forsham gave a short, angry laugh, and pushed back his chair with a grating sound. "I must be off. I've got an appointment," he said, and got up, tall and thin.

Mr. Berry got up too.

"You mentioned your brother Julian," he said. "The *Times* informs me that he is in Italy; but I rather thought that I passed him on the Embankment this morning. I won't ask any questions, of course; but if, by any chance, he is not in Italy, I should be glad if he would spare me half an hour—I will undertake that there shall be no reporters on the premises."

George Forsham's manner became distant. He looked over Mr. Berry's head, and said "Yes. Ah, yes," in a vague sort of way. Then he moved to the door. With the handle in his hand, he turned:

"To revert—er, to the—er, proposition which I put before you. You understand that it was—er, made seriously. I feel"—the door had fallen an inch or two ajar, and now, as he took half a step forward, it opened a little further still—"I feel the untenanted condition of the Dower House as a—a reflection upon my family. The proposition that I made to you was a serious proposition. I should like you to—er, take a note of it. I am prepared to pay two hundred pounds as—well, in point of fact, as a premium, to any suitable tenant—and by suitable I mean a tenant whose references and—er, social position shall be satisfactory to you. You are getting that down? I am prepared, I say, to pay a premium of two hundred pounds to such a tenant, provided—*provided* they stay six months in the house, and—er, put a stop to all these preposterous rumours. If they don't stay, they must pay the money back. You must have a guarantee to that effect. But I can leave all that to you—the power of attorney will cover everything of that sort, and—er, I shall be seeing you again, of course, before I go."

"Yes, on Friday." Mr. Berry came round the table, and shook the rather limp hand that was extended. "You don't sail till Monday, do you? I rather envy you that trip to New Zealand. I'm sure it's three months since we've seen the sun at all. Au revoir, then, and don't forget the message to your brother—if he *isn't* in Italy." Mr. Berry's dark eyes twinkled.

Mr. George Forsham turned abruptly and went out. He passed through the ante-room with no more than a momentary impression of the woman who was standing near one of the windows. He was aware that she was tall; for the rest, he was in a hurry and considerably annoyed—very considerably annoyed—both with Mr. Berry who had appeared to question him about Julian, and with Julian who had put him in what he characterized as a—well, in point of fact, a damned awkward position. He went out fuming, and as soon as the door had closed upon him, Mr. Berry came out of his office. The woman at the window turned to meet him with both hands extended.

"Oh, Mr. Berry," she said.

Mr. Berry, taking the hands in his own, was conscious of a good deal of pleasure.

"My dear Mrs. Grey, I've kept you waiting. A thousand apologies. It wasn't because I wanted to, I assure you. Between you and me and these walls, that's rather a tedious gentleman."

Amabel laughed as she preceded him into the next room. It was not till she had seated herself, and had seen Mr. Berry seated, that she said:

"It was George Forsham, wasn't it?"

"You know him?"

Amabel laughed again. Mr. Berry thought she looked charming— bright eyes, nice colour, better than half the girls. She was a little more animated than usual—he thought she seemed younger.

"He wouldn't know me," she said. "I met him years and years ago when I was a girl and he had just stopped being an undergraduate. I believe I thought him a most dreadful bore—superior, you know, and rather by way of thinking that a girl of eighteen was a sort of savage. He certainly wouldn't remember me."

Mr. Berry had no time to make the gallant reply which the occasion demanded. Amabel leant forward, and went on speaking with an eagerness which riveted his attention:

"I'm not interested in George Forsham; but I'm quite terribly interested in his house. I couldn't help eavesdropping, Mr. Berry,—I really couldn't. He pulled the door right open, you know, and then stood there, saying the most exciting things in the most dreadfully dull way, and—oh, please, Mr. Berry, do tell me all about it."

"My dear Mrs. Grey, you shock me!" said Mr. Berry with mock severity. "You shock me extremely. What a proposition! A client's confidence—"

Amabel laughed.

"Dreadful, isn't it?" she said. "But if people will make confidences while they are standing in open doorways,—besides, it wasn't a confidence, you know it wasn't; he was asking you to find him a tenant for his house. Mr. Berry, you have found him a tenant."

"Stop, stop," said Mr. Berry. "What's all this?"

"I'm going to be the tenant," said Amabel. She leaned back with an air of finality.

"But you've got a house—and besides—"

"Oh, I'm going to let mine. Clotilda Lee would take it to-morrow." She gave him a charming smile, and then said quite seriously, "Mr. Berry, I want that two hundred pounds."

Mr. Berry frowned, tapped on the table, shifted some papers.

"Mrs. Grey, you know Ethan was my oldest friend. If you would let me be of any service to you—"

The colour sprang into Amabel's cheeks.

"You're the best friend anyone ever had," she said. "If I could borrow from anyone in the world, it would be from you. But I can't—I'm just made that way. You see, I could never pay it back, because two hundred a year doesn't leave me any margin; and I should be thinking about it all the time, and not sleeping at night; and—you do see, don't you?"

When Amabel Grey looked at him like that, Mr. Berry invariably felt himself to be trembling upon the edge of a pleasant precipice. He was a bachelor of sixty years' standing. He had never asked a woman to marry him in his life, and he never meant to; but once a year, when Amabel sat in his office and smiled at him, he experienced some dangerous sensations. The precipice allured him—undoubtedly it allured him. Later in the day he would feel the satisfaction which comes from temptation safely resisted; but for the moment he was certainly being tempted.

"It is good of you," said Amabel. "You're always so good to me. But I want to earn this money. He *did* say he would give two hundred pounds to anyone who would stay six months in the Dower House, didn't he?"

"He did," said Mr. Berry, "but—"

She shook her head.

"There aren't any buts. From this moment I'm George Forsham's tenant. Why, do you know, I was coming here to-day to ask you if you could think of any way in which I could earn just that sum of money. You'll give me a good character, won't you?"

Mr. Berry looked grave.

"No, no, I don't like it," he said. "It's not the sort of thing for you at all."

"Why not?"

"Not at all the sort of thing for you—fishy sort of business—don't like the idea of it for you at all—silly stories about the house being haunted—tenants leaving one after another in a hurry. There's a screw loose somewhere."

"Well, yes, I suppose there is," said Amabel soberly. "I didn't expect to earn two hundred pounds just for nothing; and I don't suppose George Forsham is offering two hundred pounds just for the pleasure of giving it away."

"I don't like it," said Mr. Berry again. "The house has a very bad name."

"It used not to have," said Amabel. "I stayed at Forsham with the Berkeleys when I was a girl—their place is next door, you know. The two old Miss Forshams were at the Dower House then—such kind old ladies. Joan Berkeley and I used to run in and out. It was a delightful house, sunny and charming; and the old ladies were dears. What a shame to say it's haunted. Is there any story about it? Did he tell you?"

"He says there's nothing definite. People just leave in a hurry. The village is full of wild tales about mysterious noises and appearances. But there's no coherent story. By the way, I don't know how much you heard, but Mr. George Forsham and his brother spent some nights in the house about two years ago without either seeing or hearing anything unusual."

"I didn't hear that," said Amabel rather quickly, "but I heard you ask George Forsham to give a message to his brother. I wanted to ask you about that. Julian Forsham is in Italy, isn't he?"

"Don't you read your *Times*, my dear lady?" said Mr. Berry.

"Yes, I do. Mrs. Crampton passes it on to me; I read it in the evenings. They said Julian was in Italy?" Her voice made a question of the last sentence.

"Yes, yes, in Italy," said Mr. Berry easily. "In strict confidence—you won't let it go any further, of course—I believe he came to London for twenty-four hours, and was so harried by reporters that he fled. He doesn't mean to appear again till after his book comes out next month. You knew him too?"

"Yes," said Amabel, and added nothing to the single word. There was a little pause before she spoke again. "I really want to do this, Mr. Berry. I know I can count on your help, can't I?"

He pushed his chair back and got up. "I don't think it's fit for you, I don't indeed. I don't like it."

"Mr. Berry"—her tone took on a teasing shade—"you're not going to tell me that you believe in ghosts!" The dark eyes twinkled.

"Not in the day-time," said Mr. Berry briskly. "Not in the day-time, and not in this office, nor in Piccadilly Circus, or The Criterion, or Victoria Station. In all these places, my dear lady, I can count on myself to be a complete and confirmed sceptic. Pooh, I say." He blew out his cheeks. "Ghosts? Nonsense, humbug, nerves! But"—he wagged an impressive forefinger—"put me at midnight in a lonely country house, with the rain coming down, black panelling on the walls, damp under the floors, and a fine smell of mildew in the air, and I don't say that I mightn't see ghosts with the best of 'em. That's the mischief of it."

"But then you're a town-dweller, a confirmed town-dweller," said Amabel. "Now, I'm quite inured to dark nights, and pouring rain, and mildew, and things like that. They won't worry me a bit. I shall enjoy going down there. Can you tell me who is at Forsham Old House?"

"A Mr. Bronson—one of these new rich, but a very good tenant—got some money, anyhow."

"And the Berkeleys? Do you know if they are still at Forsham? Joan Berkeley is in China, married, and it's years since I heard from her. I'd like to see Edward Berkeley and Lady Susan again; they were awfully nice to me when I stayed there."

"Yes, I believe they're still in the neighbourhood. Mr. Forsham happened to mention them. But, Mrs. Grey, take my advice, don't go any further with this matter. I can't advise it, I really can't."

"But then I never take advice," said Amabel. "Nobody does really. I always think good advice just helps you to make up your mind in the opposite direction." She got up, came a step nearer, and said, as she put out her hand, "Mr. Berry, my mind is quite made up. It is really. There's only one thing—I would rather, if you don't mind, that Mr. Forsham should think of me as quite a stranger. He knew me as Amabel Ferguson, and he has probably forgotten all about it. In the circumstances, I think I'd rather take this on as a stranger. You understand?"

Mr. Berry found himself admiring the delicacy of feeling which shrank from any suspicion of wishing to trade upon an old acquaintance. He also greatly admired the way in which her colour suddenly brightened as she spoke. The edge of the precipice seemed nearer than ever before as he pressed her hand and replied that she could rely on him to carry out her wishes.

Chapter Four

"WELL, MR. BERRY?" said Amabel Grey. She shook hands with him, and then immediately began to ask him questions, her voice hurried and her colour becomingly heightened. "Have you arranged it? You know, I asked you to wire, and you didn't. You're not going to tell me that there's any difficulty, are you? I've been counting on you to settle everything before Mr. Forsham sails. It's to-morrow he sails, isn't it?"

Mr. Berry had kept hold of Amabel's hand. He patted it now, and she drew it gently away.

"My dear lady, what a lot of questions! Sit down, and I'll answer them one at a time."

Amabel moved to the fire, and stood there holding her foot to the warmth.

"I don't want to sit; I want to hear what's been happening since I saw you. The country week-end is like a desert island, you know; one is simply marooned until Monday. And when there was no wire from you this morning"—she began to warm the other foot—"well, I just had to come up. Is it settled? Will he have me?"

"Gently, gently," said Mr. Berry. He sat down, turned over some papers, and picked up a typewritten sheet. Then, swinging round with it in his hand, he smiled benignantly, and said, "There's no need to look anxious—no need at all. I saw Mr. Forsham on Saturday, and the tenancy is yours if you will subscribe to his conditions."

"Oh, Mr. Berry, you don't know how pleased I am."

Mr. Berry tapped the paper in his hand.

"Don't be pleased until you have heard the conditions. Frankly, my dear lady, I don't like them, and I can't advise you to accept them. I am speaking, you understand, in a double capacity, as your friend as well as your lawyer."

"What are the conditions?"

It was so like George Forsham to set up a neat, typewritten list of them. How little people changed. *How little or how much had Julian changed?* She crossed the room, and sat down in the armchair beside Mr. Berry's table. "What are these dreadful conditions?" she said, and smiled a little.

"Well, I don't like them, and I've had no hand in them. Mr. Forsham sat down and typed them out himself, without so much as asking my opinion of them. That's what I call taking the bread out of an honest lawyer's mouth, eh?"

"But the conditions—what are they?"

"I'm coming to them. I just wanted you to know that I had no hand in them. Now, let's see, here's the first,—only you'll understand, please, that I'm giving you the sense of it in my own words. I really can't get my tongue round the fellow's quasi-legal twaddle. Defend me from the law of the layman! This is what it comes to in plain English:

"One. You're to stay in the house for six months, unless he changes his mind and wants you to go sooner.

"Two. During the six months you're not to be away from the house for more than forty-eight hours at a stretch.

"Three. You're to get two hundred pounds down—and a fine struggle I had with him over that. I wouldn't give way because I knew you wanted the money. But I put it to him at last that it was that or nothing, and that if he wouldn't take my personal guarantee, I'd just throw up the whole business and leave him to manage his own haunted houses. He was stuffy, very stuffy; but he gave way."

Amabel nodded and smiled. There was comedy in this reversal of the ordinary procedure—the lawyer translating his client's legal verbosities into plain English. Mr. Berry gave a chuckle, turned a leaf and proceeded to number four:

"Four. You'll have to give an undertaking to return the whole of the money if you fail to stay the full six months, and,

"Five. Mrs. Brown and her daughter are to remain in undisturbed possession of the rooms allotted to them upon the ground floor of the Dower House."

"And who," said Amabel, "is Mrs. Brown?"

"Well, between you and me," said Mr. Berry, "and as a matter of complete confidence, it wouldn't at all surprise me to discover that Mrs. Brown was the ghost—Mrs. Brown *or* the daughter," he added.

"Dear Mr. Berry, you're being most dreadfully cryptic. Who on earth *is* Mrs. Brown?"

"Mr. Forsham's old nurse," said Mr. Berry. "A treasured family retainer, now bed-ridden. She and her daughter occupy two rooms in the kitchen wing. They have free lodging, free fuel, free light. They have any fruit and vegetables they like to take from the garden. And in my opinion, my dear, we needn't look very much further for the ghost—it's so very plainly to their interest that the house should not be let."

"Yes—it is—and yet—" She hesitated, and then said, "It's so obvious, that it must have occurred to the Forshams."

"Well, I put it pretty plainly to Mr. George Forsham," said Mr. Berry. "I don't know whether it had occurred to him before or not, but I may say that I put it to him with some plainness."

"And what did he say?"

"He froze," said Mr. Berry. "He put on a came-over-with-the-Conqueror sort of air, and froze—wouldn't hear a word or believe a syllable, but just froze."

"Yes, that's like George," said Amabel.

"And now we come to number six," said Mr. Berry. "That's the worst of the lot:

"Six. You are not in any circumstances to employ detectives or to send for the police. The whole of the two hundred pounds shall be forfeited if you break this condition; and you must undertake to observe it strictly and honourably, both as to the letter and the spirit."

"Why?" said Amabel.

Mr. Berry spread out his hands. "He insists," he said. "Mr. George Forsham's house is Mr. George Forsham's house. He'd rather have the worst ghost that ever walked than a single vulgar, note-taking, scare-mongering detective, or a blundering oaf of a policeman with muddy boots and a skull like an ox. These, I think, were his very moderate expressions. There were probably others which have slipped my memory—he became very angry, you know, in his stiff sort of way—he even swore once or twice. But the upshot was, and is, that he won't accept any tenant who does not accept this, to my mind, preposterous condition. Now, if you'll take my advice," Mr. Berry put down his papers and leaned forward, "if you'll take my serious advice—"

"It's too expensive, Mr. Berry," said Amabel.

"Expensive? How?"

"Dear Mr. Berry! You're going to say, 'Don't take the Dower House.' Well, if I take your advice, and don't take the Dower House, it will cost me just two hundred pounds." She laughed, and got up. "It really *is* too expensive, I'm afraid."

Ten minutes later, when she left the office with Mr. Berry's cheque for two hundred pounds in her pocket, she had the strangest feeling of excitement, anticipation. She walked down the short flight of stone steps with her head held high and her eyes bright. Just at the turn of the stair, she brushed against a man who was coming up, brushed against him and passed on. Neither looked at the other, or was aware of anything but that momentary contact with a stranger.

Amabel Grey passed out into the darkening street at the moment that Julian Forsham rang the bell of Mr. Berry's office.

"So you're not in Italy?" Mr. Berry beamed as he spoke.

"Italy!" said Mr. Julian Forsham. "Good Lord, Berry, why should I be in Italy?"

"Oh, the *Times* said you were; and I rather thought that Mr. George Forsham implied as much, if he did not actually say so."

"George is a perfect marvel at implying things," said George's brother with a dry laugh. "I'm being harried to death by reporters and all the people whose business it is to stick their noses into other people's business. I've told some of 'em I'm going to Jericho, and some of 'em that I'm going to Timbuctoo. Some bright soul has struck a happy mean and made it Italy. I'm really going down to Forsham to vegetate. That's why I'm here. What's all this nonsense about George having let the Dower House?"

"Haven't you seen your brother?"

"Not for two days until this afternoon, when he dashed in, bade me a fond farewell, and with his parting breath remarked that he'd let the Dower House, and that you wanted to see me. Is it really let? If it is, it's too bad of George."

"Yes, it's let," said Mr. Berry,—"to a Mrs. Grey, the widow of an old friend of mine."

"Unfortunate old lady!" said Julian with a grimace. "What's she done to offend you, Berry? Have you broken it to her that she won't be able to get a servant for love or money?"

"Mrs. Grey," said Mr. Berry, "is—er, prepared for certain difficulties. As to the servant question—she has, I believe, a devoted maid who has been with her for years; and I understand that Jenny

Brown, your old nurse's daughter, is prepared to give help in the house—that, I think, is the technical expression."

Julian shrugged his shoulders. He bore no resemblance to his brother George. His lean face, and quick movements; the sensitive lines of lip and nostril; the humour not untinged with sarcasm which woke suddenly in the dark eyes, transforming their melancholy—these betokened a nature and personality interesting and interested, compelling and very much alive. He shrugged his shoulders, and threw out a protesting hand.

"Oh, bother the woman!" he said. "I was going to have a peaceful ghost hunt myself. Well, I don't suppose she'll stay any longer than the others did. I shall go down to the cottage and await events. George hasn't let the cottage by any chance?"

"Not that I know of. But, Mr. Julian—"

"But, Mr. Berry—"

"The Dower House being let—"

"She'll think I'm the gardener," said Julian. "I shall wear clothes which no self-respecting gardener would be seen dead in. I shall pull my forelock and babble about asters, and antirrhinums, and salpiglossis. The old lady will only think what nice manners I've got, and what a pity I can't afford a better coat. It will be very reposeful."

"I would like to have your signature to this document, Mr. Julian." The necessity for discretion with regard to Mrs. Grey's affairs gave a touch of abstraction to Mr. Berry's manner.

Julian signed, threw down his pen, and, taking up a position by the fire, looked out at the cold, foggy evening with distaste. Rain had begun to fall in a fine drizzle; the windows were blurred with it.

"I meant to get here by three o'clock," he said, "but I ran into the only man in London that I really wanted to see—my cousin, Julian Le Mesurier—ever met him?"

"Sir Julian Le Mesurier, the head of the Criminal Investigation Department?"

Julian grinned.

"Why not call him Piggy at once, and have done with it? Anyhow, I ran into Piggy in St. James' Square, and found him gnashing his teeth over those questions in the House last night."

"Were there questions?"

"Rather! Regular snorters. All on the lines of 'Is it not the case that the French Government have made strong representations as to the alarming number of forged bank-notes imported into France from this country? Is it not a fact that these notes are known to be printed in England? Where is Scotland Yard? Have we, or have we not, a Criminal Investigation Department? Is the Government satisfied as to its efficiency?' Good Lord, Piggy *was* wild! It took me the best part of an hour to soothe him; and as I'm dining with him tonight, I shall probably have it all over again. I pine for the rural seclusion of the gardener's cottage. If anyone asks any questions about me, you can tell 'em I'm excavating a prehistoric Buddhist temple on the southern slopes of Popocatepetl."

"But, Mr. Julian, I really think—"

"Never think," said Julian, making for the door. "It's a mistake. I propose to be a vegetable for the next month at least. There's going to be an election. Piggy will probably resign. And the weather is poisonous beyond belief. Why worry? 'Books, and work, and healthful play,' as the poet Watts hath it—that's my line. A little housework; a little cooking—I'm a past master at sausages; a flirtation with Lady Susan; and all the books that I've had no time to read to keep me company in the evenings. Well, so long, Berry." He stood in the doorway and waved his hand, then turned for a last, laughing word. "By the way, if you're writing to your Mrs. Grey, or seeing her, you might just mention that the gardener is a most reliable man."

Chapter Five

A WEEK LATER, on the Monday afternoon, Amabel Grey was driving up from the minute station at Forsham Halt. Horse, cab, and cabman, all seemed relics of twenty years ago. The cab smelt strongly of mould and mice.

Amabel sat with her arm about the neck of Marmaduke, a dachshund of a certain age and a highly uncertain temper. He was engaged in snuffing the air, and at intervals he gave a short yelp and tried to lick Amabel's face; it was therefore necessary to hold him tightly. On the opposite seat sat the faithful Ellen. She would have died for her mistress; but the more cheerful virtues made no appeal to her—she wore black kid gloves, and a funereal expression.

Amabel said, "No, Marmaduke, be good!" for about the tenth time, and leaned out of the window as the cab swung round to the right and crossed the old stone bridge. She was excited, interested, in the mood for adventure. Her house was let. Daphne, in a flutter of delight, had joined her friends. And she, Amabel, was off adventuring. Her eyes were very bright as she looked out and saw all the things which she had not seen for twenty years.

The bridge was the same, and the old willow at the turn of the stream; but the trees on the other bank had been cut away. Some one had built a bungalow there, quite new, with a ridiculous bird cut out in topiary work in the middle of a tiny lawn.

They passed the bridge, and turned into the lane with its high banks. There was a drizzle of rain in the air. The banks were wet and dark. Here and there a coloured blackberry leaf or the scarlet of rose-hips. Last time she came that way there had been blue sky, and the hedges were full of blossom. Here, just here, Julian had dropped down from the bank, and, whilst the cab halted, they had looked at one another through a mist of tears. She could hear his voice now: "Amabel!" and "You promise?" It didn't seem like twenty years ago. It felt—

Amabel drew back from the window with the colour bright in her cheeks.

"We're nearly there, Ellen," she said. "I do hope you'll like it. It used to be such a pretty house—friendly—you know how some houses seem to be friends with you at once."

Ellen sniffed.

"I can't say as 'ow I do," she said. And Amabel laughed.

"Nonsense, Ellen, you know quite well what I mean. I do wish you'd cheer up. You and Jenny Brown will soon have everything as nice as possible. I remember Jenny quite well—that is to say, I remember the twins, and Jenny must be one of them. Now, what was the other one's name? Annie? Yes, that was it, Annie—Jenny and Annie. They had bright red hair, and bright brown freckles. I wonder what's happened to Annie."

"I don't 'old with red 'air myself," said Ellen.

But Amabel was not listening. The cab had turned with a lurch, just clearing a rickety gate-post, and she leaned out again, looking eagerly into the dusk.

The drive had been dreadfully neglected. The trees met overhead, and the thickly heaped leaves were like a carpet under foot. The wheels of the cab made no sound. It was only three o'clock, but the light seemed to have failed. It was a relief to come out, as from a tunnel, upon the weed-grown gravel in front of the house.

The cabman got down, rang the bell, opened the door of the cab. Marmaduke instantly hurled himself through the opening, and greeted Amabel's descent with loud and piercing barks.

"Marmaduke, be quiet! Ellen, do stop him. Yes, we'll have to ring again. I don't think they can have heard. *Marmaduke!*"

Marmaduke dodged Ellen's umbrella, cast a green and baleful glance at her, and retreating to a safe distance, sat down and continued to bark.

Amabel looked about her in dismay. Poor Miss Georgina! Poor Miss Harriet! What on earth would they have said to all this? Weeds everywhere—weeds and moss; dead shrubs; ivy fallen in long festoons; the very door-step filmed with green, and the brass knocker black! As she looked, the door opened slowly, hesitatingly.

Amabel had to take a step forward before she could see anyone; the hall was so dark.

"Is it Jenny Brown?" she said. "May we have a light, Jenny? It's so dark coming in. There is electric light in the house now, isn't there? Will you turn it on, please."

It was really very dark. Jenny, moving from behind the door, was only a shadow until light from a globe in the ceiling suddenly flooded everything. It showed the hall much as Amabel remembered it, and Jenny Brown, changed indeed beyond recognition. Amabel remembered two little red-haired girls with corkscrew curls, quicksilver tempers, and eyes that saw everything. She saw now a limp, faded woman with an expressionless face and pale eyes that blinked at the light. The red hair was still red, but dry and lifeless; it was arranged in tight, smooth plaits that almost covered the back of Jenny's head.

"Twenty years!" thought Amabel with half a sigh. She turned to speak to Ellen, and, turning, caught a glimpse of her own face in the Dutch mirror which hung, as it had always hung, above the iron-clamped dower chest. Its faceted border threw back the light. Amabel saw herself set in a brilliant ring, light in her eyes, and a warm flush upon her cheeks. The effect was strange and startling. It was as if she had seen her own youth, as if the years had been suddenly wiped out.

Jenny had set tea upstairs in the little room which the two Miss Forshams had always used.

"I thought the drawing-room would be so cold for you, ma'am," she said timidly. "And I thought perhaps you'd like your tea here; and if you please, ma'am, I've made up the bedroom opposite for you—Miss Harriet's bedroom that was;—and please, ma'am, will you like your maid next to you, in Miss Georgina's room, or will I put her down the passage?"

"Oh, I think I'll have Ellen next to me," said Amabel. "Let me see, you and your mother are downstairs, are you not?"

"Yes, ma'am. Mr. Forsham lets us use the housekeeper's room and the one next to it."

"I remember your mother quite well," said Amabel. "I should like to come and see her to-morrow, if I may. I remember you too, and your sister—wasn't her name Annie? Is she married?"

Jenny backed towards the open door. She said, "No," and then quickly, "Mother'll be very pleased, I'm sure."

Amabel drank her tea and looked about her. The wall-paper was the same wall-paper which had made a faded background for Miss Harriet's heraldic caps and Miss Georgina's woolly shawls. The chintz on sofa and chairs was the same chintz, grown limper and duller; the old-fashioned sprigged pattern could hardly be discerned any longer, but memory supplied it. The carpet was dull and grey; but there, an inch or two from her foot, was the hole which Julian had burnt in it when he dropped the poker.

The new electric light looked down on all these old things, and showed them very old, very dingy, very faded. George Forsham had put it in just before the last tenant came, and it was worked from the plant at Forsham Old House. Amabel disliked it a good deal, but was grateful for it nevertheless. With this unsparing brightness flooding every corner of the room, every inch of the passage, there was the less chance that either she or Ellen would imagine—Amabel pulled herself up short. For the first time since she had contemplated coming to the Dower House, she found herself asserting that the idea of its being haunted was, of course, utterly absurd.

She finished her tea, and went into the bedroom to unpack. Marmaduke followed her and began to make a thorough inspection of the room. When he had sniffed at everything within reach, he clung round Amabel's feet and made low, moaning noises. By the time that she had fallen over him three times his cup of wretchedness appeared to be full, and he retreated under the bed, still moaning.

Marmaduke and Ellen were not exactly cheerful companions, thought Amabel, as she hung her very few garments in the immense wardrobe which had been planned for the crinolines of an ampler age.

Ellen came in presently, with the air of one who is resigned to the worst.

"Well, Ellen," said Amabel, "you're next to me here, just through this door; and you ought to be comfortable, for it was Miss Georgina's room."

Ellen sniffed.

"If anyone wants to know what's the matter with the 'ouse, it's easy telling," she said. "Ghosts indeed! Pretty fools they was who trumped up that set of tales, and pretty fools that believed 'em. What's the matter with this 'ouse is just plain damp, neither more nor less—and quite bad enough to my mind without dragging in any silly, trumpery ghosts that's neither 'ere nor there. I never did 'old with ghosts, nor my father he never 'eld with them neither."

"Well, we'll have good fires," said Amabel cheerfully. "The house wants living in; there's nothing else the matter with it. Did you see Mrs. Brown? And have you made friends with Jenny? I couldn't make out what had happened to her twin. You might just find out before I go and see Mrs. Brown to-morrow."

Ellen tossed her head.

"Oh, I arst her for myself," she said. "Beating about the bush is a thing I don't 'old with, and I arst her straight. 'Wasn't you one of a twin?' I said. And, of course, I knew at once there was something wrong. She tried to put me off, but I arst her straight. 'Is your sister dead?' I said. And she says, 'No, she isn't *dead*.' 'Ah, well,' I says, 'least said soonest mended, and there's some that would be better dead, if that's your meaning.' And she says, 'If you'll please not to mention it to Mother, nor your lady neither.' And please, ma'am, will Marmaduke 'ave his basket in my room or yours?" concluded Ellen, without any pause or change of expression.

"Oh, I'll have him," said Amabel—and then, "Poor Mrs. Brown, I was afraid there was something." Her thoughts went to the little girls with the blue check pinafores and cork-screw curls. "Poor Annie," she said with half a sigh.

Ellen sniffed the sniff of virtue.

They went to bed early. Miss Harriet's bed was very comfortable, and Amabel was tired.

Ellen, standing in the doorway between the two rooms, bade her mistress good-night, and then lingered.

"What is it?" said Amabel at last—and was aware of offence.

"Oh, nothing," said Ellen; but she stood with the door in her hand, and did not go.

Amabel looked at her sleepily.

"It's really time you were in bed, Ellen," she said. And then enlightenment came to her. "Leave the door open if you like, and then if I want anything, I can call out to you."

Ellen rallied her dignity.

"I wouldn't like to think as you wanted anything, or was nervous," she said.

"No, I know. Oh, Ellen, I'm so dreadfully sleepy. *Do* go to bed."

"And if you should wake up—"

"I shan't. I'm going to sleep, and sleep, and sleep. But you can leave the door open."

Amabel would probably not have stirred till daylight if it had not been for the abominable conduct of Marmaduke. She was tired enough to sleep through his preliminary twistings and turnings; but when he left his basket and began to scrabble at the edge of her bed, she woke, cuffed him, and then went to sleep again. But this time the sleep was a troubled one. Through its veils she was aware of Marmaduke sniffing and whining. Then suddenly he barked, and she was broad awake, tingling all over, her hands stretched out in the darkness, feeling for the unaccustomed switch.

The light showed Marmaduke's basket overturned, his bedding on the floor, and himself leaning dejectedly against the door that led into the passage. When Amabel scolded him he growled, backed away from her, and retreated to a dark corner where his eyes looked like emeralds. Put back in his basket and slapped, he tucked his nose under his tail and appeared to be wrapped in slumber.

Amabel lay awake for an hour, listening to all the tiny sounds which edge the silence in any old house—sounds imperceptible by day, and well-nigh imperceptible by night. Sleep came back to her slowly.

Chapter Six

MRS. BROWN sat up in bed, with a very clean pillow behind her and a very clean sheet turned down over the faded eiderdown which had been a wedding present from Miss Harriet Forsham. There was a starched white cap on her head and a cross-over shawl of crimson wool about her shoulders. The shawl had a white crochet border done in shell pattern.

Mrs. Brown herself was pale and plump. She had mild, kind eyes, and a surprisingly firm mouth.

"Now, just to think of its being you!" she said. "When Mr. Forsham wrote and said that a lady had taken the house, I no more thought of its being the young lady that we was all so fond of—and then last night, when Jenny come down and said that you remembered us—well, I *was* puzzled! And now, just to think of its being you!" She paused, beamed upon Amabel, and said, "I should have known you, my dear,—yes, I should have known you for sure."

"That's very nice of you," said Amabel. "Twenty years is a long time."

"Oh, my dear, *yes*. The old ladies gone; Forsham Old House let—and that's a thing I never thought to see; and you a widow—deary me! Have you any children, ma'am, may I ask?"

"One," said Amabel. "Daphne is just grown up. She has gone to Egypt for the winter with some friends."

Mrs. Brown sighed heavily.

"Ah well, children's a trouble," she said. "If we don't have 'em we fret for 'em, and if we do, they're just a trouble. There was a time when I thought I'd go to my grave single—I married late, you know, when Mr. George and Mr. Julian was out of the nursery, and the longing for children come over me so that I couldn't bear it. And I took Brown, and many's the time. I've wished I hadn't."

"Oh, Mrs. Brown," said Amabel, "but you wouldn't be without Jenny, would you?"

Mrs. Brown's mild eyes filled with tears.

"Jenny's a good girl—I'm not saying a word against Jenny," she said. "But, oh, my dear, I can't look at her and not think of Annie."

"I remember Annie," said Amabel gently. She took Mrs. Brown's hand and held it. The fingers closed hard on hers.

Only sixteen—and he didn't marry her—and she ran away—and we've never heard since." The words came in a slow whisper. The pressure on Amabel's fingers increased. "It's hard, my dear, it's hard," said Mrs. Brown.

Amabel came away feeling sad and a little conscience-stricken. Mr. Berry's suspicions of Mrs. Brown and Jenny were too ridiculous for words. She was ashamed of having listened to them. The two women seemed to her extraordinarily simple and pathetic in their isolation and the sorrow which brooded over them. Ellen's explanation of the tenants' flight seemed every moment more reasonable—the passages smelt of blue mould; the garden rotted in the rain; the rooms were darkened by curtains of neglected ivy.

"George Forsham always was a fool. How in the world he *expected* to let a house in such a state of neglect! I think I'll write and tell him that new wall-papers and chintzes will exorcise his ghosts."

There was a good fire in the little sitting-room, but she stirred it and added another log. She was surprised at the absence of Marmaduke, who adored a fire. Presently she went in search of Ellen.

Marmaduke had had his dinner and been turned into the garden for a stroll.

"And seeing 'e 'asn't been tearing the doors down, I made certain that you'd let him in, ma'am."

"No, I haven't seen him. Ellen, he'd never stay out in the rain like this. Where can he be?"

"'E's a dratted nuisance, neither more nor less," said Ellen gloomily. But she went to the door, nevertheless, and stood there calling for ten minutes or more. "He'll come back presently," she said at last.

But the hours passed, and Marmaduke did not come back.

Whilst Amabel and Ellen were searching high and low for Marmaduke, Julian Forsham was tramping along the muddy lane between the gardener's cottage, in which he had that morning installed himself, and Wood End where the Berkeleys lived. He reflected as he walked that if Forsham still held for him a hint of home, it was thanks to Susan and Edward Berkeley.

He found them in the smoking-room, and felt his welcome, though neither of them offered him any conventional greeting. Edward Berkeley looked up from a treatise on earth-worms and said, "Hullo, Julian!" Lady Susan, sitting cross-legged in front of the fire with six rose catalogues spread out before her and a much corrected list in her hand, merely nodded and said, "You're just in the nick of time. Come and disentangle this horrible list with me. You needn't sit on the floor unless you like."

"Hullo, Edward!" said Julian. "I don't believe you've moved since I saw you last—three years ago, isn't it? Susan, not *more* roses!"

Susan Berkeley moved two catalogues, and he sat down on the floor beside her.

"It's the new sorts," she said.

"It's vice," said Julian.

"But I don't buy any clothes."

Julian threw back his head and laughed.

"My dear Susan, that makes it worse, not better. You ought to buy clothes. A woman who doesn't buy clothes is a monster of virtue."

Lady Susan patted her worn tweed skirt affectionately.

"Pre-war," she said. Then, with the chuckle that Julian loved, "You see, if I spend money on roses, there's beauty—months and months of it,—the sort of thing that makes you say 'Thank God' right out loud in front of your gardener; whereas no one's going to say 'Thank God' if they see me in a new dress. It's all a question of values."

Julian looked at the square figure and strong, plain face, and smiled suddenly, charmingly.

"My dear Susan, I always say 'Thank God' when I see you," he said; and Susan Berkeley actually blushed.

When they had straightened out the list, Julian took the catalogues and put them firmly away in a drawer.

"From duty to pleasure," he said. "Gossip is now the order of the day. As a returned wanderer, I am naturally thirsting to know who is born, and married, and bankrupt. To begin with"—he sat down on the floor again and made himself comfortable with a cushion—"to begin with, I hear George has jockeyed some unfortunate old lady into taking the Dower House."

"Susan is going to call on her," said Edward Berkeley.

"What Edward really means," said Lady Susan crossly, "is that I've had a letter from George in his most eighteenth-century grand seigneur style, ordering me to go and call on her. She's a Mrs. Grey, by the by; and she'll probably have run away from the damp and the general discomfort long before I get the length of calling."

Edward Berkeley turned a leaf.

"Did you know that there were fifty known varieties of British earth-worms, and that in 1865 only eleven had been identified?— Susan will go and call on her to-morrow," he added.

"You shall come with me, Julian."

"I? Jamais de la vie. To all intents and purposes, my good Susan, I'm not here at all—I'm in Italy."

Lady Susan snorted.

"Don't you flatter yourself. Do you imagine there's a single soul in the village that doesn't know you're here? When did you come? This morning? Well, old Bell told Mary all about it when he came with the milk at three. So that's that!"

Julian ran his hands through his hair.

"I shall not call," he said firmly. "No one shall make me. By the way, who's been building the comic bungalow by the bridge?"

"People of the name of Miller—brother and sister. He's an artist—away a good deal. She gardens. I like Anne Miller."

"Any other new comers?"

"There's Nita King," said Lady Susan in a gloomy voice.

"Who is Nita King?"

"She's a widow. She says she's a cousin of Edward's."

Edward lifted his eyes from his pamphlet.

"My dear," he said quietly. "Since I had eight great-uncles, and they all had families of fifteen and upwards, why should she not be my cousin? Personally, I see no reason to suppose that she is not a grand-daughter of my Uncle John's ninth son. I believe his name was Albert."

"Well, hers is Nita. She's a red-haired serpent," said Lady Susan.

Julian grinned.

"I have a passionate adoration for red hair," he declared.

"Tell her so. Tell her the first time you meet her. She won't mind; she's that sort. Only don't blame me if you find you've got engaged to her without quite knowing how."

Edward Berkeley turned another leaf, and spoke without looking up:

"She has most undeniable ankles."

Julian's eyes danced.

"Where does this exciting lady live?" he inquired.

Lady Susan got up, opened the drawer which Julian had shut, extracted all her rose catalogues, and came back with them to the hearth-rug.

"Mr. Bronson lent her the Lodge for a time. He seemed to think he was obliging Edward. At the moment, I believe, she's staying up at the Old House."

"And the Bronsons?"

"The girl's just grown up—a handsome, shy lump at present. Mr. Bronson is just the same. People like him, you know—he's generous without making too much of a splash. As a matter of fact, he's a great deal better liked than George ever was. Pity you weren't the elder brother, Julian." She opened one of her catalogues, became immersed for a moment, and then inquired, "Do you know Mabel Morse?"

"Good Lord, no! How should I? Is she another of Edward's cousins?"

"She's a rose," said Lady Susan in tones of indignant scorn. "I'm sick of people, and I'm going to talk roses. I give you fair warning. If you don't like it, go and talk to Edward. He's just joined a thing called the Incorporated Vermin Repression Society and College of Pestology, and he can't find anyone who will listen whilst he explains its aims."

"I'd rather talk about Mabel," said Julian hurriedly.

He dined with the Berkeleys, and came back to his cottage late. The rain had ceased. The moon looked down on rising mist. As he paused at the door for a moment, he heard a woman's voice calling in the distance, and stood still to listen.

What queer tricks memory plays us. Years pass. The silted dust of every day gathers upon old thoughts and feelings, and the incidents with which those thoughts and feelings were associated. And then suddenly, after ten years, fifteen, twenty, the past may come alive again at a word, a touch—a who knows what?

Julian stood, and heard a woman calling; and the sound took him back twenty years. The brief, long buried romance of his boyhood came vividly to his memory. All the romantic side of his nature thrilled to it pleasantly, whilst that other Julian, man of the world—a little tired, a little blasé, a little disillusioned—stood by, as it were, and made sarcastic comment.

The voice called again, and Julian began to move towards the sound. He remembered a May night, all moonlight and apple-blossom. He remembered Amabel Ferguson, and how desperately he had cared for her then. Moonlight and apple-blossom, and Amabel's voice calling to the old retriever beloved of his aunts. The memory, robbed of pain, was as pleasant as a dream. Strange how the pain went out of things, leaving just a ghost behind. He came to the very tree where they had kissed—that one unpremeditated kiss which had lain so heavy on Amabel's conscience. The branches had been weighed down with their drifts of scented blossom then. They were almost leafless now, and the rain dripped from them.

He wondered a little about Amabel as he stood there. She had married the old professor; but beyond that he knew nothing. Joan

Berkeley, who had been her friend, had gone to China, and there was no link. That was as it should be. One should certainly never meet one's first love again. Moonlight and apple-blossom are the right setting for romance. The anti-climax of twenty years after is its destruction. He had never had the slightest desire to see Amabel again.

It was at this moment that he took a step forward and saw her coming down the path towards him.

Julian stood, shocked into a stillness so absolute that his very breath halted. For one instant it seemed to him that what he saw must be a projection of his own thought; and then, hard upon that, the realization that this was not the girl Amabel whom he had kissed under a May moon, but Amabel, the woman and the stranger. She was bare-headed, and the moonlight showed every feature. It was she past all doubt, and yet not Amabel Ferguson, but this new Amabel of whose very name he was ignorant.

He made a movement, and she stood still. One hand held a dark cloak about her. She put up the other to push aside a drooping bough, and spoke.

"Is anyone there?"

He came forward, still in the shadow of the tree.

"I hope I didn't startle you."

"Who is it?" said Amabel.

"I'm afraid I have no business here. I'm living in the gardener's cottage, and I heard somebody calling."

"I was calling to my dog. You haven't seen him, have you—a dachshund? He has been away for hours, and I'm afraid he may be lost. I am Mrs. Grey," she added. "I have just come to the Dower House."

"Mrs. Grey—George's old lady—Amabel! Good Lord, what a surprising trick for fate to play them all!"

Julian came nearer with more than a little reluctance. His incognito must go by the board; and he regretted it frankly. He said,

"I really must apologize. The fact is, I recognized you at once, but I suppose you will hardly recognize me."

He was about to name himself, but a spice of malice made him pause.

"Who is it?" said Amabel in a bewildered voice.

He turned to face the light. Her hand dropped slowly from the apple bough. Julian saw her face change. He felt a queer excitement, and still that hint of malice. But Amabel's discomposure was momentary. She said quite simply,

"It Julian Forsham, I am sure," and held out her hand—the pretty, slim hand that he remembered.

At its touch the sarcasm passed from Julian's mood. He experienced real pleasure, real emotion, both in a degree which surprised him, and which made speech difficult. He said,

"Yes."

It was she who withdrew her hand.

"But I thought you were abroad."

"Only officially," said Julian.

"I thought you were in Italy."

"Or you wouldn't have come here? Quite right. One should always keep one's old illusions."

Amabel gave a little, shaky laugh.

"I think I would rather keep my old friends," she said; and Julian's heart went out to the dignity and simplicity with which she spoke. That was the old Amabel. He said quickly,

"You'll find more than one down here—the Berkeleys—"

"Yes, I know. I want to see them so much." And then, "Julian, I'm so distressed about Marmaduke. He's been away for such hours. Does anyone in the neighbourhood set traps?"

"Not that I know of. He'll turn up all right. Dogs always do."

She turned to go.

"Ellen will think I'm lost too," she said with a little laugh. "Will you come and see me?"

"May I? To-morrow?"

"Yes, to-morrow. Come to tea."

Chapter Seven

IT WAS VERY LATE before Amabel slept. The open door between her room and Ellen's irked her. She would have liked to shut herself in and be alone, really alone. Her hearing, always acute, was tonight distressingly so; every movement that Ellen made fretted it. She felt disturbed and troubled, almost afraid, and the thought of Marmaduke astray and frightened weighed on her continually.

It was just as she was falling asleep that she heard the sound for the first time. She sat up and listened, switching on the light. Next moment she was out of bed, thrusting her feet into slippers, and pulling her dressing-gown about her. The sound was the unmistakable sound of a dog thudding against the front door. As she came out into the passage and turned on the lights there, it came again—scratch, scratch, rattle, thud. And then thud, thud it came once more.

She ran down the stairs without troubling about the light in the lower hall, struggled with bolt and chain, and pulled the door open upon an empty porch. The silence, the blackness, the emptiness were like a blank wall. She called, "Duke! Duke! Marmaduke!" and heard the rain drip from the eaves.

"But he was here—he *was* here—he *was*," she said, speaking aloud to the emptiness; and as she spoke she moved across the threshold out into the porch, and stood there, searching the darkness, listening.

From the wet darkness in front of her there came a sound, but it was not the sound that she expected to hear. The sound that came was a laugh, shaky and thin. It seemed to come from so near at hand that she stepped back sharply and slammed the door. As she leaned against it, panting a little, she heard behind her a very faint mewing cry. It seemed to come from the foot of the stairs. "It was a cat—it must have been a cat," she said to herself. But when she crossed the hall and came back to the stairs the sound ceased.

She was frankly glad to come back into the full light. At her own door she stood for a moment, listening, before turning out the passage light. There was not a sound anywhere. But, as her fingers touched the switch, and the darkness fell, she heard the cat mew again with a long, wailing cry.

Amabel shut her door. She laid her dressing-gown over the back of a chair, set her slippers ready to put on if she should need them, and was about to get into bed, when she noticed that the door between her room and Ellen's was shut. After a moment's hesitation she opened it. She could hear Ellen's deep, regular breathing; and now she no longer felt worried by it or wished to be shut in by herself. She put out her light, and in ten minutes was asleep.

Ellen came in at half-past seven with a cup of tea, and a grievance.

"I'm sure, ma'am, that I'm the last person to wish to impose myself," she said. "And I'm sure, ma'am, that you need only to 'ave mentioned it and not just took and done it, which I know there's people that can't take a hint, but I'm not one of them and never 'ave been, and it's a thing that I don't 'old with."

Amabel sat up and straightened her pillow.

"Good gracious, Ellen, what do you mean?" she said.

Ellen stood rigidly by the bed and sniffed.

"I'm sure my meaning's plain enough," she said. "Seeing I never was one to beat about the bush, and brought up to believe that a double meaning was an abomination to the Lord, I thinks what I says and says what I thinks."

Amabel laughed.

"Well, you'll have to say it again this time, Ellen. I'm not there—I'm not really."

Ellen sniffed again.

"I'm sure I spoke plain enough," she said. "And if the door shut is more to your liking, I'd be the last to say a word."

"What door?" asked Amabel.

Ellen pointed to the door between the two rooms.

"I'm sure I'm more than willing to 'ave it shut," she repeated.

Amabel looked surprised.

"But I don't want it shut. I opened it in the night."

"I left it open when I went to bed," said Ellen reproachfully.

Amabel saw the shut door, and herself opening it.

"Wasn't it open this morning?" she asked, and tried to make her tone as casual as possible.

Ellen stood still, looking at her, her face suddenly frightened.

"Didn't you shut it? It was shut when I woke up." Her voice wavered and fell to a whisper. "Who shut it?" she said.

Julian Forsham came to tea. He was not at all sure that he wished to come; but he came. Last night's encounter had disturbed him strangely, but he had the feeling that, after all, it fitted well enough into his old romance. What he dreaded was the cold light of common-sense and everyday. To meet an old love in the dusk of a ruined garden is one thing; to confront her over a tea-table by electric light is another. Nevertheless, after the briefest period of mental adjustment, he found himself very glad that he had come.

Amazing how some women bring to any place that they are in the atmosphere of a home. Julian remembered the few days that he and George had spent in the Dower House three years before. They had used this room, and very dreary and bleak they had found it. Now, after three years of added neglect, the room was suddenly not only tolerable, but homelike. Amabel's smile and voice; the firelight on her hair; her pretty hands touching the tea things—all these things had their intimate charm.

They talked, filling in the twenty years' blank with light touches.

"I have a daughter, you know—Daphne. She's just grown up and very modern—not a bit like me. She has gone to Egypt for the winter."

"Why do you say 'not a bit like me'?"

"Because I'm Victorian. You are, you know, if you've lived in a village for fifteen years. Daphne teases me about it."

Julian made an impatient movement. Fifteen years in a village smaller than Forsham on next to nothing a year! He said impulsively,

"Good Lord, how did you stick it?"

She smiled.

"I minded at first. But one makes interests. I wasn't unhappy."

Julian felt strangely touched. He had a glimpse of her building her life resolutely. He began to talk about his travels, and presently found himself using her name after the old boy and girl fashion. Her expression changed, and he caught himself up.

"Ought I to say Mrs. Grey? It's not easy."

Amabel coloured, and laughed.

"I don't think I could say Mr. Forsham," she said. "After all, we are pretty old friends." He nodded, and she went on speaking. "I'm going to treat you like an old friend if I may. I want to talk to you about the house."

"This house?"

She stretched out her hand for his cup, and as she put in the milk and sugar, she said seriously,

"Yes, I want to tell you how I came to take it, and to ask you some questions. To start with, your brother George is paying me two hundred pounds for being here; and I feel it's up to me to earn it. I want to earn it. If I can live here for six months, the stories about the house will all die away—at least that's what he thinks."

"And if you don't stay here six months?"

"Then I have to give back the two hundred pounds," said Amabel.

Julian drank his tea with a gulp and put the cup down.

"But it's preposterous!" he said. "What on earth was old Berry about, that he let you in for such an arrangement?"

"He didn't," said Amabel—a dimple showed in her cheek—"he hated it. But don't let us begin about that. What I really want is to ask you some questions."

"Berry oughtn't to have allowed it," said Julian. "What questions do you want to ask me?"

Amabel left the tea-table and drew in a chair to the fire.

"Well, I want to know,"—she paused, picked up a small log, and bending forward, placed it carefully on the fire. Her face was very near him as she turned—"Julian, what is the matter with the house?"

"I don't know," said Julian. "It used to be all right."

"Yes."

She drew back; there was a silence; then Julian said quickly,

"What's worrying you? You'd better tell me."

"Yes, I want to. It's difficult to put into words—it comes to so little, really. And yet"—her laugh had a little shake in it—"I think I can understand why the other tenants ran away."

"What's been happening?"

She hesitated; then spoke with her candid eyes fixed on his face:

"It's so little, really. I thought I heard Marmaduke at the door in the night, and ran down. When I got the door open he wasn't there, but—but something laughed. Julian, it was horrid—it was, really."

She saw his face relax.

"An owl," he said.

"No, *really*. I slammed the door. And then there was a cat mewing somewhere; but I couldn't see anything. I didn't like it a bit."

Julian laughed outright.

"Brownie has probably got half-a-dozen cats." He stopped suddenly and whistled. "No, by Jove," he said under his breath; and Amabel met his eyes and nodded.

"Yes. I asked Jenny this morning, and she told me—Mrs. Brown can't stand cats, and they never have one in the house. Jenny said her mother would be taken ill at once if a cat came into the room."

"You don't suppose Jenny's playing tricks?" He pulled himself up. "No, that's a shame. I'd bank on Jenny."

"I know—she gives you that feeling", said Amabel. "I did think, before I came, that perhaps she and Mrs. Brown wanted to keep the house empty, but after I'd seen them I simply couldn't think it any longer; there's something about them—oh, no, it's not Jenny; I think she's frightened too."

"Yet they've been here all these years."

"I know, but,"—Amabel hesitated, leaned nearer, spoke lower—"Julian, she's frightened all the same. She brings my tea, and clears it away, and then she doesn't come upstairs again. She—she won't.

I asked her why, and she just drooped and said she couldn't. Ellen brings me my supper on a tray."

As she stopped speaking the door opened and Jenny herself appeared, a drooping figure with downcast eyes.

"Mrs. King," she said in her spiritless voice; and there came in a little person, in a vivid orange-checked coat.

Amabel saw red-brown hair and hazel eyes under a jaunty felt hat. Julian observed the ankles commended by Edward Berkeley.

Nita King advanced, all smiles.

"It is Mrs. Grey? I'm sure it is. And I must apologize for coming at such an hour; but I went to the station to inquire about a parcel, and they kept me an age, simply an age."

She shook hands, and looked inquiringly at Julian, breaking into fresh smiles as soon as Amabel mentioned his name.

"But, Mr. Forsham, fancy meeting you *here*!"

"And why not here?" thought Julian crossly to himself as he handed tea and cake and listened to an unceasing flow of conversation delivered in a high, silvery voice:

"I felt I must come and call at once, because really, I am a stranger here too, and I know how *desolate* one feels in a new place. I came here, of course, to be near my cousins, the Berkeleys. I shall ask Lady Susan to come and see you too. Such a dear creature, Susan Berkeley, but not really very sociable, I'm afraid. I know some people think she gives herself airs, but I *don't* think it's that, I don't *indeed*. Do you?" She turned the rather fascinating hazel eyes upon Julian with a look of appeal.

"Red-haired serpent!" he said to himself, and remarked aloud that Susan Berkeley was one of the best women on earth.

"Exactly what I've always said. Just a little more sugar please, Mrs. Grey. Yes, the Berkeleys are charming, and I do hope you'll meet them soon. You know, Mr. Forsham, I'm staying at your old home just now. Mr. Bronson has been *so* kind to me. He let me have the Lodge—such a ducky little place. But the rain certainly did come in through the roof, so he insisted, *absolutely insisted* on my coming to stay with him. You see"—turning to Amabel—"his daughter is only just grown up, and perhaps he finds it a little bit dull. Of course there's Angela's governess, Mademoiselle Lemoine—you'll meet her, I expect. She goes everywhere—a charming person." She paused, and gave a little conscious laugh. "Some people *have* said that they thought she was just a little too charming—you know what I mean, a widower's household. People are so unkind about that sort of thing. Don't you think so?"

"Some people are," said Amabel. She looked straight at Mrs. King as she spoke, and received a beaming smile.

"Yes, *indeed*. But I always think it's so horrid. Why shouldn't poor Mr. Bronson have a charming governess? It's much nicer for Angela. And, as to there being anything *wrong*—I think it's dreadful of people to think of such things. Don't you? I think they *must* have *horrid* minds."

"Yes," said Julian.

"I think one should try and see good in everybody," said Nita King sweetly. "Oh, thank you, Mrs. Grey,—yes, just half a cup—such delicious tea. Now, there are some other neighbours of ours, the Millers. They've built a little bungalow down by the bridge, and when they first came, *really*, people said the unkindest things about them. I used to get furious about it. Why should everyone assume that they are Germans just because Müller and Miller are so much alike?"

"It doesn't seem quite an adequate reason," said Julian, meeting an appealing glance with gravity.

"No, *indeed*. That's what I kept on saying. Of course her name is Anne—so like Anna—, and some people think that he has a slight accent. But I do think one ought to be charitable. Don't you? Why, if one believed everything one heard—" She broke off and threw a glance about the room. "People have even said things about this *charming* old house," she declared with a ripple of laughter. "Too absurd, of course—just because it has stood empty for so long—such ridiculous stories!"

"Ah," said Julian with sudden interest. "Now, I wonder what *your* stories are. They're all different, you know. Is yours the one about the tenant who ran away, or the much better one about the postman meeting the stray donkey in the drive? That's my favourite, really."

Nita King gazed at him with a hint of reproach.

"Oh, Mr. Forsham," she said, "I don't think one ought to—mock at the supernatural, I don't indeed. Mrs. Grey, *you* agree with me, I am sure. We women are not such scoffers as the men. Not, of course I mean, that one need believe everything one hears. For instance, I don't think it really can be true that—but perhaps I'd better not repeat it; it might make you nervous."

"I'm not a nervous person," said Amabel.

"No, of course you're not, or you wouldn't be living here, would you? So brave of you! Tell me,"—she glanced over her shoulder and dropped her voice—"you haven't *seen* anything, have you?"

Amabel laughed and shook her head.

"Not—not anything at all?"

"Not a thing," said Amabel.

Mrs. King's voice fell to the merest whisper.

"Or—or *heard* anything? They say—oh, it's all nonsense of course—they say that you hear wings, and something that cries in the night." She shuddered violently, and sprang to her feet. "How stupid of me to talk about it. I haven't frightened you, but I've frightened myself; and now I'm afraid to go home in the dark. Mr. Bronson did say that he would call for me, but he must have been kept."

She turned with an appealing gesture to Julian.

"Would you just see me down the drive, Mr. Forsham? It's so dark there, and if I saw anything,"—she broke off with another shudder—"I'm not *nearly* so brave as Mrs. Grey."

It ended, of course, in Julian walking back with her to Forsham Old House. On the way he heard that Edward Berkeley was considered *peculiar*; that the vicar was breaking up *very* fast; and that some people said—but of course it wasn't true—that Mr. Bronson drank. He fished in vain for any definite story about the Dower House.

Ten minutes after Julian and Mrs. King had left, Jenny announced Mr. Bronson. He came in, shook hands, and seemed surprised that his guest had not waited for him. Amabel looked at him with interest, and decided that the Old House might have fallen into worse hands.

Mr. Bronson had good manners and an agreeable voice. He was a strongly built man in the late forties, with a pale, clean-shaven face, very straight eyebrows, and the lightest of light grey eyes. He wore rough tweeds, and they seemed a little incongruous; one would, somehow, have expected broadcloth and a heavy gold watch chain. He sat down, and talked pleasantly enough for about quarter of an hour. He hoped that Mrs. Grey was comfortable, didn't find the house damp or—er, anything. Presently he took his departure, and Jenny crept in to take away the tea things.

Chapter Eight

AMABEL WAS READING that evening when Ellen came in with the tray. She finished a paragraph before she looked up; but what she saw brought her quickly to her feet.

Ellen was leaning against the wall, the tray sloping at a highly dangerous angle, and her face—

Amabel rescued the tray, set it down, and half pulled, half pushed Ellen into a chair.

"I come over so queer. Oh, my dear ma'am, shut the door!" Ellen's lips were very white, and the words came in gasps.

"Yes. I've shut it. What's the matter? No, don't try and speak for a minute. It's all right; there's nothing to be frightened of."

Ellen held her hand painfully tight.

"Oh, my dear ma'am!" she said, and burst into tears.

Amabel let her cry, and busied herself with pouring out a cup of tea. When Ellen had drunk it she said in a sobbing whisper,

"All the way up the stairs behind me, and I never dropped the tray. I don't know 'ow I 'eld it, but 'old it I did. Oh, my dear ma'am!"

"That was splendid of you," said Amabel. "Now, do you think you could tell me what happened—just from the beginning, you know, quietly?"

"I never turned my 'ead to look, because I dursn't," said Ellen. "I never turned my 'ead, but I know'd that it was there."

Amabel was conscious of an answering shudder, but she kept her voice firm and cheerful.

"Now, Ellen, do begin at the beginning. You got my tray—and then?"

Ellen shivered.

"I got your tray same as I always do, and I come along with it, and as I come past the Browns I calls out to Jenny, and she says 'all right.' And then I come into the 'all with the tray, and when I was 'alf-way up the stair I thought I 'eard Jenny come after me. Well I just stood with the tray in my 'and, and I says 'Is that you, Jenny?' And all at once I knowed it wasn't Jenny. And I took and come along just as fast as I could, and I 'eard it come after me, and I *dursn't* turn my 'ead."

"But perhaps it was Jenny," said Amabel.

"It wasn't no yuman being," said Ellen. "There's yuman things, and there's things that isn't yuman." She paused. "Don't ask me how I knowed, for there's things as I couldn't put into words—but it wasn't Jenny."

Amabel went to the door, opened it, and stood in the lighted passage. It was empty and shadowless. She walked as far as the stair-head and looked down into the hall below. To right and left the closed doors of the dining-room and drawing-room. There was a red and blue Indian rug, very faded; the old chest with the Dutch mirror above it; three or four chairs standing primly against the panelling; the portrait of a great-uncle of Julian's in wig and gown—these familiar and peaceable objects alone met her gaze. She switched off the light in the lower hall, and turned back to the sitting-room. As she closed the door, there came to her faintly the mewing of a cat.

She and Ellen ate their supper together, and left the tray in the sitting-room until the morning. When they went to bed Amabel opened the connecting door between the two rooms, and set a chair against it to keep it in position. It was just as they were getting into bed that they heard the sound of something thudding against the front door.

Ellen was in the room in a moment, an odd figure in a red flannel dressing-gown, her hair in tightly plaited tails. She caught Amabel by the arm and held her with stiff, bony fingers.

"Oh, ma'am, you'll not go down!" she cried.

"Ellen dear!"

The thudding came again—scratch, scratch, thud, thud; and then a thin, faint sound, half whine, half howl.

"If it's Marmaduke—" said Amabel.

She was sitting on the edge of the bed, her long fair hair thrown back, one hand at her throat. Ellen clutched her tighter.

"You mustn't go down. Oh, you mustn't!"

"If it's Marmaduke—if he's hurt or ill—"

"It isn't Marmaduke," declared Ellen fiercely. "It isn't a yuman, natural thing at all, and you shan't go down, my dear. Why, if it was Marmaduke, 'e'd bark same as 'e always 'ave done. It stands to reason 'e would, and not go making that there creepsy, 'owling sound."

"If he's been hurt—" said Amabel again.

She spoke just under her breath, and they both stayed motionless, listening. A minute passed, and another. Ellen's grasp had begun to relax, when, for the third time, something thudded against the door, and a faint crying followed. Amabel started to her feet.

"Ellen, I must go down. He may have been caught in some trap and have dragged himself loose. No, it's no use. I really must go."

She was out on the landing turning the lights on before Ellen could stop her, and without giving herself time to think, she ran down the short flight into the hall, and heard Ellen follow her. They stood by the door for a moment, and then Amabel turned the key with a jerk. She meant to open only an inch or two, but the door swung back as heavily as if someone had been pushing against it. She began to say, "Duke, are you there?" but the words never passed into sound, for, with a suddenness that was like a blow, all the lights went out. She heard herself give some sort of a cry. She heard Ellen scream. And then something passed between them in the dark, and the door swung to with a slam. Some one touched her. She thought it was Ellen, and said her name; and as she fell against her, a dead weight, the mewing of a cat seemed to fill the hall.

Amabel never quite knew how she got Ellen upstairs again. The mewing went on all the time, sometimes faint and pitiful, sometimes long-drawn out and with a horrid note of pain.

Ellen was not quite fainting, but very near it. In Amabel herself, thought, energy, and feeling had narrowed to one single aim—to get upstairs, to get to her room, to get into the light. Once on the level, it was not so hard—about fifteen steps to the bedroom door. They managed it, and she guided Ellen to the bed.

There were candle and matches on the chest of drawers, she knew; but, before feeling for them, she tried the switch by the head of the bed. Instantly the light came on; the whole room showed at once—Miss Harriet's bureau; the great press which filled all the wall space opposite; the bed with poor Ellen sunk in a heap against the foot of it; and one thing more—in the middle of the floor a chair lying over on its side. Amabel looked beyond it, and saw what she had known that she would see. The connecting door between her room and Ellen's was shut.

When Ellen had recovered a little they brought in her mattress and bedding from the next room, and spent the rest of the night together, after locking both doors.

It was after breakfast next morning that Ellen presented a tearful ultimatum.

"If it was just a plain, ordinary ghost, I'd put up with it," she declared. "My Aunt Ellen that I was named for was 'ousekeeper in a real big 'ouse that 'ad an 'aunted wing. Many's the time that she've told me of it. A lady in 'er night-dress, with 'er 'air down 'er back, that one was—and never did no 'arm to nobody, pore young thing.

That's what I call a yuman ghost. 'Er name was Lady Sapphira, or Sophia, or some such. But as for these 'ere 'orrible 'owlings, and footsteps, and cats where there ain't none—it's not in nature, and you can't get from it. Oh, my dear ma'am, you won't stay, will you?"

Amabel turned rather a white face upon her old servant.

"I must stay, Ellen. But you needn't," she said.

Ellen produced a large and very neatly folded handkerchief with her name embroidered across one corner. She shook it out and buried her face in it. Through muffled sobs she could be heard protesting her willingness to "do anything in yuman power, only another night like last night is what I can't do, not for nobody, not even for you, ma'am."

"I won't ask you to," said Amabel. "You shall go back to the cottage. Miss Lee will be very glad to have you, I know."

The scene lasted a long time, prolonging itself, indeed, until the moment of Ellen's tearful departure. Amabel had to combat Ellen's own plan which was to have a room in the village and "come up every day and do for you, ma'am." Ellen could not see that this was likely to raise a new crop of stories about the Dower House. She wept, protested, argued, and then wept again. If Amabel felt a lonely sinking of the heart as she watched the cab disappear down the weed-grown drive, she felt also a certain relief. As it turned out of sight, a telegraph boy on a bicycle shaved past it, swerved, and came zig-zagging up the slope towards her.

She took the orange envelope with a little feeling of dismay. What could it be? Then with sudden relief she read, "Marmaduke has turned up here. Shall I keep him?" It was signed "Lee."

"Any answer, ma'am?"

"Yes," said Amabel. "Oh, yes."

She wrote, "Please keep Marmaduke," and watched the boy out of sight with a frowning gaze that did not really see him at all.

Marmaduke had turned up at the cottage which she had let to Miss Lee. Little Middle-bury was forty miles away! Marmaduke who lay down and growled if a walk lasted for more than half an hour!

She went back into the house, and sat with her head in her hands, thinking, thinking, thinking.

Chapter Nine

"LADY SUSAN BERKELEY," said Jenny at the door; and Amabel jumped up with a quick smile and her hands out. Lady Susan caught them in her own and pressed them warmly.

"Julian told me it was you—came in last night on purpose. My dear, how nice of you not to be a fat old lady. I don't know why we thought you were going to be, but we did; and I was simply groaning at having to call. Let me look at you. I asked Julian if you'd changed, and he said 'Go and see for yourself.'"

"What did he mean by that?" said Amabel, laughing.

"Couldn't say, I'm sure. I should have known you, anyhow. Personally, I don't think it's any compliment to a woman to say she looks the same at forty as she did at twenty It's either a downright lie, or else it means she's got the sort of face that don't show anything, chiefly because there isn't anything to show—no heart, no feelings, nothing of that sort. You're just as nice looking as you were; but you've grown."

"Well, yes, I suppose I have," said Amabel.

They fell to talking about old times; and in the end Lady Susan carried Amabel back to tea with her.

"Edward wants to see you," she said. "And Julian's coming in. He can take you home afterwards."

As they came out upon the road, two women passed with a large Airedale.

"The Bronson girl and her governess," said Lady Susan quickly. "I'd better introduce you."

She called "Angela!" The other two turned, waiting, and she put her hand on the girl's arm.

"I want you to meet Mrs. Grey—Mademoiselle Lemoine, Miss Bronson."

Angela Bronson was certainly too tall. In ten years' time she would be handsome, perhaps beautiful. She stood now, the picture of awkward embarrassment, obviously uncertain as to whether she ought to shake hands or not.

Mademoiselle Lemoine presented a very complete contrast. Wings of smooth black hair under a close black hat; a delicate fair skin; eyes between grey and green. Without being beautiful, she certainly put the handsome heiress in the shade; pose and manner were distinguished and assured. She acknowledged the introduction smilingly, and laid a hand on the Airedale's head as he pressed against her grey tweed skirt.

"You do not introduce Forester," she said, "and yet he is so much the most important of us three."

Amabel thought that she had never heard a Frenchwoman speak such good English—just the faintest suspicion of an accent and no more.

"Forester is last year's Crystal Palace Champion," said Lady Susan. They walked on, talking of dogs, until they came to the corner where their ways parted.

Later on, at tea, Lady Susan turned to Julian and said gravely, "I suppose you know that the name of Forsham has become famous. No, don't begin to look modest, because it's nothing to do with you." She gave her deep chuckle—"It's the Bronson girl's dogs— she breeds prize Airedales, and they're all Forsham something or other. Amabel and I met her with Forester just now. He's last year's Champion. And then there's Forsham Favourite, and Forsham Fantasy, and goodness knows how many more besides."

"Why not Bronson's Bloomer?" inquired Julian. "Why drag in the Forshams?"

Susan Berkeley chuckled again.

"I'll ask Angela, if you like," she said. "She's not a bad child really—just a little lacking in perception perhaps, but no vice. And, in case you know of anyone who wants a real good watch-dog, she's got two she wants to sell just short of show form and going cheap. I've seen one of them about with her—quite a nice dog. He is Forsham Fearless," she added with a twinkle.

"Thanks," said Julian, "one may want a dog; one never knows. Were you thinking of my lonely and unprotected state?" He turned to Amabel. "I meant to ask you before. Have you heard anything of your dog?"

Amabel did not look at him; she was cutting a piece of cake into little bits. Her manner was abstracted as she said:

"Oh, yes, he went home. I heard from Miss Lee this morning."

"Home!" said Julian. The word escaped him as a sharp exclamation.

Amabel did not raise her eyes.

"Yes," she said; and there was a little pause which Susan Berkeley filled with a question as to Julian's plans for the winter.

Presently, when they were walking home together, Julian broke the silence that had succeeded their good-byes with an abrupt, "What's the matter with you? You look horribly tired."

"Well, we didn't have a very good night," said Amabel.

"I knew that as soon as I saw you. What's been happening?" His shoulder just touched hers in the darkness. His voice sounded angry.

The heaviness at Amabel's heart lifted a little. Julian was angry for her. She felt warmed and cheered.

"Well, it's been rather horrid," she said. "Ellen and I had a dreadful night, and I've had to send her away. She couldn't have stood any more."

"What happened?" said Julian.

"There was that banging sound again at the front door, and a sort of whining. And I thought it might be Marmaduke, hurt in some trap, poor old boy. And I went down, though Ellen didn't want me to. She—she'd had a fright earlier in the evening, and she was very nervous, but she followed me down. And when I opened the door something rushed between us, and all the lights went out, and Ellen fainted." Amabel was a little breathless; the words came low and fast.

Julian slipped his hand through her arm, and felt it quiver.

"I don't know how I got her upstairs. It was pitch dark, and there was that horrible mewing which seemed to come from everywhere at once. Ellen could only just walk, and she kept crying and moaning. Julian, it was horrid."

"I'm sure it was. But—you say something rushed in when you opened the door. It must have been some stray cat."

"It—it wasn't a cat," said Amabel. "It touched my shoulder as it passed."

"It might have jumped."

"My shoulder and my knee, like a person brushing past. And the lights—Julian, what made the lights go out?"

Electric lights do not go out in the draught from an open door. This thought was in both their minds; but neither spoke.

At last Julian said, "Ellen's gone, you say?"

"Yes, I packed her off this afternoon. She didn't want to go, poor thing, but she couldn't have stood any more."

Julian's hand tightened on her arm.

"And you?"

Amabel laughed a little shakily.

"Oh, I'm all right. Telling you about it has done me good."

"It's not fit for you to be there by yourself. Let me take you back to the Berkeleys. Susan will put you up for the night."

"I've got to earn my two hundred pounds," said Amabel. "You forget that."

"Well, will you let me come up and camp out in the drawing-room? I should be within call, and—er, all that."

"I'm afraid it wouldn't do,' said Amabel regretfully.

"Why?"

"Well, Mrs. Grundy—"

"I thought Mrs. Grundy was dead."

"No, only left town for the country. I haven't lived in a village for fifteen years without acquiring a very high respect for her. You've no idea of how a village can talk."

"Why should anyone know?"

Amabel's head lifted a little. He felt the movement, and understood. He said, "Damn Mrs. Grundy!" under his breath, and they walked on in silence.

The air was still and heavy with damp, the lane wet and slippery under foot. On either side high banks made a black wall. After a while, Julian, who had been looking straight in front of him, turned a little.

"Are you going to have your dog back?" he asked.

Amabel hesitated.

"I don't think so. No, I don't think I shall have him back."

"Why?"

"I don't know." But she used the tone which means, "I don't think I want to say why."

"Why not?" said Julian again. "You ought to have a dog."

Amabel was silent. Julian's thought grew angrier. How obstinate women were, and how incalculable—floods of talk when they ought to hold their tongues, and this capacity for gentle, impenetrable silence when you wanted them to talk.

"Why don't you have him back?" he repeated, and felt her pull her arm away with a little jerk.

"I don't know. Julian, there's something most awfully queer about the whole thing."

"About your dog?"

"About Marmaduke. To start with, his going off like that—it worried me a lot. Why, he never leaves me at all. He hates the cold and the wet, and adores a fire; but if I'm gardening, for instance, he won't leave me, however horrible the weather is. He hates it like poison, but he won't go in. I wish he would, because he whines all the time, and it's most distracting; but he won't leave me. Yet—"

"Yes?"

"Yet he left me *and* a fire, and went off on a most horribly cold, wet day all by himself. And—and, Julian, my cottage is forty miles from here. I simply can't understand it. He couldn't have done it, he couldn't really."

"And why won't you have him back?"

"I don't know. I can't get it into words. I feel as if—as if something might happen; and it's all very well for me, but it doesn't seem quite fair to drag my poor old Marmaduke into it."

"You ought to have a dog," said Julian stubbornly.

They walked in silence till they came to the house.

"May I come in?" he said. "I want to look at something, if you don't mind."

She let herself in, and he followed her upstairs. When they were in the sitting-room and he had shut the door, he said,

"There used to be a telephone to the cottage; it was put in a year or two before my aunts died. Brownie's husband was the gardener then, and they liked to feel that they could send him off for the doctor or call Brownie up here if they weren't quite the thing. There were only women in the house."

"I haven't seen a telephone," said Amabel.

"It was working all right when George and I were here three years ago. It's just a private line to the cottage, you know. It used to be in the room opposite to this."

"I haven't seen it," said Amabel again.

She led the way across the passage to the room that she was occupying.

"It was there, by the window," said Julian. "They've moved the bureau in front of it." He crossed the room, shifted the bureau, and disclosed a speaking tube fixed in the wall, the receiver hanging limply from a cord. "Here you are," he said. "Now do you mind holding on here whilst I run down to the cottage? We'll just see if it's in working order. I expect the battery wants gingering up a bit. That's down my end, I know. Brownie used always to think it was going to blow up. She simply hated having it in her kitchen."

Amabel sat down to wait. It had cost her a good deal to refuse Julian's offer of camping out in the drawing-room. Dread of the night had been gathering about her steadily as the day wore on. If the telephone would work, it would be the next best thing to having Julian in the house; to feel that he was within call, to know that she could, at a moment's notice, come into touch with him, would be most extraordinarily assuaging and supporting. Her thoughts drifted as she sat and waited. Behind their changing flow there was still the pressure of an unchanging necessity. She had to earn George Forsham's two hundred pounds. Whatever happened, she had to stay on at the Dower House.

The telephone bell rang, suddenly, sharply. She started up, held the receiver to her ear, and heard Julian's voice say, "That you?" Her answer shook a little:

"Yes."

"It's working all right? You can hear me?"

"Yes, perfectly."

"All right. You've only to ring, and I can be with you in two minutes. Look here, I've got a job I want to do; and then, if I may, I'll just look in and see you for a moment. Mrs. Grundy won't mind that?"

Amabel laughed.

"Mrs. Grundy must be reasonable," she said.

Chapter Ten

ABOUT AN HOUR later the front door bell rang. Amabel heard Jenny pass through the hall; and then a step on the stairs that was not Jenny's.

She was prepared for Julian, but not for his companion. Julian wore an air of triumph. He had with him, on a lead, one of the largest Airedales that Amabel had ever seen.

"Forsham Fearless," he said. "Warranted free from vice, house-trained, and a perfect watch-dog. He's an out-size, isn't he? Too big for the show ring, I gather, but rather a nice beast."

"Julian, you haven't bought him!"

"She looks the gift-dog in the mouth. As a matter of fact, he's on approval." He touched the Airedale on the shoulder, and dropped the lead. "Go and speak to the lady."

Fearless came forward, his peat-brown eyes fixed gravely on Amabel. She said "Well, Fearless?"—and he snuffed her outstretched hand, and then slid his head under it with a funny sort of jerk.

"You are approved. Is he?" said Julian, smiling.

Amabel looked at him, her hand on the dog's head, a little mist before her eyes.

"Oh, Julian, he's a beauty! But you shouldn't—you really shouldn't."

Julian came forward.

"What does that mean? You wouldn't have me, so I was bound to find you a substitute."

"It means 'Thank you,'" said Amabel.

"I should keep him on the lead, you know—for the present, at any rate. And don't go a step without him. The Bronson girl says she's had him in her room, and he's no trouble—sleeps like a baby. Look here, what about your supper? Have you arranged with Jenny to bring it up, now Ellen's gone?"

"Oh, I'll get it myself. Jenny won't come up again once she's cleared the tea."

"Let me talk to her," said Julian grimly.

"No, don't. Please—I'd rather not. Besides she won't—she's frightened."

"And you?" His tone was rough.

"Oh, I'm frightened too; but then, you see, it's my supper."

It ended in their leaving Fearless shut into the sitting-room whilst they went down together into the kitchen, where they scrambled eggs, fried bacon, and made coffee. It was very pleasant and gay; and so was the informal meal upstairs which followed. Mrs. Grundy or no Mrs. Grundy, it is impossible to deny one's fellow-cook his supper. Fearless lay with his nose between his paws, and seemed to slumber; but the instant that Julian moved from his chair a brown eye opened and an ear twitched.

They carried down the tray, and Julian took his leave unwillingly.

"Keep Fearless with you, and call me up if you want me," he said as they parted at the front door.

Amabel nodded. He saw her face change.

"What is it?" he asked quickly.

She tried to smile.

"I'm stupid. It was the thought of last night. We were standing just like this, Ellen and I, when the door blew back on us and the lights went out."

"How do you mean the door blew back on you?"

"I'll show you." She put one hand on the catch, the other on the handle, and opened the door a bare three inches. "I meant just to see if it was Marmaduke, but the door was pushed back—I don't know how to describe it—I couldn't hold it."

"And the lights went out?"

"The lights went out." She was leaning against the wall now, looking at him with a serious, troubled gaze.

"You said Ellen had had a fright before. What was it?"

Amabel grew a little paler.

"She said something followed her up the stairs," she whispered, and then grew paler still. It came to her that she would have to lock the door on Julian and go up those stairs alone.

Julian's hand was on her arm.

"My dear girl, don't look like that. Go and get the dog. I'll wait here."

The quickness with which he had read her thought startled her. It was as if one of those many veils which separate us from our fellows had been torn away. She felt his eyes on her face, and could not meet them; they saw too much. And, if she looked, it might happen that she, too, would see something that she was not ready to see. The colour rose to the roots of her hair, and without a word she turned and ran upstairs. When she came back with Fearless, the veil was between them again; the intimate moment had passed.

They shook hands and said good-night. Then Amabel locked and bolted the door, and went back to the sitting-room, Fearless walking beside her in the most sedate and comfortable fashion.

At ten she went down again to take him for a run. The hall had lost its terrors. It was raining a little, but not cold. As they came in, she saw Jenny at the far end of the passage leading to the kitchen, and called out a cheerful good-night. Then she and Fearless went up to bed. Before putting out her light she surveyed the room. The great, dark press that filled the whole wall opposite the door gave it a gloomy look. Amabel remembered paying a visit as a child and being put to sleep in a room with just such another cupboard in it; it had haunted her childish dreams for years. If this room were really hers, she thought she would have bright-coloured curtains, yellow or orange, and a warm brown carpet instead of the cold washed-out chintzes and grey Axminster of Miss Harriet's bequeathing. To spend money in imagination is one of the harmless dissipations of the poor, and one which had often given Amabel a good deal of pleasure.

She locked the door which led through into Miss Georgina's room, and got into bed. The telephone and Fearless were really more satisfying companions than poor, gloomy Ellen.

Fearless had curled himself into a ball in front of the bureau, and was already asleep. Amabel's heart warmed to him. She put out the light, and fell asleep with grateful thoughts of Julian.

It was about two hours later that something woke her. Her eyes opened on the darkness, and, for a confused moment, though she was aware of sound—sound that had awakened her and still continued—, she did not know what sort of sound it was. Then it came to her that Fearless was growling, with a little whimper thrown in now and again. She heard the pad of his feet as he moved in the room, and she put out her hand and switched on the light. He just turned his head, and she saw his eyes, big and anxious. Then he was at the door, head cocked on one side, nose to the crack, snuffling and whining. Amabel sat up and spoke his name:

"Fearless, good boy, lie down."

Again that quick, anxious glance at her.

"Lie down, Fearless!"

But the whimpering increased, and he began to scratch at the door. Amabel got out of bed, flung her dressing-gown about her, came to the door, and stood there listening. At first she could hear nothing. The dog's excitement grew. She tried to hush him, and caught—or thought she caught—a distant sound impossible to define. It was not the thudding which had brought her downstairs before, but something else.

She put her hand on the Airedale's head, and strained to hear. It came again, like something moving, like something being dragged, something heavy—the whole sound so blurred that she could hardly catch it. But Fearless was becoming frantic and beyond her power to control; he was on his hind legs now, tearing at the door and uttering sharp yelps; every now and then he turned, licked Amabel's hand, caught at her dress, her wrist. She picked up the end of the lead, gave it a double turn round her hand, unlocked the door, opened it, and reached for the switch that controlled the passage lights. The dog's upward bound and furious rush forward brought her to her knees before she could touch it.

The high, strained wail of a cat rose up from the black hall. The lead was wrenched from her hand. She lost her balance completely and fell. Fearless was gone. She heard him go clattering down the stairs, and as she stumbled up and got the light turned on, the crying of the cat came again.

Amabel had a moment of indecision. She could go back into her room and lock herself in, or she could go forward to the stair-head and turn on the light in the hall. The moment lasted only long enough to draw a quick breath. "It must be a real cat—it must. And of course Fearless is crazy. I must get him back." She ran to the head of the stairs, and as she pressed the switch and saw the hall leap into light, there came to her ears the sudden, violent crash of breaking glass. She stood, her hand on the wall, and stared down.

The drawing-room door just opposite the foot of the stairs was wide open; the room showed dark beyond; and from that darkness there came the tinkling sound of falling glass. It ceased. No other sound came.

Amabel stood there without moving, her eyes on the open door. A very deep silence settled on the house. She tried to speak, to break it, to call to Fearless; but no sound would come; the stillness was unbroken; it was very cold, it was very, very cold. With one of the greatest efforts she had ever made in her life she withdrew her hand from the wall. She did not know how to turn and get back to her room, but she knew that she must turn and get back. If something were to come up the stairs behind her! The momentary panic passed into numbness; she could not turn, she could not move. She stood there for a long time, and there was never another sound at all. At last she drew a long breath, and went slowly, stiffly, back to her room. She left the lights burning, and locked her door, then turned, and stood wide-eyed and rigid.

There was the window on her right; the bureau pulled out a little with the telephone behind it; the dark press opposite. To the left, the table with the lamp upon it; the big, old-fashioned bed; and, beyond the bed-foot, the door into Miss Georgina's room.

And the door into Miss Georgina's room was open.

Chapter Eleven

JENNY BROUGHT UP a cup of tea in the morning, opened the curtains, set hot water. Amabel looked at her keenly.

"Did you hear anything last night, Jenny?" she asked.

"No, ma'am," said Jenny. "Did it blow, ma'am? Mother and me are heavy sleepers."

"I think," said Amabel, still looking at her, "I think there's a window broken somewhere. Have you been into the drawing-room yet?"

"No, ma'am," said Jenny. Then, by the door, she turned and said in her usual gentle, depressed manner, "Did you know as all the lights was on, up and down? They must have been on all night."

"Yes," said Amabel, "I'm afraid they were." Just as Jenny was disappearing she called her back. "Was the drawing-room door open as you came upstairs?"

Jenny stood on the threshold and drooped.

"Not that I took notice of," she said.

Amabel dressed, and came downstairs. The drawing-room door was shut. She opened it, and came into the half light of a curtained room. There was a mouldy smell, and something else—a fresh draught blowing; it stirred the heaviness which it could not lift.

Amabel crossed the floor and pulled back the heavy, brocaded curtains which had, perhaps, been new when Julian's mother was a bride. As she stepped forward to pull them, she trod on a piece of glass and felt it break. The light showed a gaping hole in the window about four feet from the floor, the whole pane splintered, the edges jagged and irregular; outside on the moss-grown gravel a litter of shivered fragments. She stood and looked for a moment, and then turned back into the room. There was another window at the far end. She drew this curtain also, then went to the door and shut it.

Ten minutes later she heard the sound of footsteps, saw Julian coming across the gravel, and heard him check and exclaim. She came up to the broken window, and they looked at one another across the debris.

Julian gave a long whistle.

"Hullo! What's this?" he said.

She told him dryly and briefly.

"Why didn't you ring up?"

"Nothing more happened."

He stirred the fragments of glass with his foot.

"I hope he hasn't cut himself to bits. He probably went straight home. I think I'll just go and find out." With no more than this he turned away.

Amabel felt a little depressed. She went slowly upstairs and had her breakfast. She was dusting the room when Julian returned, and he asked impatiently,

"Doesn't Jenny do that?" His tone astonished her a little.

"I've told Jenny that I'll do these two rooms if she'll do the cooking," she said. "I like house-work, you know. But—have you found Fearless?"

"Yes. He's all right—not a scratch. He must have gone straight home. Mademoiselle Lemoine heard him at the door, and let him in."

"Not a scratch!" said Amabel.

Julian stood over the fire.

"That's nothing. If he went for it bald-headed, he probably wouldn't be cut. I've seen a man push his fist through a pane of glass and never break the skin." He frowned as he spoke.

Amabel had scarcely to look at him to know that he was in a black bad temper. She looked, all the same, half indulgently. The boy of twenty years ago had frowned just like that when anger took him—mouth all on one straight line, and brows drawn hard together over eyes that seemed almost black.

He kicked a half-burned log, and said,

"If you ask my opinion, the whole thing is a lot of ado about nothing. What does it come to, when all's said and done?"

Amabel set down a china figure, and took up another. She suppressed a little desire to smile. Why on earth should Julian be angry like this? What babies men were!

"I don't know," she said sweetly. "Suppose you tell me—then we shall know just where we are."

He threw her a suspicious glance. Something in it set a spark to her temper too.

"In my opinion, it all comes to precious little. A stray cat gets in, or doesn't get in; but you hear it. Fearless hears it too, and naturally goes off his head with excitement."

"The drawing-room door was shut when I came upstairs," said Amabel.

"Then he pushed it open. He must have heard the cat outside and gone bang through the glass to get at it."

Amabel pressed her lips together. The little kindled spark danced in her eyes.

"When I came back to my room," she said slowly, "the door into the other room—your Aunt Georgina's room—was open. Do you suppose the cat opened it?"

"You probably left it open."

"I shut it; and I locked it before I went to bed. I can swear to that."

"Then the lock's defective. Will you let me have a look at it?"

"Certainly."

Odd how the antagonism seemed to be growing between them. It was as sudden a thing as last night's sympathy. Neither thought of calling it reaction.

Julian fiddled with the lock of the connecting door, turned and re-turned the key without getting any evidence to support his own theory. The lock appeared to be perfectly sound; when the key was turned the door remained shut in spite of any amount of shaking.

They went back into the sitting-room.

"You must have forgotten to lock it," was Julian's last word on the subject. Amabel let it pass in silence, and he burst out with:

"Well, will you have Fearless back? I told them I'd let them know if I wanted him."

"What did you tell them?" said Amabel.

"Just the truth—that he'd gone through one of the windows. Will you have him back?"

"No," said Amabel.

"Why not?" His tone was sharp.

She threw out her hand.

"What's the use? He was crazy—I couldn't control him. It would happen again; he wouldn't stay." She turned away from him, and leaned on the mantelpiece. "Marmaduke wouldn't stay either," she said very low.

"Fearless will stay all right if you chain him up."

She shook her head.

"It's no use." Then her tone changed; it was not Amabel who spoke, but Mrs. Grey, a charming stranger. "You have been most kind. Please do not trouble yourself any further. I shall be quite all right."

Julian was aware that he was being snubbed, a fact which did not improve his temper. He experienced a very strong desire to quarrel openly and violently with Mrs. Grey who had snubbed him. Civilization deprives one of these solaces. He therefore made his farewells, and had reached the door, when he heard his name. He half turned, and saw that Mrs. Grey had disappeared; it was Amabel who was saying, "Julian, don't quarrel. That was horrid of me." There were tears in her eyes. He came back.

"Julian, there's something I didn't tell you. I think I ought to. I think you ought to know."

"What is it?"

"Fearless didn't break that glass."

"What?"

"Fearless didn't break that glass at all."

"What on earth do you mean?"

She put her hand on his arm.

"Come downstairs. Come into the drawing-room, and I'll show you."

There was surprise and excitement in the air. They ran down the stairs, and Julian tried the shut drawing-room door with his shoulder. The latch held firm. If Fearless had opened it last night, it must have been already ajar. They came into the room, which was just as Amabel had left it. She shut the door carefully behind her, and led the way to the big, deep sofa which stood facing the empty hearth. There were cushions on it of faded brocade, one pink, one green, one blue, the colours fast merging into indeterminate grey. The blue cushion was nearest, propped against the sofa corner. Amabel lifted it gingerly, turned it over, pointed.

The silk on the under side was ripped and burst. A long needle-like splinter of glass hung entangled amongst the shreds.

Chapter Twelve

THEY STOOD in silence and looked at the splinter of glass. Neither of them spoke; there seemed to be nothing to say. After the first few moments of stupefaction Julian turned, looked from the sofa to the window, and from the window to the sofa. He whistled softly, and looked again. The distance was about fifteen feet. He touched the splinter, frowning deeply, but not this time in anger.

"You found this?"

She nodded.

"How?"

"There was a tiny flake of glass on the floor just here, a few inches from the sofa." She touched the place with the point of her shoe. "I saw it shine. Then I looked about, and found another little bit on the sofa. After that I took up this cushion to shake it, and saw what I've just shown you. I put it back again carefully so as not to disturb the glass. I wanted you to see for yourself."

There was another long silence. Then Julian said,

"Look here, I want to think. I'll go for a tramp, and come back this afternoon. I was a brute just now—regular black dog. I don't know why. You're not angry, are you?"

She shook her head, smiling, and they came into the hall together. Julian halted there.

"I think I'd like to see Jenny," he said. "Do you mind?"

"No. Where will you see her? I'm going out—I've got to get some things in the village. Shall I send her upstairs?"

"No," said Julian, "I'll find her. I want to see Brownie too. She'll be hurt if I don't.'

They parted at the foot of the stairs, and Julian went along the kitchen passage.

"Jenny was in the kitchen, bending over the large, old-fashioned range.

"Morning, Jenny," he said, and she straightened up and faced him, very white, in a colourless lilac print, her eyes startled, her reddish hair rather ruffled.

"I'm not a ghost, Jenny," said Julian of design.

She said, "Oh, no, sir," and came forward to the table. Julian took a seat on the corner of it.

"You look just as startled as if I were," he said teasingly.

"Oh, no, sir," said Jenny again.

Julian let his foot swing, watched it swinging, and then with a sudden, sharp turn asked:

"What's all this about your not going upstairs after you've cleared the tea? That's something new, isn't it? Why on earth don't you take Mrs. Grey's supper up to her?"

"Ellen took it." Jenny was a little breathless. She didn't look at him; but he looked at her.

"Well, Ellen's gone. I suppose you'll take it up to her now."

Jenny took hold of the edge of the table drooped, shook her head.

"Why not?"

No answer. Julian just touched the hand that held the edge of the table. It was cold enough.

"Come, Jenny, why not?" he repeated.

Jenny shook her head again. He saw her eyelids moisten and a tear run down her cheek. He swung himself off the table, and came round it until he was standing beside her.

"Come, Jenny, what's your reason? I suppose you've got one. Mrs. Grey says she thinks you're frightened to come upstairs at night. Is she right? Is that your reason? Has anything ever frightened you in this house, Jenny?"

Jenny began to draw quick, sobbing breaths. The tears ran down freely.

"Oh, Mr. Julian," she said. "Oh, Mr. Julian, don't ask me."

"Has anything frightened you? Have you seen anything? Have you seen anything upstairs that frightened you?"

Jenny let go of the table, and hid her face in her hands.

"Mr. Julian—oh, please, Mr. Julian!"

He laid his hand on her shoulder. She was trembling all over like a nervous animal.

"What did you see, Jenny?" he said, bending nearer, and felt her pull away from him.

"Oh, Mr. Julian, Mr. Julian!"

"What did you see, Jenny?"

She was sobbing violently now.

"Oh, you won't tell Mother? Oh, Mr. Julian, it 'ud kill Mother, It 'ud kill Mother for sure."

"Jenny, what *did* you see?"

"It was Annie." The words were just a trembling breath, scarcely to be distinguished as articulate sound, "It was Annie as I saw."

Julian took her kindly by the arm.

"My dear girl, don't be so upset. Just tell me about it. You'll feel better when you've told someone. Where did you see her?"

"In Miss Georgina's room. It was dark, and I hadn't thought to put the lights on."

"And how did you see?"

"I'd my candle in my hand—and I come past Miss Georgina's room—I saw Annie."

"Where?"

Jenny trembled.

"The door was half open, and I saw her face."

"Only her face?"

"Looking at me," whispered Jenny. "Oh, Mr. Julian, you won't tell Mother? She were looking at me, and I knew it come for a sign. Oh, you'll please not tell Mother, or for sure I'll lose her too."

Julian was very gentle with her. He patted her shoulder, promised discretion, and changed the subject.

"Did you hear a cat last night, Jenny? That dog went off after one, and I wondered whether you heard it."

"No," said Jenny, wiping her eyes, "not to take any notice of, I didn't. Mrs. Grey was asking me too, and I told her that we never had a cat in the house because of Mother. You remember, Mr. Julian, how she comes all over queer if there's a cat in the room—so we never have one. Of course they come into the garden now and again. Father used to say they tore up his flower beds something cruel."

Julian went in to see his old nurse before he left the house. He found her in her neat room, with everything in apple-pie order—a geranium in the window, a bright little fire on the hearth, and her hands folded on a large, clean pocket handkerchief. She was very pleased to see him, and said so.

"And to see you alone, my dear," she added with a glance over her shoulder. "The other times you came here there was Jenny in and out. And there's things I want to say, and things I want to ask you, Master Julian."

Julian sat down by the bed, and patted her hand.

"All right, Brownie," he said. "Go ahead."

"It was to ask you if there was any news—if you had found anything—about Annie," she whispered.

Julian shook his head.

"I'm afraid not, Brownie dear," he said.

There was a pause.

When Annie Brown had disappeared a dozen years before, he had done his best to trace her. Long ago he had given up hope of gathering anything that would comfort the heart-broken mother. Yet, whenever he returned to Forsham, the same question was asked, the same answer given. Mrs. Brown's lips were quivering. Her eyes filled with tears that did not fall.

"Twelve years is a long time," she said.

After a moment Julian got up.

"Have you got a photograph of her anywhere?" he asked. "There used to be one on the mantelpiece, I thought."

"Jenny took it away," said Mrs. Brown. "She thought it set me grieving, and she took it away."

"Haven't you another?"

Mrs. Brown glanced over her shoulder again; then she beckoned him nearer, and, still without speaking, put her hand under her pillow and produced a worn, old-fashioned Bible. She fluttered the leaves a little nervously until they opened upon a lock of hair and a faded photograph. Julian bent nearer to look, and saw a snapshot which he himself had taken—Annie and Jenny gathering apples, a loaded basket between them, both faces turned to the camera. For the moment he was not sure which was which, and Mrs. Brown seemed to read his thought, for she pointed with a trembling finger.

"Like as two peas they was then, but Annie always quicker and prettier—more alive-like than Jenny," she said; and then, as a step sounded in the passage, she shut the book in a flurry and pushed it under the pillow again.

Chapter Thirteen

AMABEL MET the postman on the door-step, and turned back into the hall to read her letters. There were three—one from Daphne, one from Miss Lee, one from her sister Agatha.

Two of the letters dropped unheeded whilst she tore open Daphne's envelope and read the hurried scrawl that had been posted at Marseilles.

"It's *heavenly*," Daphne wrote, "simply heavenly. I do *adore* travelling. And it's hot, really hot, and I'd nearly forgotten what it was like to be hot. Jimmy was *frightfully* pleased to see me. He joined us here, and we're going on in his yacht. Isn't it simply too scrumptious for words? If this weather lasts, we shall cruise about a bit." There was more in the same strain—Jimmy and the yacht; a halcyon, sapphire sea, and cloudless skies; youth and pleasure. There were two postscripts: "I want another hank of white silk to finish my jumper. I will put in a pattern. Please match it *very* carefully, because there are five shades of white, and they always try and give you the wrong one." Amabel looked the letter over, shook it, looked inside the envelope. There was no pattern. She turned to the second postscript: "Please send me some of my nail polish—I forgot it. It's the sort you hate and always say smells of prussic acid. *Don't get any other sort.*" There followed a childish row of kisses. Amabel smiled at them, and felt her eyes blur. After a while she picked up the other letters and read them. Miss Lee first:

"The weather is really—" Amabel skipped the weather.

"The kitchen chimney—" She skipped the chimney too with an impatient, "Well, I *told* her it smoked in an east wind."

"Marmaduke"—yes, this was what she wanted to hear—"Marmaduke turned up here this morning. We found him when we opened the front door. I have wired to ask you if you want him back. He seemed rather tired, but he is quite well. About the kitchen chimney—"Amabel very nearly used an un-Victorian expression caught from Daphne. "Isn't that Clotilda Lee all over? As if I cared about the wretched chimney! And she hasn't even the sense to say whether Marmaduke is footsore or not." She tore the letter up. "If he'd really run forty miles, his feet would have been raw. Rather tired indeed!"

She opened Agatha's letter, and found it short and to the point:

"How are you getting on? Would you like to have me for the week-end? If so, wire, and I'll come down on Saturday afternoon. Cyril's away and I'm at a loose end."

Amabel considered the question of Agatha for the week-end. It might do rather well. It would placate Mrs. Grundy, and—it would be nice to have Agatha; there was, after all something solid about Agatha. She gathered up her letters and set out for the village.

The post office was also the general shop. It had over the door in rickety letters the name G. Moorshed. Against the right-hand wall there leaned a black-board upon which might be read such pieces of information as "Onions are plentiful," "Lard is cheap to-day," "Lodger wanted single lady or gent." Inside one might buy ready-made trousers for men, infants' comforters, soap, bacon, candles, and cheese; also peppermint bull's-eyes and pork chops.

Amabel looked around her, and was shaken by a spasm of inward laughter as she thought of Daphne's commissions. She sent her telegram to Agatha. She then bought three common paraffin lamps with tin reflectors, a drum of oil, and three stout iron bolts. The oil and the lamps were to be sent up before dark; the bolts she took away in her pocket together with a handful of screws done up in the blue paper which had come off a packet of candles.

She walked home. The world seemed a good deal brighter than it had been in the morning. The row of crooked kisses had been very fortifying—and it would be nice to have Agatha. Never before had a visit from Agatha presented so pleasant a prospect.

When Julian appeared at tea-time, he found her in very good spirits, and firm in her refusal to have Fearless back.

"I wish your sister were coming to-night," he said. The concern in his voice pleased her, though she laughed it away.

"I was foolish and strung up this morning. I feel quite different about it all now, I do really. I think I was getting rather intense. After all, as you said, the whole thing was probably due to a stray cat—and I got fussed. I'm rather ashamed of myself. I'm going to turn over a new leaf and start fresh."

There was no response from Julian. He stood by the hearth, looking gravely into the fire.

"Go down to the Berkeleys for to-night," he said, and frowned at her "No, I'd rather not."

"I wish you'd give the whole thing up and go home." This was after a pause of some minutes' duration.

"Thank you," said Amabel. "My house is let, and I haven't got a home to go to."

Julian relapsed into thought.

"Will you let me come and sleep here tomorrow night?" he said after a while.

"Yes, of course."

When he was going he asked again:

"You're sure you won't go to the Berkeleys?"

"Quite sure. I've been putting bolts on the doors, and I shall simply bolt myself in and refuse to open my door whatever happens."

"Where have you put the bolts?"

"On this door,"—she pointed to her bedroom—"and the one through into your Aunt Georgina's room. I'll see if I can't make it stay shut to-night." A little shiver crept over her, and she laughed to drive it away.

Julian seemed loth to go.

"I see you've put oil lamps in this passage and the hall," he said.

"Yes, I want light, and electric light is too expensive to keep on all the time. Besides, it seems to have a trick of going out at the critical moment, so I thought I'd try these. They're hideous but useful."

Julian said good-night, and then turned back again.

"You'll call me up if you want anything?"

"Yes, I will, really; but I shan't need to; I'm going to sleep."

Amabel watched him down the stair and heard the front door close behind him. Then she went back into the sitting-room and read Daphne's letter again.

Chapter Fourteen

AMABEL'S PROPHECY was fulfilled. She went to bed at ten, leaving an oil lamp burning in the passage, and a second one turned down low in the corner of her room. She bolted both doors, and slept from the moment that her head touched the pillow until Jenny's knock woke her.

"Please, ma'am, Ellen's here," said Jenny, putting down the cup of tea which she had been carrying at rather a dangerous angle.

"What!" said Amabel.

"Please, ma'am, Ellen's here," said Jenny, obviously flustered. And, before she could say more, Ellen herself pushed past her into the room—Ellen in workaday attire, hatless and gloveless.

"Ellen!" gasped Amabel.

With a lofty air, Ellen waved Jenny from the room and shut the door. She then came close up to the bed and observed in a low, thrilling voice:

"Sooner than 'ave it on my conscience, I come back."

"But when? How?"

Just for a moment it seemed to Amabel as if some mysterious agency were picking up her dogs and her maids, and just dropping them again promiscuously.

"Sooner than 'ave it on my conscience, I come back last night," said Ellen in still deeper and more thrilling tones. She paused, and a look of pride overspread her features. "*Lodger wanted single lady or gent,*" she added.

"Look here, Ellen," said Amabel, "begin at the beginning. I can't keep my head when you start at the end. When did you come?"

"Last night I come," said Ellen with some offence. "Miss Lee being suited, and a widow with a child is what I wouldn't take into my 'ouse, though I know there's many that does it nowadays—"

"Do you mean that Miss Lee wouldn't keep you?"

Ellen tossed her head.

"Glad and thankful she'd be to keep me, and gladder and thankfuller she'll be before she's anyways through with that widow woman and her child, which Gwendoline is a name I 'ates."

"Was the child's name Gwendoline?"

"Victorier Gwendoline," said Ellen gloomily, "and as much at 'ome as you please. So when my conscience says to me 'Why did you leave 'er? Why did you go and leave 'er, Ellen?' I takes it as a sign. I thinks to myself 'None of your bare-faced brats for me. I'll 'ave a room in the village, and come up and do for you, ma'am.' *Lodger wanted single lady or gent*—it struck my eye when I was a-driving to the station, and I come back last night and took it." She paused for breath, caught Amabel's hand in both of hers, and changed her tone. "Oh, my dear ma'am, I couldn't leave you, really." A tear dropped on the eiderdown.

Agatha Moreland arrived by the three o'clock train. Amabel met her, and they drove up together in the mouldy cab. On the bridge they passed Julian, walking. Mrs. Moreland, who had been leaning out to look at the Millers' bungalow, exclaimed:

"Who's the frightfully good-looking man?"

Amabel glanced out of the other window.

"Mr. Forsham."

"Any relation of Julian Forsham?"

"It is Julian Forsham," said Amabel.

"Do you know him?"

"Of course I do. I'm living in his brother's house." She paused and added, "Julian is coming to stay for the week-end."

"With you?" Agatha's surprise was rather amusing.

"With *us*," said Amabel, laughing a little. She thought it better to continue after a while with, "He's an old friend, you know. Both he and the Berkeleys were here when I was here before. It's very nice to meet them all again."

Once they had arrived at the house, Agatha's own concerns were too much to the fore to admit of an undue curiosity about Amabel's. She made no confidences, but talked incessantly, and with a scarcely veiled uneasiness, about her husband. Cyril liked this, and Cyril liked that, and Cyril thought it was a mistake to do the other, and so on, and so forth. It transpired that amongst the things which Cyril liked were race-meetings and night clubs. "And I do loathe races—so horribly cold and draughty, the weather always simply beyond words—, and of course I don't dance."

Amabel suppressed a smile because of the real trouble underlying this rather self-evident statement. Agatha Moreland was a handsome and imposing person, with a figure built on rigidly massive lines. She was five years older than Amabel, and looked fifteen, in spite, or perhaps because of, beautifully tinted golden hair.

Amongst the things of which Cyril disapproved was what he termed the bourgeois habit of husband and wife paying visits together; hence his absence and Agatha's week-end with her sister.

Julian came up to dinner—a meal shared by Agatha could never be supper. He found Amabel alone, and was glad to get a few words with her.

"I wanted to ask what your sister knows about the house and your tenancy."

"Oh, nothing," said Amabel quickly, "nothing at all, except that I was offered the house on very favourable terms and was glad of the opportunity of seeing some old friends."

Mrs. Moreland came in before there was time for more. She wore a jetted tea-gown, black but magnificent; and, like most fair women of ample proportions, appeared at her best rather décolletée. "Agatha always makes me feel as if I had been ironed out flat," Amabel once told Daphne. She had rather that feeling now. There was so much of Agatha—hair, pearls, shoulders—and assurance of manner.

They waited on themselves, and the meal was a friendly one. When they had cleared away, Julian opened Miss Georgina's piano.

"It's been kept in order, I know," he said. "I was thinking this afternoon that perhaps you would play on it—you used to."

"I hardly ever play now. Nobody does unless they're frightfully good."

"Are you fond of music, Mr. Forsham?" asked Agatha.

"I don't know," said Julian. "I hate concerts, and people doing things frightfully well—it's all so public and unreposeful. I like the sort of music my mother used to make in the firelight—I always think firelight and music go together."

He turned to Amabel and said, "Please," and, rather as if he took her answer for granted, he turned out all the lights except the one by the piano.

Amabel sat down and played old scraps of songs, old fragments of dance music, a piece of a nocturne, Scotch and Irish melodies, just as they came. She had a pretty touch, and, though she did not know it, she made a pleasant picture with the light falling on her through a soft yellow shade.

As a log fell and the flame leaped on the hearth, Agatha caught a glimpse of Julian's face. He was looking at Amabel, and it was this look which arrested her attention. In the course of her prosperous life Agatha had been a good deal deferred to, admired, and courted; but no man had ever worn quite that look for her—the look that sees the woman and the ideal, and sees them as one. It was a look at once unmistakable and revealing.

Agatha Moreland felt an odd pang of envy. Her thoughts went to the man of whom she was not sure. She forgot Julian Forsham altogether. If Agatha forgot Julian, Julian had certainly forgotten Agatha. The shabby room was full of the enchantment of home, an enchantment at once simple and potent—not the Book of Verses underneath the Bough—not the far land and the unclouding sun, but England and the drip of rain from the eaves. The room he had known from boyhood; the old melodies; and the glow of wood-ash on the open hearth—these things were romance. He had certainly forgotten Agatha, for he said,

"You've played—now sing. Sing the thing that you sang the night before you went away. I've never heard anyone sing it since."

Amabel did not speak. She touched a note or two softly. It did not come into her mind how much it would confess if she sang the song that he had not named. It was part of a memory which had never grown old. She sang Brahms' Cradle Song softly and just as she might have sung it to a sleepy child—as she had often sung it to Daphne:

"With the dawn, if God will, thou shalt waken to joy."

The words sounded a second time, and died away. Amabel was thinking of Daphne now, of Daphne wakening to joy. Nothing mattered—everything was worth while if it meant happiness for Daphne.

Later on that evening, Agatha came into her sister's room, handsome and mountainous in pale blue satin and white fur. She leaned on the foot of the bed.

Amabel put down Daphne's letter. She had not been exactly reading it, for she knew it by heart.

"I told you I'd heard from Daphne."

"Yes," said Agatha firmly. "Once at the station, twice in the cab, and about two dozen times since."

"Nonsense, Agatha!" But Amabel coloured and laughed.

"Daphne is all right," said Agatha Moreland. "I haven't come in here to talk about Daphne, who is about the luckiest girl I know. Jimmy Malleson has taken this trip simply and solely on her account. I happen to know that he really means business; and he'll be a son-in-law after your own heart."

"You're sure?"

"Absolutely. But, as I said, I've not come in here to talk about Daphne." She put her elbows on the rail of the bed, clasped her hands under her chin, and looked meaningly at Amabel. "I've come in here to talk about you. I want to know all about Julian Forsham."

Amabel felt at a serious disadvantage. It is very difficult to be dignified in bed.

"*Who's Who* will tell you." She told herself furiously that she ought to have outgrown blushing years ago.

"*Who's Who*? Fiddlesticks!" said Agatha. "As if I cared a threepenny bit about Hittite tombs and Chaldæan thingumabobs! What I want to know is, is he the old romance come to life again?—the man you turned down to marry Ethan? I never knew his name. Was it Julian Forsham?"

Amabel's head lifted. Really, Agatha could be very ill-bred.

"We're very old friends," she began.

Mrs. Moreland laughed aloud.

"Good gracious, Amy, how Victorian you are! Anyone can see that the man's in love with you." She stopped there because of what she saw in her sister's face.

"Agatha! Really!" Her voice was not quite steady.

All at once Agatha sighed heavily.

"Well, my dear, it's your affair," she said, "and I won't butt in. At any rate, you'll have the satisfaction of being *sure* that it's you he wants and not your money—*sure*," she repeated. She stood up straight and looked aside. "You don't know what it is not to be sure. You'll never know—and you may thank God for it. No, please don't say anything. I'm a fool; but you're safe." She pressed a handkerchief to her face for a moment and went quickly to the door; but, just as she reached it, she turned, came back again, and spoke, her voice amazingly softened:

"I really only wanted to say that I'd be very glad if it was Julian Forsham. You—you haven't had much of a show up to now. That's all."

When she was gone, Amabel lay for a long time, thinking. The fact, patent to all the world except Agatha, that Cyril Moreland—described by Daphne as "that little worm"—had married her in order to be comfortably provided for for life, had now begun to dawn upon Agatha herself. Poor Agatha!

Just on the edge of sleep, Amabel remembered that she had not bolted the door between the two rooms. She hesitated; then got out of bed and shot the bolt.

Chapter Fifteen

"How DID you sleep?" said Julian in the morning.

"Perfectly. So did Agatha. And you?"

"Oh, I never moved—but then I never do."

They walked up to Forsham Old House in the afternoon.

"A special tea-party in your honour," suggested Julian.

"Or in yours. Are you prepared to be lionized?"

"No, I'm safe in Forsham. Nobody bothers about the lion when they've known him from a cub."

"Mr. Bronson didn't know you when you were a cub. Has he changed the house much?"

"I should think he had."

"How?"

"I shan't tell you. I want to see how it strikes you."

When they came into the drawing-room Amabel found it striking enough. She remembered it very stiff, with polished tables and gilded mirrors, the whole effect rather colourless except for an atrocious crimson carpet. To come into it now was like entering a black and white engraving. She had never been in a room at all like it. The floor was black, dull black, with here and there on its large expanse some very dark-toned Persian rug. The walls were white. There were no mirrors. The three long windows that looked upon the terrace were hung from ceiling to floor with draperies of inky violet. The Adam mantelpiece held three exquisite pieces of black Wedgwood. There was one very fine engraving on each wall. The sofas and chairs were covered in some lustreless black stuff.

Amabel wondered very much whose choice these things had been. Not Angela Bronson's, she thought as she shook hands with her. Angela, in the roughest of tweed skirts and the most staring of jade-green jumpers, looked a good deal out of place against this mausoleum-like background. Mademoiselle Lemoine, on the other hand, fitted into it as if it had been designed for her—perhaps it had. Amabel was human, and the thought certainly sprang into her mind, though she dismissed it. Mademoiselle was in black like the room, black of a singular and expensive elegance. Seen without a hat, she gained from the contrast between a very white skin and the black hair, satin-smooth, which swathed her head like a tight turban, quite hiding her ears. An odd type, and attractive; yet Amabel was conscious of preferring Angela.

She was very pleased to see the Berkeleys come in. The Millers followed; he fair and indeterminate looking, she very large and untidy, with a friendly smile. Lady Susan annexed her immediately, and they appeared to pass without effort into a highly technical argument on the proper preparation of rosebeds; at intervals such words as basic slag, bone-meal, and kainit reached the outer world. Nita King came in late, and fastened upon Edward Berkeley. She was all smiles and fluffy black frills, her hair as red as burning wood. She wore a string of very large sham pearls.

Amabel found herself beside her host, and rather at a loss for a subject. He asked her again how she liked the Dower House; and when she said that she liked it very much, he had the same air of surprise which she had noticed on the occasion of his call.

"You don't find it damp?"

"The ground floor rooms are rather damp, but I am not using them."

"Every house ought to have proper cellars," said Mr. Bronson. "And you are really quite comfortable? Other tenants have not stayed as long as you."

"No?" said Amabel.

"No," said Mr. Bronson.

She broke the silence by admiring the engraving on the opposite wall, and was amazed at the sudden change in the man's face.

"You like engravings? Do you understand them at all? They are my hobby. I have a portfolio over here which might interest you—if you care for such things."

"I don't understand them, I'm afraid; but I like them."

He nodded, crossed the room, and came back with a large portfolio.

"I have them out one at a time," he explained. "I won't put more than one on each wall—it spoils them. That's something we had to learn from Japan." He dropped his voice. "You've no idea what the room was like—the crowd!"

Amabel dropped her voice too.

"I remember it." She felt like a detected conspirator as Julian and Mr. Miller joined them.

Mr. Miller pointed at the engraving on Amabel's knee. The subject was a wood—black pine trees with straight stems in endless perspective.

"I saw the fellow of that in Paris the other day," he said. "Fleury has it."

"Have you just been in Paris?" Amabel asked the question quite idly.

"I got back yesterday."

"And how's Paris?" said Julian as idly as Amabel.

"A little fussed," said Mr. Miller—he stooped and pointed again, "Just look at that shadow. You can't get the depth by the photographic process—This bank-note business, it's fussing them a good deal. There's an absolute flood of forged notes, and they can't stop it. And it's hitting their credit, besides making no end of a feeling of unrest everywhere. Talk about engraving—the man who did that job must be pretty useful!"

Mr. Bronson nodded.

"I'd like to meet him," he said. "But what beats me, is how they've managed the water-mark."

There was a little crash of china, a woman's sharp exclamation; and then apologies and protestations.

"So stupid of me, so careless! Your lovely china! And Angela's—"

"It doesn't matter a bit. It really doesn't matter."

Three women were standing at the tea table, and it was the middle one of the three, Miss Miller, who had dropped her cup.

It lay, rather hopelessly broken, in the midst of a puddle of tea on the dull black floor. Nita King, on one side, bent to pick up the fragments, whilst Mademoiselle Lemoine, on the other, echoed Angela's assurance that it didn't matter at all.

Chapter Sixteen

THERE WAS A little changing of seats after that, and Julian, after supplying Miss Miller with a fresh cup of tea, found that he was expected to take a vacant chair between Mrs. King and Miss Lemoine.

"Tell me," said Nita King, "do tell me, Mr. Forsham, how does one forge a bank-note?"

"I haven't an idea," said Julian. "You must find a really competent forger, and get him to explain exactly how he does it."

She looked up at him through her eyelashes.

"You're laughing at me. People always do—I can't think why. I heard you talking about forged notes, and I did so want to know how it was done. You know, I never can understand why it's wrong to do it. It always seems to me that everybody gets into trouble because there isn't enough money. Just look at the things in the papers about unemployment, and trade depression, and there not being enough to go round anywhere. And it seems to me that if you can make more money, why, there'll be more to go round and everybody will be better off. Yes, I knew you'd laugh at me if I said that, because I said it to Mr. Bronson and he laughed. But, really and truly, I do think that your mysterious forger is a public benefactor, and I can't see why anybody should try and stop him."

"He's not my mysterious forger," said Julian.

Mrs. King came a little nearer, and assumed a confidential whisper:

"Mr. Forsham, I've been simply dying to ask you what you think of your old home. It must be so strange for you to come here and find it all quite different. This room, for instance—do you really *like* it?"

"Well,—it's impressive," said Julian.

Nita King shivered, came nearer still, and dropped her voice to a thread.

"It's like a *tomb*. But then I'm a sensitive—I feel these things directly. Are you psychic?"

"I hope not," said Julian. "I've never shown any signs of it. But you know, you're the last person who ought to complain of this room; it's simply made for a red-haired woman."

He had a wicked desire to see whether Susan Berkeley had misjudged the lady or not, and was rewarded by a distinctly flirtatious glance.

"My poor hair that so many people dislike!" sighed Nita.

"Soul-less beings! I adore red hair."

"Do you really, Mr. Forsham?"

"Passionately!" declared Julian. "I always have; I always shall."

Mrs. King looked up and then down again; and a curious thing happened. Something in the look, something in the angle at which the movement presented her features, brought another red-haired woman to his mind. The impression was gone in a moment, but it had been quite startlingly vivid. Jenny and Nita King—no, not Jenny—Annie. The likeness was to Annie, to the snapshot he had seen yesterday in Brownie's Bible. "It's the type. All red-haired women are alike," he said to himself. But the malicious desire to tease Mrs. King had departed. He got up, gave his place to Agatha Moreland, and took a chair on the other side of Miss Lemoine.

He found her very easy to talk to. She had read his first book, and spoke with real insight and interest of the problems it had raised. To his surprise, Julian found himself talking to her as if they were old friends.

Nita King was finding plenty to say to Mrs. Moreland. She began by glancing across the room at Amabel and observing in her sweetest tones, "I *do* admire your sister," and hardly waited for Agatha's non-committal murmur before she went on eagerly. "I mean her courage. I think it's so wonderful."

Agatha's expression here faithfully reproduced her inward thoughts. "My good woman, I haven't the faintest idea what you mean," was what she was too polite to say in so many words.

"I think she's too wonderful," Nita continued. She clasped her hands, and gazed at Agatha very much as she had gazed at Julian.

"Why?" said Agatha a little brusquely.

"Of course, I know everyone's not so sensitive as I am. I'm really *too* psychic. I feel these things at once—pressing upon one, you know, from beyond the veil."

"And why is Amabel wonderful?"

"My dear Mrs. Moreland, you don't mean to say that you don't know!"

"Know what?"

"The Dower House," said Nita in a thrilling whisper. "Yes, haunted. Oh, I hope I haven't been indiscreet."

"No, Amabel didn't tell me. I expect she thought I'd be nervous. As a matter of fact, these things interest me enormously."

Nita nodded. "I *know*," she said. "I could feel it. I think one always knows. There's a perfectly marvellous medium that I go to in London—simply *wonderful*—, and I shall never forget her saying to me the very first time I went to see her, 'You are psychic—a true sensitive.' One knows at once." She paused, and Agatha inquired:

"What's the matter with the Dower House? Amabel seems quite comfortable there."

"Oh, don't *ask* me. I'm afraid I've said too much already, but I'd no idea that you didn't know. Of course, if I was Mrs. Grey, I'd try and get right to the bottom of it. I should get Mrs. Thompson to come down and have a séance. She's so marvellous—Mrs. Thompson, I mean. Why, a friend of mine went to her a few weeks ago because she was most awfully unhappy about her husband—she wanted to divorce him, you know, and she couldn't be sure or get enough evidence. And Mrs. Thompson just looked in the crystal for her, and told her the whole story from beginning to end. It was wonderful, and, as Jacynth said, much, *much* cheaper than having a detective—because Mrs. Thompson's fee is only two guineas, and detectives run you in for goodness knows what. And then another friend, Muriel Weston, she went to her when she lost her pearl necklace, and—oh, really she's wonderful. If you're interested in those sort of things, you ought to go and see her—you really ought. *Do* let me give you her address."

Mrs. Moreland hesitated. There was no harm in having the address—she needn't go and see the woman. She said, "Thank you. It might interest a friend of mine." She put the address away carefully in her bag, and found that Nita King was addressing her as Mrs. Moorland. She corrected her, and Nita exclaimed,

"Any relation of Cyril Moreland's? Not his wife! How strange! Why, I used to know him ever so well."

It was just as they were all going that Mrs. King advanced upon Julian with an autograph book. It was heart-shaped, bound in pale blue suède, and bore upon it in silver lettering the words, My Friends' Names.

When he had signed the book with as good a grace as possible, of course everyone else had to sign it too—the Berkeleys; the Millers; Angela; Mrs. Moreland; Amabel; and Mademoiselle Lemoine.

"What a lot of A's," said Nita. "I don't think I know what they all stand for." She ran her finger down the page: "Angela; and Miss Miller is Anne—or is it Anna; and you are Amabel; and your sister?"

"Agatha. We have very old-fashioned names, I'm afraid."

"And I'm A too, because Nita is only short for Anita."

"So is Mademoiselle an A," said Angela in her loud, clear voice—she pointed at the last name on the page—"only she's cheated, and put just M. She is really M. A."

"And what does her A stand for?"

"Guess!" said Angela with rather a boisterous laugh. "You won't though, so I'll have to tell you. It's Anastasie—Marie Anastasie. Now, I'm sure you'd never have guessed that."

There was a little laughter. Mademoiselle Lemoine stood by, smiling faintly, but with a hint of constraint. Julian thought her distressed at Angela's loudness.

"And what is Mr. Miller's F?" said Nita gaily. "Come, Mr. Miller, confess. Is it Frederick, or Fergus, or—I can't think of any other F's except Philip, and that's not one really."

"It is Ferdinand," said Mr. Miller. He touched his sister on the arm. "Come, Anne, we must be going."

In the middle of their walk home Edward Berkeley surprised his wife by asking:

"What was that thing that Amabel was wearing under her coat? A lot of women wear them now, and I suppose I ought to know what they are called."

"It was a yellow jumper," said Susan Berkeley. "She knitted it herself."

"It was a very pleasing colour—rather like the old rose on the north wall, the one my mother was so fond of—I'm afraid I've forgotten the name."

"It's a Gloire de Dijon."

"Yes," said Edward, "that's it. My mother used to call them Glories. It's a very pleasing colour. I remember, Susan, that you had a dress of that shade when we were engaged. When I was looking at Amabel this afternoon I remembered that it suited you very well. It is a colour that I am fond of. You don't ever wear it now."

"My dear Edward, you forget that I haven't got Amabel's complexion."

"No, no, of course not," said Edward innocently, "and you are older, some years older. Amabel is a very charming person—don't you think so, my dear?"

"Oh, yes," said Susan Berkeley.

"Yes, I thought a good deal about Amabel this afternoon. I felt sorry for her." He put his hand inside his wife's arm and patted it. "We're so happy. It makes one sorry for all the other people."

Half-way down the lane that led to the bungalow Mr. Miller said sharply to his sister, "One of those two women pushed you. Which was it?"

"Ferdinand, when?"

"At tea, when you dropped your cup. Mademoiselle was on one side of you, and Mrs. King on the other. One of them pushed you. Which was it?"

Anne Miller's voice sounded distressed,

"Oh, Ferdinand, it sounds so stupid, but I really don't know."

"You don't know?"

"No, I really don't. I was thinking about the front of the herbaceous border—and then something seemed to push against me, and I dropped my cup. It was dreadfully careless."

Mr. Miller heaved a sigh of resignation. "You'd be a lot more use to me if you weren't half asleep all the time," he said.

Chapter Seventeen

"I DIDN'T KNOW you'd got a haunted house on your hands, my dear." Agatha was very comfortable in a chair before the fire; her tone was lazy.

"Who told you I had?" said Amabel. "No, I needn't ask—I saw Mrs. King talking to you at the Bronsons'."

"King—is that her name? I didn't catch it. Everyone seemed to be calling her Nita."

"What did she say?" Amabel was sitting on the floor, her elbow on the fender-stool, her chin propped in her hand. She looked quite self-possessed and amused.

"Oh, not very much. She thought I knew, and she seemed to think you deserved a V.C. for staying here." She paused, then asked, "Is there anything wrong with the house?"

"It has stood empty for a good many years."

"But is there anything really wrong with it? If there is, I must say I think you ought to have told me."

"You see, I know how strong-minded you are," said Amabel, laughing.

"Well, I hate weak-kneed people," said Agatha. "You know—the sort that are afraid of everything. But you haven't told me anything. Is there really a ghost?"

"I haven't seen one," said Amabel cheerfully.

"My dear Amy, how horribly secretive you are. I shall ask Julian Forsham—I can see that I had better get accustomed to calling him Julian."

Amabel flushed, and was angry with herself. Mrs. Moreland was still laughing at her, when the door opened and Julian came in. She turned to him at once.

"Mr. Forsham, we've been talking about this delightful old house of yours."

"It's not mine, it's my brother's."

"It's the same thing. I mean you'll know all about it. Do tell me, is it very old?"

"The original house was, but there isn't much of it left. There was a fire in my great-grandfather's time."

"And which are the old bits?"

"This room—and the room I'm in—the two bedrooms opposite— the hall and kitchen—I think those are all part of the old house. I know the dining-room and drawing-room are new."

"Is that why there are no cellars?" said Amabel. "Mr. Bronson was saying that it was odd that an old house like this shouldn't have proper cellars. They generally do, don't they? And of course the ground floor would be drier if there were cellars under it."

"Oh, there are cellars all right," said Julian. "They haven't been used for years—not safe, or something. I remember that George and I got into a fearful row for going into them and playing treasure-hunts. I think they only use the two under the kitchen now."

"When you came in," said Agatha, "I was asking Amy if the house was haunted."

"And why did you ask that?"

She laughed her comfortable laugh.

"Well, I *might* say that it looked as if it were, or felt as if it were; but I'll be honest and admit that Mrs. King put the idea into my head."

"My dear Mrs. Moreland, if you start believing what Mrs. King says, you'll have a busy time in front of you. She told me that it was so nice of people to issue forged notes, because it made more money for all the poor people who hadn't got enough."

They all laughed.

"No, but about the house—is it haunted? You see, I am dreadfully pertinacious; but these things do interest me. Is it?"

"I don't know," said Julian. He had dropped his light tone.

Agatha was sufficiently woman of the world to be aware that she had come up against a blank wall. She turned gracefully aside and changed the subject.

That night Amabel certainly bolted the door that led from her bedroom into the corridor; but she was never afterwards quite sure about the door between her room and Agatha's. She thought that she had bolted it, but the memory was a hazy one, and not to be depended on. She slept well, and when Jenny called her she went into Agatha's room to say good-morning. The door was certainly not bolted then. She looked at it with a little, puzzled frown as she turned the handle.

"I wish you weren't going, Agatha. It's been very nice having you."

"Get someone else—you'd really better. The occasion demands a chaperone. Oh, Amy, I do love to see you blush! None of the girls can do it nowadays, and there's no doubt it's quite becoming. Anyhow, I'd stay; but I'm dining with the Amberleys to-morrow, and doing a theatre with Hilda Langton to-night. She's only up for a couple of days, or I'd put her off. I don't know when Cyril will be back." Her brow clouded, and she looked away. "Of course, he's got simply heaps of friends, and there's no earthly reason why he should give them up just because he's married."

Amabel said nothing. There seemed to be nothing to say. She took Agatha's cup, set it down, and prepared to go. She was half-way to the door, when Agatha said,

"That maid of yours is an odd bird, Amy."

"Who? Ellen?" Amabel half turned, ready to smile at something quaint that Ellen had said or done.

Mrs. Moreland shook her head, its golden waves as miraculous as ever.

"No, not Ellen. That poor run-in-the-wash sort of creature who belongs to the house—I forget her name."

"Jenny. What has she been doing?"

"Well, I thought it odd of her to come walking through here in the middle of the night."

"Jenny! In the middle of the night!"

"I don't know what time it was—I didn't look. I always have a night-light, you know; I can't sleep in the dark. And when I woke up and saw your door open, of course I thought it was you, and that you wanted something."

If Amabel put her hand on the connecting door, it was partly to steady herself.

"This door, Agatha?"

"Yes, that door. It opened, and, to my surprise, I saw that Jenny creature."

"Agatha, you dreamt it."

"Not a bit of it. She came in a little way and drew back again; then she shut the door and I went to sleep. What was she doing in your room? Had you called her?"

Amabel shook her head.

"No," she said. "No. Perhaps—perhaps she was walking in her sleep. What was she dressed in?"

"I don't know—her black afternoon dress, I think, but no apron."

Amabel made an effort, and forced a laugh.

"It's very odd of her. I'll ask her about it. Did you bolt your door last night?"

"Yes, I did."

"And was it bolted this morning?"

"Yes, I had to get out of bed to let Jenny in when she came with the tea."

"Then she didn't go out that way," said Amabel.

"Little glimpses of the obvious!" said Mrs. Moreland, laughing.

Amabel went into her own room and shut the door. She found Ellen waiting for her—an Ellen very anxious to be of service, to get out her things, to brush her hair, and above all else to talk.

Amabel said "Yes, Ellen," and "No, Ellen" at intervals; but all the while, in her own mind, she was wrestling with Agatha's story.

If Agatha had found her door bolted in the morning, Jenny could not have gone out that way. ("Little glimpses of the obvious, my dear Amy!") But her own door had been bolted too. She, too, had had to get up and let Jenny in. She remembered as a strange thing that Jenny never *had* used the connecting door when she came with the tea, but always went round by the passage. If Jenny had really been in her room last night, how and when had she left it?

She said aloud, "Yes, my old, grey tweed skirt, please," and heard Ellen conclude something that she had been saying with a fluttered. "And I knew as 'ow you would be pleased."

"I'm so sorry. I was thinking about something else. What am I to be pleased about?"

"There's no *call* to be pleased." There was subtle offence in Ellen's tone.

"Oh, Ellen, don't be silly. I'll be pleased as soon as I know what to be pleased about; but you'll have to tell me what it is."

"It takes the 'eart out of anything," said Ellen gloomily. "But, since you wish for to know, I'm not one to keep things back, nor yet to crawl and spy like some that I could name—and not a 'undred miles from 'ere neither—, which is a thing I can't abide and don't 'old with. Red 'air and crawlingness I 'ates with all 'atred."

"Ellen, really!" said Amabel. "I don't seem to know what you're talking about. Do you mind explaining?"

"That there Jenny," said Ellen. She stripped the bed with a vicious jerk and nearly upset a chair. "As Mrs. Moorshed says to me: 'Mark my words,' she says, 'that there Jenny is one of the crawlingest'—and, being my own cousin, I should 'ope that she wouldn't deceive me."

"Ellen *dear*! You know you're not explaining—not really. Is Mrs. Moorshed Jenny's cousin?"

Ellen tossed her head and sniffed.

"She wouldn't demean 'erself," she said. "Come of real good people, she does, same as I do myself—and a cousin of my own as it turns out, which is what I was telling you, and what I thought as you'd be pleased to 'ear."

"Oh, but I am. I'm very pleased. Did you know she was a cousin?"

"I know'd that a cousin of my father's was married to a Moorshed, and I won't deny as the name struck me when I went in about the lodging. So after supper last night I says to 'er, 'What might your grandmother's Christian name 'ave been?' and when she looks funny, then I know'd where I were. 'Was it Pistles?' I arst—and sure enough Pistles it were."

"Pistles?" said Amabel faintly. "Ellen, what *do* you mean?"

"Matthew Mark Luke John Acts and Pistles," said Ellen very rapidly. "Acts and Pistles was a twin of girls—the others was boys," she added.

"Ellen *dear*!"

"Pistles was 'er grandmother right enough, and own niece to my great-grandfather, which I thought as 'ow you'd be pleased."

"I think it's very nice for you," said Amabel.

"That's as may be," said Ellen with dignity. She folded Amabel's nightdress, and said,

"What's wrong with this 'ouse is just plain Browns, neither more nor less. And if Mrs. Moorshed *is* my cousin, she's got as much sense as others, I should 'ope."

Amabel felt a certain sense of fatigue.

"Look here, Ellen, don't quarrel with Jenny, there's an angel. She's rather a poor thing, but there's no harm in her, I'm sure."

"Least sure of, soonest mended," said Ellen.

Chapter Eighteen

MRS. MORELAND departed by an afternoon train. After seeing her off Amabel walked home through the damp lanes. The ruin of the hedgerows was now almost complete. Brambles still flaunted a tattered rag or two of finery, striking a note of gold or scarlet, and there were berries of all sorts and hues from green to crimson. Everything was sodden with wet, and the smell of rotting leaves hung in the air.

As she crossed the bridge she met Mr. Miller. Rather to her surprise, he stopped and entered into a desultory conversation. When it was evident that she did not wish to be kept, he turned and began to walk beside her in the direction of the Dower House.

"It is fortunate that I met you, because I really had a message to give to Lady Susan from my sister, and I had quite forgotten it," he explained; and then, "Is your sister making a long stay?"

"I've just been seeing her off."

Mr. Miller turned pale, vague eyes upon her. "Dear me, I'm sorry for that. It must be rather lonely for you at the Dower House."

"I'm used to being alone," said Amabel.

"Yes? But all the same, it is not very good for one to be alone. In the day-time it is all very well—one has one's occupations, one goes out, one sees one's friends—but in the long, dark evenings, when one is quite alone and the house is still, one is apt, I think, to fancy things; one sits by the fire and hears footsteps that are not there—especially in an old house like the Dower House."

Amabel had an impulse towards resentment. It leapt in her, and then died before something of melancholy kindness in the man's voice and manner. She laughed a little, and said,

"You speak like someone who is accustomed to living in a town."

"Do I?" said Mr. Miller. "Well, perhaps. I have lived in towns most of my life. I couldn't stand the country, in winter at any rate, if I didn't go away so much. I came here on my sister's account, you know."

Just before they parted at Amabel's gate he asked the question which she had begun to expect.

"And you are really comfortable at the Dower House?"

"Oh, yes. Why shouldn't I be?"

"I don't know. People don't seem to stay there. It is said to be haunted."

"Yes, that's what everyone says, but so far nobody has been able to tell me who is supposed to haunt it."

"No," said Mr. Miller dreamily. "No, I've noticed that too."

Amabel turned into the drive, and was out of sight almost immediately.

Mr. Miller walked as far as the corner, and then turned back. It is to be supposed that he had again forgotten his sister's message to Lady Susan. Anyone who had overheard his conversation with Anne Miller the evening before would have been struck at the contrast between his manner then and his manner this afternoon. Ferdinand Miller talking to his sister had had a sharp, matter-of-fact way with him. Ferdinand Miller walking in the lane with Mrs. Grey had seemed a gently dreamy person, amiable and rather absent-minded.

Amabel came upstairs and found Ellen in coat and hat preparing, as usual, to depart before dusk.

"And I don't like leaving you alone, ma'am," she said, fidgeting in the doorway whilst Amabel took off her hat and changed her shoes.

"Oh, Ellen, don't *gloom*!" said Amabel with a little impatience.

"Me going 'ome to my tea in a comfortable 'ouse where there wouldn't be room for a ghost if such *was* to be the case—the Moorshed boys being three in a room as it is, and me in what you might call a bit taken off of the droring-room."

"I shouldn't have thought there was room for a drawing-room."

"A droring-room was what Eliza Moorshed was brought up to," said Ellen with dignity, "and a droring-room she would 'ave in whatever 'ouse she was in. She've got it lovely too—I will say that for her—with a plush suite, and the best Brussels, and her Aunt Arabella's stuffed birds on the mantelpiece."

"Well, that's very nice. I'm glad you're so comfortable."

Ellen sniffed vigorously.

"Me going 'ome to me comforts, and you staying 'ere all by your lone self—oh, my dear ma'am, I can't a-bear it. I'd stay, but what's the use of my staying? There's things you can bear, and there's things you can't bear, and this 'ouse at night is just what I can't a-bear, and no blame to me neither, for it's not in yuman nature."

"But, Ellen, I don't want you to stop, I don't really. And I do wish you'd cheer up and not be so dreadfully depressing. You know"—she laughed teasingly—"this morning you said that there was nothing the matter with the house but the Browns. Well, I like the Browns, so there's nothing to worry about, is there?"

"There's many a thing we says in the morning that we don't 'old with at night," said Ellen with the air of one making a Scriptural pronouncement. "Browns I may 'ave said in the morning, and Browns I may 'ave felt in the morning, seeing that that red-'aired Jenny must needs take it on 'erself to twite me with my sleeping out when I come to-day. 'We're all still 'ere,' she says when I come in; 'we're all still living,' she says—and 'I 'ope you slept well at Mrs. Moorshed's,' she says—the red-haired upstartness of her!"

"My poor Ellen, what did you say?"

Ellen drew herself up.

"I says, 'Miss Brown, I was brought up a lady'—and I come upstairs."

Amabel did not dare to laugh. She bent and re-buttoned a shoe.

"Well, Ellen, you ought to be going; it's getting dark. And you needn't worry about me, because I really do think we let ourselves be frightened by a stray cat. The house has been as quiet as possible the last three nights."

"And so it would be," said Ellen. "So it would be so long as Mr. Julian Forsham was in it. Why I'd stay 'ere 'appy and sleep like a hinfant if 'e was going to be in the 'ouse tonight. It stands to reason there wouldn't be nothing 'appening with Mr. Julian 'ere."

"What do you mean, Ellen? Why won't anything happen with Mr. Forsham in the house?"

Ellen tossed her head.

"Why should it?" she inquired.

"Well, I don't know—why shouldn't it?"

A superior smile crossed Ellen's face.

"Those that 'aunts this 'ouse won't 'aunt it when there's Forshams in it—it stands to reason they won't. 'Why,' says Eliza Moorshed to me last night, 'can anyone say as ever there was 'air, 'ide, or 'oof of a ghost whilst there was Forshams at the Dower House? It stands to reason,' she says, 'that ghosts don't 'aunt unless they *wants* something. And plain as a pike-staff it is,' she says, 'that they wants the Forshams back, and the more the Forshams don't come the spitefuller they gets,'—though by all that's said it isn't Mr. George Forsham that anyone wants to see back. It's Mr. Julian as they love, ma'am."

She turned to go, and then asked with an innocent assumption of carelessness:

"You didn't meet Mr. Julian or anyone whilst you was out, did you, ma'am?"

"I met Mr. Miller."

Amabel put a little distance into her tone. Ellen was obviously disappointed.

"They do say as 'e's a German," she said with a relapse into gloom—"not much liked 'e isn't."

"Poor Mr. Miller, why not?"

"Very sharp in 'is ways," said Ellen, "and always a-coming and a-going to foreign parts—and to my mind there's always something double-faced about folks that their own country's not good enough for. I says to Eliza Moorshed last night, 'If we'd been meant to 'ave lived in foreign parts, we'd ha' been born foreign.'"

"Perhaps he *was* born foreign," said Amabel, laughing. "Do run along, Ellen, or it will be quite dark—and then you'll say I kept you."

Ellen glanced at the window, and a change came over her. It was a subdued and humble person who said,

"If you would just come as far as the door with me, ma'am. It's that 'all that I 'ates."

Amabel went to the front door with her.

Chapter Nineteen

The house felt very empty as Amabel went upstairs. She got her three oil lamps and lighted them, putting one in the lower hall, one in the passage, and one in her bedroom. The one in the passage stood on a small table between the two bedroom doors. All three lamps gave quite a good light. She noticed that the wicks were nice and level, with no uneven jags.

The telephone bell rang just as she was wondering why Jenny was late with the tea. She put the receiver to her ear, and heard Julian say, "Is that you?"

She said, "Yes—Amabel," and then had the feeling that, said like that, the name had a very intimate sound. There was no one to see her quick change of colour, and she was glad of it.

"Are you all right?"

"Yes, quite all right." There was a pause. She was not sure whether Julian was still there or not until she heard him say, with just a trace of hesitation, "I did rather want to see you."

Amabel laughed.

"You've done nothing but see me,"

Another pause.

"Well, I wanted to talk to you. We've never really had a talk since that broken window business—I couldn't very well discuss it in front of your sister."

"No."

"Well, I do want to talk to you."

"I believe you really want to be asked to tea. Is that it?"

"May I?"

"Yes, of course."

Tea was ready when Julian arrived. They talked of trifles until Jenny had taken away the tray. Then Julian leaned forward in his chair and said, "Well?"

"It's for me to say 'Well?'"

She had taken up some knitting. The needles clicked gently to and fro.

"All right, I'll lead off. To begin with, I agree with you that Fearless didn't break the window. Somebody broke it with the sofa cushion, and Fearless may, or may not, have gone through the hole afterwards."

"Oh, he must have done that."

Julian made a quick gesture with his hand.

"Unless somebody let him out by the door."

"Do you think that they did?"

"I don't know. Well, that's that. It comes to this—there is somebody who is playing tricks."

"Yes, but who?"

"Well, we agreed not to suspect poor old Brownie, and Ellen was away when the window was broken; so that leaves in the house at the time only yourself and Jenny. I suppose it wasn't you, so—we come back to Jenny. Are we equally sure that it wasn't Jenny?"

"Julian, I can't think it." She laid down her work, and looked at him in soft-eyed distress. "Besides, what possible motive—"

"Oh, as to that, the motive would be plain enough—to get you out of the house."

"I can't believe it—unless—"

"What?"

"Unless—well, do you know, I've wondered if she walks in her sleep."

"What made you think of that?" He was very intent.

"I thought of it this morning because Agatha would have it that Jenny came into her room in the night."

"How? When? Tell me exactly."

She told him, adding, "What puzzles me is the bolted doors. Otherwise I should be sure that it was just Jenny walking in her sleep."

"And if it wasn't Jenny?"

"I—don't—know," said Amabel.

Julian did not speak. He was remembering Jenny's sobbed-out story: "I seen Annie—I seen her in Miss Georgina's room." He weighed the question of whether to tell Amabel—then thought of the lonely night in front of her, and held his tongue.

"I shouldn't wonder if you hadn't hit the right nail on the head. It's an idea, anyway. Of course," he went on in a lighter tone, "what we really ought to do is to take all the people in the neighbourhood and pick out the most unlikely one. That is what is always done in the best detective fiction."

"I should think that the most unlikely one would be Susan Berkeley," said Amabel. She smiled and showed her dimple. "I'd love to see Susan being a ghost."

"Well, I think I should vote for Edward," said Julian, "or old Bronson, or that harmless little beggar, Miller. That's the worst of a place like this—everyone is the most unlikely person; you couldn't put your hands on a likely one to save your life."

"The village wouldn't consider Mr. Miller an unlikely person," said Amabel.

"Miller!"

"Yes, poor Mr. Miller. Ellen tells me that they don't like him because he goes to foreign parts."

Julian laughed.

"How like the village! But if that damns Miller, it damns me deeper still."

"Oh, but they love you," said Amabel quickly.

"Did Ellen say that too?"

"She did."

"But they don't love Miller?"

"No. You see, his name is Ferdinand. Mrs. King, I'm sure, thinks that very suspicious."

"Poor Miller," said Julian. He got up. "Look here, Amabel, I want you to give Fearless another trial—not in your room this time, but chained at the top of the stairs where he could stop anyone going up or down. If he raises Cain, let him. And,—and if you did happen to want him, he'd be handy. Only I don't think I'd let him off the chain this time. If he does behave as if there were somebody about, I think you'd better call me up. I want to get at the bottom of all this."

"Very well," said Amabel. The idea of having Fearless with her for the night was not altogether unpleasant. When Julian had gone, the prospect of companionship became even pleasanter; the house was so very still, and so very empty.

Julian walked up to Forsham Old House, and asked for Miss Bronson. He was shown into what had been his mother's morning-room, and found it less changed than the drawing-room. The linen chair-covers with their bunches of lilac and wistaria were the natural descendants of the shiny rose-patterned chintzes of his schoolboy days. The walls were pale grey, it is true, instead of being festooned with flowery garlands; but the room had an obvious air of being lived in and used, and was without any touch of the macabre. There was a bright fire burning, chrysanthemums in pots near the window, and a huge bowl of Russian violets on the low table that held also a woman's work-basket.

He was still looking about him, when the door opened and Mademoiselle Lemoine came in.

"Angela is away for a day or two," she said, "She has gone to London. Did you especially want to see her?"

"Oh, no. I only came about Fearless. I should like to give him another trial, if I may."

Miss Lemoine moved a little nearer to the fire. She laid a pretty hand upon the mantelpiece, and warmed a pretty foot. Seen thus, in profile, she appeared almost beautiful; there was so much of grace, so much of the charm of severe and simple line.

"Ah, I'm sorry," she said. The "r's" trilled faintly.

"For me, or for Fearless?"

She just lifted her eyes.

"For you, evidently, since you must go away without what you came for."

"What? Can't I have him?"

She shook her head very slightly, and made no other reply.

"And am I allowed to ask why?"—Julian was rather intrigued.

"One may always ask, Mr. Forsham,"—again that trill of the "r." She had so little accent in a general way that he found himself watching for it with a certain sense of fascination. He smiled and said,

"Well, then, I will ask why I may not have Fearless."

Miss Lemoine's manner changed. The hint of coquetry went out of it—the subtle something which reminded him that he was a man, and she an attractive woman. She looked, and spoke seriously, frankly.

"I'm really sorry, Mr. Forsham, because I know that it is for Mrs. Grey that you want Fearless; and it is not right at all that she should be in that house alone. So I am sorry that Fearless is gone."

"Gone!" he exclaimed sharply.

"Yes. Angela had an offer for him, and I am afraid that I urged her to take it. Since that night when he broke your window and ran away, Fearless has not been at all himself. One would have said, 'Impossible that this should be Fearless. It must be another dog.'"

"How?"

She spread out both her hands.

"How to describe it? So quiet, so frightened—he will not prick his ears; he will not wag his tail; he has a look of melancholy that goes to one's heart. And I say to Angela, 'Better take this offer, and send him away. In a new place he will be distracted, he will forget.'"

Julian glanced at her rather quizzically.

"And what do you suppose he has to forget?" he asked.

Miss Lemoine made another gesture.

"How can I tell you? If I even say what I think, perhaps you will be offended."

He shook his head.

"No. Please tell me what you think."

"Well,"—she gave him again that profile view, looking down and away from him—"I have thought that something frightened him there in that house. I do not talk about 'sensitives' as Mrs. King does,"—there was a spice of malice here—"but I say that animals sometimes see things that we do not see, and hear things that we do not hear. And they are dumb; they cannot tell us. I think that Fearless has seen something in that old house of yours, Mr. Forsham. Perhaps I am wrong—that is my thought."

Julian looked into the fire, his face without expression.

"Well, he's gone, and I can't have him," he said at last. "I'm sorry, but it can't be helped. There isn't another dog that I could have, I suppose?"

"I'm afraid not."

"I thought Lady Susan spoke of two. I mean she thought that there were two to be disposed of."

Miss Lemoine shook her head again.

"No, none that Angela would part with." She looked full at him, and he saw that her eyes were hazel, very dark hazel. "A dog is a good friend, is he not? Men—one cannot make friends with them. They misunderstand—always they misunderstand, and wish to play the lover." Julian had the feeling that those hazel eyes were asking him some question, their gaze was so direct, so insistent. She paused, sighed, and said in quite a low voice,

"A dog is the safer friend."

Julian came away with his mind in rather a disturbed state. He found Miss Lemoine both interesting and unusual.

At the Dower House gate he hesitated, but presently turned up the side path to the gardener's cottage. It was in darkness. He lit up, and went to the telephone.

Chapter Twenty

AMABEL HEARD the bell ring sharply, and put down her book. As she took up the receiver the thought just passed through her mind that it was pleasant to know beforehand what voice she was going to hear. The sense of pleasure faded, however, when Julian said,

"Look here, I couldn't get Fearless; they've sold him."

She tried to keep the disappointment out of her voice.

"That seems rather sudden."

"Yes, it's a bit of a muddle. But Angela Bronson's away and, you see, my first deal was entirely with her—Miss Lemoine wasn't there—, and I expect there's been some misunderstanding. Anyhow, the dog is sold, and there's an end of it. But I'm sorry about you."

"That's nice of you. But I'm all right."

A pause.

"I'll come up in the morning," Julian said at last, and rang off.

The evening passed, not exactly slowly, but rather drearily. Amabel had made a new arrangement about her supper. At half-past seven she rang the bell, and went downstairs to fetch the tray which Jenny had ready for her. When she had finished, she put the tray on the table in the passage for Jenny to take down in the morning.

She sat by the fire with a book when supper was over, and Mr. Miller's words kept sliding into her thoughts: "You sit by the fire, and you hear footsteps that are not there."

The house was very still; but twice the stillness was broken by that sound of light footsteps. Jenny, of course, moving about downstairs. She turned a page, and forced her mind to follow the words. They remained words to her, separate words with no connecting thought to string them together. On other nights there had been a hundred sounds—the wind in the chimneys; the pattering of the rain; the unkempt ivy buffeting the window pane; the faint scuttering of mice. To-night there were none of these sounds. The house was very still. It was like the hush before a storm.

Amabel threw down her book, and stood up.

"If you're going to be this sort of fool, you'd better go home," she said. "After all those years at the cottage! You're behaving exactly like Ellen!"

She went to the piano and opened it. She played the old waltz tunes which are not really forgotten, though nobody dances to them now—*Estudiantina, Doktrinen, Eldorado, The Blue Danube, The River of Years*—

"Stay, Steersman, oh, stay thy course,
Down the River of Years,

Turn, turn to the far off Time,
Free from sorrow and tears."

Miss Georgina had hummed the words in a sweet, cracked voice as her fingers beat out the melody, not on this piano, but on the Broadwood grand in the drawing-room downstairs. The scene came back like the little coloured picture that one sees on the screen of a camera—the polished floor stripped of its carpet; the old-fashioned chandelier hanging down in the middle of the room, with all its candles lighted and all its lustres gleaming; old Miss Harriet in her best China crêpe shawl with the little worked roses on it; Susan and Edward; Joan Berkeley and George—George Forsham had had a lordly fancy for Joan in those days; herself and Julian.

"Stay, Steersman, oh, stay thy course,
Down the River of Years."

She closed the piano, went back to the fire, and stood there, looking down at the glowing bed into which it had settled. There was a log almost charred through. She touched it with her foot, and saw it break into tiny blue and golden flames. The fire, too, was full of pictures—the Julian of long ago with his beautiful boy's face and the look of eager worship in his eyes; Julian, the man, offering friendship, loyalty, service. The flames died, and the glowing embers faded. With a start Amabel realized that it was growing late. The evening had passed quickly after all. "Old friends make good company," she said to herself.

She opened the door, and switched off the light. The room fell into darkness behind her. Standing on the threshold, she had, on her right, the stairs which began their rather sharp descent a couple of yards away; on her left, the door of the room which Julian had occupied; immediately opposite, the other two bedroom doors, with a small table placed between them, and an oil lamp burning on the table. A narrower passage ran on past the stair-head to the bathroom and other bedrooms which were over the dining-room and drawing-room.

Amabel's first thought as she came out of the sitting-room was that the lamp was not burning properly; the flame had a feeble look, and the passage seemed dark. She glanced involuntarily to her right to see how the light in the lower hall was burning. As she looked, she took a step forward and turned. The hall was as dim as the passage. But there was something more than that—there was something strange about the dimness. It was as if there were a mist rising—a thick, white mist such as one sees spread over water-meadows at dusk.

Amabel came to the head of the stairs and looked down, puzzled and frowning. The hall was full of mist—mist or smoke. The last thought startled her out of the puzzled frame of mind in which she had looked at this strange dusk. Smoke—where could it be coming from? It must be smoke; and yet there was no smell of fire, but rather the soft, damp smell that comes from wet, rotting, undergrowth. Yet it must be smoke. Impossible that mist should rise like this in an inhabited house—quite, quite impossible. Jenny must have let something catch in the kitchen—she might have been burning greasy paper or—or anything—(there was no smell of fire, no smell of burning, only the soft breath of a rising mist).

Amabel's hand closed hard on the pomegranate which crowned the newel-post. The whiteness, the smoke—it must be smoke was rising softly and steadily. Impossible to go to bed and lock one's door, with who knew what of smothered burning ready to break out in the house below. She took hold of her courage, steadied herself, and forced coherent thought. If she were to run down the stairs without stopping to look or think, a very short spurt would take her as far as the Browns' door. Once there, she would, at any rate, be near some other human presence; and if she knocked, Jenny could not fail to open. Then she would get Jenny to come into the kitchen, and they could find out what was causing the smoke (it must be smoke).

The mist had reached the picture of Julian's great-uncle which hung on the panelling midway between the dining-room and drawing-room doors. Across the mist, his eyes seemed to look at Amabel—queer, malicious eyes, too light for the dark, thin face. The mist came up to his chin. Below, on the hall table, the lamp showed faintly with a nimbus round it like a street lamp in a fog.

Amabel took her hand off the pomegranate and ran quickly down the stairs. The mist met her half-way. She ran, reached the bottom, turned to the right.

It wasn't smoke. It couldn't be smoke. It was heavy and damp to breathe, and it pressed upon her eyes. It wasn't smoke.

She reached the Browns' door, and clung to the handle, her head against the panel, her breath coming in quick gasps. And, as she leaned there, she heard Jenny's voice within—Jenny reading aloud, the words flowing smooth and evenly. Here and there one came to her—words from a psalm. Then old Mrs. Brown's voice, nearer than Jenny's, every word distinct: "Thank you, my girl, we'll be getting to sleep. You're a good girl, Jenny."

Amabel lifted her hand and knocked hard upon the door—and knocked again. She felt as if she were drowning—so hard to breathe, so hard to think. She heard a chair pushed back, steps crossing the floor. A key was turned, and a bolt withdrawn. The door opened a very little way, and she pushed at it, only to feel it held against her. At that feeling of human resistance, Amabel's self-control returned. She straightened herself and said, "It is I, Jenny,—Mrs. Grey." And with that, the door opened widely, and she stepped into the room.

Mrs. Brown turned anxious eyes upon her. "Is anything wrong?" she asked.

Amabel drew a long breath. The room was so clean, so comfortable, so cheerful. There were two lighted candles on the mantelshelf, with a big pink shell between them, and a row of photographs behind the shell. The fire had been raked out. Mrs. Brown's eiderdown was folded back.

Amabel shook her head.

"I thought—there seemed to be smoke, or mist, or something in the passages. I thought perhaps Jenny would come with me and see that everything is all right in the kitchen."

"To be sure!" said Mrs. Brown. "But I don't smell any smoke, my dear; and I've got a wonderful nose for it. I expect it's just a bit of damp rising. But Jenny'll go along with you and make sure."

Amabel turned to Jenny—a Jenny that she had never seen before, with long red plaits to her knee and a magenta flannel dressing-gown which gave her pale face a ghastly tinge. Jenny made no movement.

"It's nothing," she said. "It will be the damp rising after the rain, nothing more." She had closed the door after Amabel had come in, and now stood in front of it with her arms folded; her fingers moved all the time.

"But just look!" said Amabel.

Jenny did not move.

"There's no call to look," she said in a low voice. "If you don't look for trouble you won't find it."

Amabel drew herself up.

"I think you are behaving very strangely, Jenny," she said, "and I shall mention it to Mr. Forsham."

Jenny's lips twitched, and Mrs. Brown said in a distressed voice,

"Don't take notice of her, ma'am. Why, Jenny, you're standing right in Mrs. Grey's way. Open the door, and no more nonsense, my girl."

Amabel felt herself dismissed. She saw Jenny open the door and stand away from it. The light from the room showed the passageway a little dim, but no longer thick with fog.

"Just leave this door open until I've got upstairs, Jenny," she said. And with a hasty "Good night, Mrs. Brown," she went out.

Before she had gone a yard along the passage the mist was thick about her again, and she heard the slam of Jenny's door and the grinding sound of the bolt being driven home in a hurry.

She had reached the foot of the stairs, when some one laughed in the hall beyond. It was the same sound that she had heard that first night when she ran down to let Marmaduke in, and found the empty porch—darkness—and that laugh. Just for a moment she halted. The sound came from her right—the Browns' room lay to her left along the passage. She caught at the bannister, and went up, three steps, four, five, making herself walk slowly. As her foot touched the sixth step, she heard what Ellen had heard, a footstep on the stair that was not her own, a footstep that followed hers; and, like Ellen, it was more than she could do to turn her head and see what was following her.

There were eighteen steps. Amabel walked slowly to the top, and heard behind her the other step—as light a footstep as her own. When she had reached the top, she turned with a sudden, desperate courage and looked back.

There was nothing there. The mist hung thinly in the hall. The stairs, with their polished treads and broad strip of dull green carpeting, lay empty. She could see the mat at the stair-foot. She could see the whole length of the stairs. There was no one there.

Amabel went into her room, and locked and bolted the door.

Chapter Twenty-One

JULIAN FORSHAM stood at his cottage door and looked out. A clear night and very still, the stars actually visible—a little soft and blurred with mist, but still stars that one could see and recognize.

"One wouldn't go so far as to say that it will be fine to-morrow; but, at any rate, for the moment it isn't raining." With half a laugh he reached for a pocket torch, stepped outside, and pulled the door to behind him. He did not mean to use the torch if he could help it. Walking by night in this queer, overgrown garden had a certain charm for him. He moved towards the house, and met damp branches of trees which hung low and sprinkled him, and huge encroaching bushes which covered half the path they were meant to edge.

He came on the small terrace outside the drawing-room, and walked up to the windows. The broken window had been boarded up pending the arrival of a new pane, and the shutters were fastened inside.

That was a queer thing now; he had not thought of it before. Shutters—why, of course all the ground-floor rooms had shutters. Then why on earth hadn't they been fastened the other night? Jenny ought to have fastened them—there was no doubt about that. Julian stood still in the darkness, frowning. It all came back to Jenny. Jenny ought to have fastened the shutters. Perhaps she had fastened them. The person who broke the window could have opened the shutter too.

He passed to another window. To-night, at least, there had been no negligence. The house was well secured. He walked slowly round it, his mind busy with the problem of what Jenny had seen upstairs, and of what Amabel had told him.

Supposing, just supposing, that Annie Brown had come back to the neighbourhood, and, stealing into the Dower House for a glimpse of her mother, had been seen and recognized by Jenny. It was all right as a theory; but, when it came to detail, it wouldn't do, it simply wouldn't do. Impossible to fit in Marmaduke's departure or any of the Fearless episode. It simply wouldn't do. And Annie was probably dead years ago, poor soul. He had traced her to Paris and lost her there. Twelve years was a long time, as poor old Brownie had said.

Sharply across his thoughts there came a sound. It was a sound inside the house, deadened by distance. It was the sound of a laugh. He ran back round the house to a point close under the shrubbery from which he could see the windows of his aunts' rooms. The one on the left was Amabel's. A light showed through the curtains. He stood there waiting and listening; but the sound was not repeated.

Five minutes passed, and he was just about to move on, when the window above him opened. The parted curtains showed Amabel's silhouette against the background of the lighted room. She stood there, looking out, her face invisible, her figure motionless. The first impulse to speak, to call her name, passed quickly. Instead, he watched for what seemed to be a long time. At last she moved, stepped back. The curtains fell together. The window showed as a faintly luminous square in the blackness of the wall.

Julian moved away, treading softly. On the damp surface of what had once been gravel, it was easy to walk without noise. He completed his circuit of the house, and decided that to-morrow he would explore the inside very carefully from garret to cellar. Those disused cellars—yes, those would do with a thorough search if there were any way of getting into them. He had some idea that they had been bricked up.

As he came down from the terrace, he heard, not far away, a sound which brought him to a standstill. It was the sound which is made when a loose stone moves under foot. Julian's own feet were at the moment on moss; the sound had certainly not been made by him. He stood absolutely motionless, a black cypress towering overhead, and listened until he caught a soft movement on his right.

At the first sound he had put his hand on his torch. He swung it up now, a level beam of light, pointing in the direction from which the sound had come. An intricate pattern of holly leaves, each prickle sharply defined, sprang into view. He shifted the beam an inch or two to the left, and, through a gap in the bush, found a face unnaturally white. The eyes blinked rapidly. A voice said, "I'm afraid I'm fairly caught." Most astonishingly, Mr. Miller emerged from behind the holly bush.

"Miller! Good Lord!" said Julian—he was considerably startled.

Mr. Miller dodged out of the beam.

"Excuse me—just a little dazzling." And then, "Good evening, Mr. Forsham."

"What on earth—" Julian began, and was suavely interrupted.

"Oh, yes. Quite so, quite so. I'm as well aware as yourself that my presence here must require a little explanation."

"My good sir, I should damn well think it does!"

"Yes, yes, of course." Mr. Miller's tone was more than common calm. "Perhaps, if we walk on together—yes, as I was saying, my presence here—Mr. Forsham, I know quite well that it requires an apology as well as an explanation. Only the apology should really be made to Mrs. Grey, and I should much prefer that she should never know of any occasion for it."

"Naturally." Julian's tone was very dry. "Meanwhile, will you kindly explain yourself."

"Now, Mr. Forsham, you're angry. I will not say that you have no right to be angry, but it makes my explanation rather difficult because—well, as an explanation, it leaves a good deal to be desired."

Julian's temper was rising.

"Will you stop beating about the bush, and say what you were doing!"

"I'm afraid I was taking a liberty," said Mr. Miller gently. "The fact is that I'm greatly interested in psychical matters—I belong to the Society for Psychical Research, by the way. As you know, there has been a great deal of talk about the Dower House being haunted. The whole village believes that certain manifestations occur as soon as anyone but a Forsham attempts to live there. I ask you most earnestly to believe that I had no intention whatever of intruding on Mrs. Grey, a lady for whom I have a deep admiration and respect. I was merely watching the house, in the hope that if any manifestations occurred, I might, as a conscientious investigator, be privileged to observe them."

"Bunkum!" said Julian to himself. "Damned bunkum!" Aloud he remarked stiffly, "You had no right to do any such thing—you must know that perfectly well. It was a most infernal liberty."

"I'm bound to agree with you, Mr. Forsham. I can do no less, but I can do no more."

They had reached the gate, and both halted.

"I beg that you will accept a most sincere apology; and I shall be very grateful if you will not tell Mrs. Grey. I should be sorry indeed to lose her good opinion."

After a pause Julian said,

"I've certainly no desire to go out of my way to tell Mrs. Grey something that would be sure to annoy her; but I can give no undertaking on the subject. I think that, in future, you'll have to curb your zeal for investigation. Good night, Mr. Miller."

"Oh, good night, Mr. Forsham."

Ferdinand Miller walked down through the muddy lanes to his bungalow beside the river. He let himself in with a latch-key, and went into the living-room where a light still burned.

Miss Miller had fallen asleep in her easy-chair, and was snoring gently. She looked very large, comfortable, and untidy in a loose gown of dark brown woollen stuff, with strange conventional flowers worked on it in emerald green. A huge, black Persian cat lay on her lap and snored too, in a slightly different key.

Anne Miller woke up with a start. The cat slept on.

"Dear me, I've been asleep," she said, and put up a hand to her wispy, light brown hair.

"Yes," said Mr. Miller. "Look here, Anne, I want you to do something for me."

Miss Miller yawned.

"Oh, Ferdinand, what?" she inquired anxiously.

"I want you to go and see Mrs. Grey tomorrow."

"Oh, well, that's easy. She has promised me a jumper pattern, and I can go and ask for it."

"That's not all. In fact, I may say that that is only the beginning. I want you to offer to go and stay with her."

Miss Miller sat up and woke the cat.

"Really, Ferdinand! What a thing to ask me to do! How can I?"

"I want it done, Anne. I don't care how you do it." This was the Ferdinand Miller who had "such a sharp way with him."

His sister looked distressed.

"I don't see—oh, Ferdinand, indeed, I couldn't do such a thing. Why, I don't really know her at all."

"You don't know her enough, or you know too much about the Dower House—which is it?"

She flushed at that, but did not speak.

Ferdinand Miller took off his wrist-watch and began to wind it.

"It's time we went to bed," he said. "You'll go to the Dower House bright and early to-morrow so as to make sure of catching Mrs. Grey before she goes out. And you won't come away till she's asked you to stay. It won't be as hard as you think. I have a feeling that Mrs. Grey will be hospitably inclined."

Chapter Twenty-Two

ON THE MORNING after her return from Forsham Agatha Moreland was breakfasting in bed according to her usual habit. She wore a blue crêpe de chine négligé, and a most elaborate boudoir cap. All the colours in the room were pale and delicate; they were, in fact, a little too pale and delicate for its owner, but of this she was most comfortably unaware. Nevertheless, she frowned as she drank her coffee and looked at her letters.

Nothing from Cyril. Not a line since he went away on Friday. Of course, that was nothing, really. One wouldn't expect one's husband to write every time he went away for a week-end. But she didn't even know his address. That wasn't right. Suppose she wanted him in a hurry. She ought at least to know where he was. It wouldn't do to nag, of course; but she must try and get him to see that she ought to have his address.

She ran through one or two invitations, and came to an envelope with a typewritten address. She opened it carelessly, unfolded the sheet of paper which it contained, and found herself reading the first anonymous letter which she had ever received. It was quite short, and like the address it was typed. She stared at it, and read:

"Where is Cyril? Don't you wish you had second sight? It might be worth while. It is sometimes better to know the worst."

That was all. There was no signature.

Agatha pushed it aside with a look of disgust. How *nasty*! How insufferably impertinent! For the moment she was too angry to take any other view; but presently, when she was dressed, she read the letter again very carefully and then burnt it. This time instead of anger there came a feeling of dull, resentful misery. Cyril had no business to expose her to this sort of thing. People must be talking, pitying her—or perhaps laughing and saying that, after all, she had brought it on herself.

She went and looked at herself in the glass, and the picture pleased her. She was a handsome, well-preserved woman of the type that men admire. The letter was all nonsense. Cyril was in love with her—they had only been married three months. Her own words to Amabel came back: "If one could only be sure." And suddenly she saw herself talking to Nita King, and Nita pressing her to go and see some medium. What was the woman's name?—Thompson. The address was there in her bag. Of course, she didn't mean to use it. But if this Thompson woman could *really* satisfy her about Cyril— the words of the anonymous letter danced mockingly before her eyes: "Don't you wish you had second sight?"—if she went to Mrs. Thompson, perhaps all this load of suspicion would be lifted.

She took up the bag, and found the address. No, it wouldn't do. Supposing Mrs. Thompson were to tell her dreadful, unendurable things. She wouldn't risk it. Besides, she had never meant to go and see the woman.

In the end she went.

She took a taxi, dismissed it at the corner of the street, and walked slowly up the pavement, looking for No. 13. All the houses were exactly alike—small, narrow, and built of yellow brick. The street had a mean, neglected air.

Arrived at No. 13, her courage nearly failed her. It had, if possible, a drabber, dingier look than its neighbours. After a pause she rang. It seemed a long time before anyone came to let her in. The door was opened by a girl in her teens, a girl in a bright pink blouse with a string of blue glass beads about her neck and a shock of untidy fair hair. She indicated a room on the left, and shut the door on Agatha without more ado.

Agatha sat down on a chair upholstered in American cloth, and looked about her. There was certainly nothing occult about her surroundings. The room was like half a million rooms in the meaner streets of London. Nottingham lace curtains were looped across the dirty window. There was an aspidistra in a magenta pot on a bamboo table. The wall paper had probably once boasted a floral design, but it now resembled a cabbage field in some advanced stage of decay; photographic enlargements of half a dozen singularly unattractive people hid a good deal of it from view. There were only two things which made the room different from other rooms of the same sort. In the middle of it stood a small round table covered with a piece of black velvet such as photographers use. In the middle of the table was a crystal ball. That was the first unusual thing. The second was the door into the back room. Instead of being a folding door, as is usually the case, it was narrow, and the top part of it was filled with panes of clouded glass. One of the bottom panes had a broken corner.

Agatha found the room cold and stuffy. It smelt of onions and kippers. She began to wish that she had stayed at home, and she made an impatient movement.

Whilst Agatha waited, a woman was looking at her. To do this she had to kneel at the far side of the glass door and look through the broken pane. At Agatha's impatient movement the woman got up, went to the window, and turned the pages of a small note-book until she found a very accurate description of Mrs. Moreland. She read it through, slipped the book into her pocket, dusted the front of her dress, and went through the glass door into the front room. Agatha got up as she came in.

"I'm afraid I can't wait after all," she said rather crossly. "Are you Mrs. Thompson?"

She saw a small woman in a loose black dress. The woman had fair, damp hair with streaks of grey in it. Pale, prominent eyes looked indifferently at Agatha out of a pasty face.

"How do you do?" She put out a limp hand and said, "Yes, I am Mrs. Thompson." Her voice sounded very tired.

Agatha shook hands, though she had not meant to do so.

"A friend of mine told me about you," she began.

"Yes?" said Mrs. Thompson. "Please do not tell me her name. People come to me because they are sent. It is not any human agency that sends them. I do not wish to know your friend's name." She sighed, and added, "Do you wish me to look in the crystal?"

"I don't know," said Agatha. "I wanted some information—to be sure about something—and my friend told me that you—"

Mrs. Thompson put out a hand in a gesture that invited silence.

"Do not tell me anything," she said. "If there is a message for you, you shall have it. Please do not tell me anything." She spoke with just the trace of cockney accent which first strikes the ear and then eludes it; one could not say that any word was mispronounced, but there was an indefinable something. All the same, Agatha was aware that she was being impressed, that the desire to go was melting into a desire to stay.

"Do you want to know my name?" said Agatha. Insensibly she had dropped her voice a little.

"No," said Mrs. Thompson. "No, I do not want to know anything—from you. If there is a message, I will give it to you. Will you have the trance or the crystal?"

Agatha felt quite sure that if this little woman went into a trance, here in this shoddy, ordinary room, and began to speak with strange voices, that she, Agatha, would dislike it very much indeed. She said hurriedly, "Oh, the crystal"; and Mrs. Thompson nodded.

Then she walked to the window, pulled down a dark blind, and drew heavy curtains across the tiny bay. They were made of crimson chenille and finished with a woollen ball fringe. The room was now quite dark. Agatha put her hand on the black velvet of the table-cover, and stood there, waiting. Mrs. Thompson touched a switch and turned on the light in the long pendant, which hung down over the table. The green cardboard shade kept the upper half of the room in darkness. The light fell on the crystal globe.

"Sit down," said Mrs. Thompson. "There is a chair behind you."

Agatha sat down. She saw Mrs. Thompson draw a chair to the other side of the table and pull down the pendant light until it was only about a foot above the globe. Then she seated herself, drew the crystal a little nearer to her, and, bending forward, began to stare into it with those pale, tired eyes. Agatha watched her, fascinated.

With the disappearance of the ugly room the impression made upon her by Mrs. Thompson had deepened. There was nothing attractive about her, but she impressed. Everything about her seemed to be ordinary and rather unpleasant—the flabby skin, the damp hair, the awkward, high-busted figure; but behind all these things there was something that was not ordinary.

Agatha looked at the crystal, and then looked away because it dazzled her. She stared instead at Mrs. Thompson's hands, spread out on the black velvet with the light shining down on them—such ugly hands, not large, but square and fleshy, with all the nails cut straight across.

Quite suddenly Mrs. Thompson began to speak in a very low voice. She said,

"You have been very troubled and anxious. I can see the clouds of suspicion, jealousy, and mistrust. They have been making you very unhappy and poisoning your life. The trouble has all been about one person. It is a man. His name begins with a C. Shall I describe him to you?"

"Yes," said Agatha, with a gasp.

Mrs. Thompson proceeded to describe Cyril Moreland.

"I see him in the crystal," she said. "And I can see his thoughts. He is thinking of you. You fill his thought. There is no one else there."

"You're sure?" said Agatha breathlessly.

Mrs. Thompson made no protestations.

"I tell you what I see in the crystal," she said in her even voice. "His thoughts are all of you. They are thoughts of truth and devotion. But he is a little sad, I think, because of the clouds that have come between you. If you do not banish them, they will separate you, and you will have a great sorrow."

"You're sure that he only cares for me?" said Agatha. Her hands held one another tightly.

"His thoughts are full of you. They are thoughts of devotion and truth," said Mrs. Thompson.

There was a pause. Agatha got out her handkerchief and dabbed her eyes. She felt absurdly happy, absurdly young. She thought Mrs. Thompson the most wonderful woman in the world. The tears rose again to her eyes. She leaned back in her chair with the feeling of an intolerable weight removed. Mrs. Thompson was speaking again:

"Your anxieties have all been about C," she said. "But there is another person in the crystal. It is a woman. Her name begins with an A."

"Yes?" said Agatha. "What about her?"

"You have been with her lately. She has been much in your life. There is some tie between you—something that links you together. Your anxiety should be for her, not for C."

Agatha sat up.

"For her? Why?"

"Some danger threatens her," said Mrs. Thompson. "I do not understand what. Perhaps you can help me here. I see her in the crystal very plainly. She is in a room—a bedroom. On the right there is a window with chintz curtains. On the left the bed, and by the foot of the bed a door. One side of the room is quite filled with a big, dark cupboard. The woman I have described is standing in the middle of the room in her nightdress. She looks towards the door at the foot of the bed. The door begins to open slowly of itself. She looks at it, and she is very much afraid. Oh, she is quite terrified. She opens her mouth to scream, and she sways as if she would fall down. I can see the open door, but I cannot see what is beyond it. There is a thick mist. I have seen this three times in the crystal—the picture breaks up and forms again. Can you help me here? Do you know such a woman and such a room?"

Agatha had begun to feel very much agitated.

"Yes, I do," she said. "Can't you tell me anything more?"

"Some great danger is threatening her. I cannot tell you what it is. She should be warned of her danger. If she is in a house with a room such as I have described, she should leave it without delay. The danger is there."

"Can't you tell me what it is?" said Agatha.

Mrs. Thompson sighed.

"The pictures are getting fainter," she said. "I can see her coming up a steep stair. The house seems to be an old one. The post at the top of the stair has a round, carved fruit on it. The woman is coming up the stairs. The danger is there, behind her. Oh!" said Mrs. Thompson. It was not a word, but a sharp sound of terror. Her hands moved convulsively in the circle of light; her head fell forward between them.

Agatha felt as if she were choking—as if the darkness were choking her. She pushed back her chair and stumbled to the window. With shaking hands she wrenched back the curtains and released the spring of the blind. Then she took Mrs. Thompson by the shoulder and shook her.

The daylight showed the aspidistra, the bamboo table, and the photographic enlargements. They were the most comforting objects Mrs. Moreland had ever beheld.

Mrs. Thompson came to herself with a gasp. She leaned back in her chair, put one hand to her forehead in a vague sort of way, and said,

"What happened?"

"You saw something in the crystal, and you fainted," said Agatha. "What did you see?"

"I don't know," said Mrs. Thompson in a low, trembling voice. "I don't know what I saw."

"You described my sister coming up the stairs of a house she has taken," said Agatha, "You said, 'There is danger there'—and then you screamed and fainted. What did you see? You must tell me what you saw."

Mrs. Thompson's pale eyes stared at her.

"I don't know what I saw. It's all gone," she said. "That's the way with the crystal. I tell what I see—and then it is all gone, and I don't remember it." She put her elbows on the table and leaned her head on her hands. "I can't tell you any more. Your sister had better leave the house at once. I've never fainted before. I must have seen something very bad to make me faint. She ought to leave the house at once. Will you go now, please. The fee? Oh, anything you like—it doesn't matter."

When Mrs. Moreland had left the room, Mrs. Thompson did not move until she heard the front door shut. Then she got up, took the notes which Agatha had put down beside the crystal, counted them, turned out the electric light, and went back into the room beyond the glass door. There was a telephone fixed to the wall by the fireplace. She sat down in an easy chair, leaned back, and closed her eyes. Some little time later the telephone bell rang. A man's voice answered her "Hullo." She said, "Who is it speaking?" in a sharp matter of fact voice, and waited for the answer. When it came she said,

"It's all right, she's been. Didn't lose much time about it, did she?" She laughed—Mrs. Thompson had not at all a pleasant laugh.

"Well, what happened?" said the man on the line.

"Oh, it all went off A1—couldn't have been better. She lapped it all up about her precious Cyril. I told her he never thought of anyone but her." Mrs. Thompson laughed again. "All right, don't be so impatient. I'm coming to the rest of it. I described the sister and the house, like you told me to, and said I saw the most horrible danger threatening her, and she'd better look sharp and clear out. And when I couldn't think of anything more to say I threw a faint, and scared my lady stiff. One of the best jobs I've ever done—and I'd like my money all in ten shilling notes by to-morrow morning, first post. Pay on the nail's my motto, and no credit."

She hung up the receiver, and locked away Agatha's notes in an old black tin cash-box.

Chapter Twenty-Three

JULIAN FORSHAM came up to the Dower House in the morning, and went in to see Mrs. Brown. The idea that Annie might be somewhere in the neighbourhood kept recurring to his mind, and when it recurred he could not help remembering the queer, fleeting likeness which had startled him at the Bronsons—Nita King, Anita King, and Annie. Preposterous—she was Edward Berkeley's cousin. But, even as he dismissed the thought, he could hear Lady Susan saying, "She *says* she's a cousin of Edward's." He thought he would have another talk with Brownie. He found her a little troubled.

"Jenny, she spoke hasty to Mrs. Grey last night, and I'm hoping that she didn't take it amiss. Jenny's a good girl, but there's times when she's hasty. And if you could speak a word for her to Mrs. Grey, I'm sure I'd be grateful, Master Julian."

"All right, Brownie, don't upset yourself. If Jenny said anything she oughtn't to have, she must just tell Mrs. Grey she's sorry. There's nothing for you to worry about."

Mrs. Brown had her Bible out on the coverlet. Julian picked it up and turned the pages.

"May I have another look at that photograph?" And when he had found it, he turned it to the light and looked at it for a long time. "How tall was Annie?" he asked suddenly "I seem to remember her and Jenny just the same height."

"Not later on, they weren't," said Mrs Brown. "Inch for inch they grew till they come to their teens; and then Jenny, she went on and left Annie a matter of two inches behind."

Anita King was small. The thought would come. He frowned, and asked abruptly,

"When did I see Annie last? I don't seem to remember her any older than this,"—he touched the photograph—"but I was at Forsham again a couple of years later."

"And Annie was away visiting her grandmother. No, my dear, you never saw her after she was twelve, and the last time you saw her at all was the day Miss Georgina give a treat to the Sunday school and took 'em all a picnic up in Forsham High Woods. You and Mr. George was here, and Mr. George wouldn't go—proud, you know, Master Julian, like he always was—wouldn't go and play with a peck of children; and fine and vexed his poor aunts were. But you went, my dear; and a fine time the children had till the storm come up."

"Of course!" said Julian. "I remember quite well. It *was* a storm, too."

Mrs. Brown nodded.

"And poor Annie so frightened of storms. Jenny never minded them at all, but the least mite of a storm, and Annie would be like a wild thing. Just crazy she was that day—and never forgot how good you was to her. She fair worshipped you after that."

Julian remembered it all very well—the picnic; the romping children; the fire they had built; and even the squirrel which had sat in the tree above and chattered furiously at them. Miss Georgina, benevolent and pleased; Brownie terribly busy over the teacups. Then, after tea, hide-and-seek in the woods, and the storm coming up from the other side of the hill and catching them unawares. It was rather a bad storm too—soon over, but violent while it lasted.

So that was when he had last seen Annie Brown. He could look back and see her now, quite white, with staring eyes; and he could feel how she had trembled and clung to him when he put his arm about her.

"Always like that in a thunder-storm, Annie was," said Mrs. Brown. "Just out of herself with fright."

Julian put the photograph back, and let the leaves flutter down upon it, the fly-leaf last. Mary Ann Brown he read, and exclaimed, "That's not you, Brownie!"

"It were Brown's mother's Bible," said Mrs. Brown, "And then it were Annie's because of her name being the same."

"I'd forgotten she was Mary Ann," said Julian.

He went upstairs and found Amabel.

"I meant to come up earlier; but I'd a huge post. If I don't answer letters at once, I never answer them at all. Did you sleep all right?"

"Not frightfully well," said Amabel.

"Why not?"

"I don't know—just stupidity."

He looked at her sharply, and saw that she was pale.

"Did anything happen? I walked all round the house before I went to bed, and I thought I heard someone laugh."

"You heard it? You *did* hear it?"

"I certainly heard something. What was it?"

"I don't know. It's what I heard the first night. Oh, Julian, I'm so thankful you heard it too. I began to wonder—" Her voice trembled and stopped.

"Of course I heard it. Tell me exactly what happened."

"Oh, nothing much. Nothing, really. Just that horrid laugh—and a sort of mist in the passages—and footsteps coming upstairs after me."

"My dear—"

She put her hand quickly to her eyes.

"It's nothing—I'm stupid. And—and, Julian, I've been thinking. The things seem to happen in the hall. Well, I've made up my mind that, whatever happens, I simply won't go down into the hall at night. If I stay in my room and bolt the door, I shall be quite all right—I'm sure I shall. And besides,"—she looked up at him with a smile—"I'm going to have a visitor to-night; I shan't be here by myself."

"Mrs. Moreland is coming back?" His tone was eager.

"No, it's not Agatha. It's someone here, someone in Forsham."

"Not Mrs. King?" said Julian quickly.

"Good gracious, no! The poor little thing would die of fright. No, it's Miss Miller."

"Amabel, you don't mean that!"

"I do."

"Miss Miller?"

Amabel nodded. She was a good deal amused.

"Miss Miller," she said. "She arrived at ten o'clock this morning to ask me for a jumper pattern which I'd promised her. I gave it to her, and she sat. She didn't talk, you know,—I don't think she does talk much—she just sat, very large and rather shy. And at last she turned very red, and said she'd been so glad to hear my sister had been staying here. And when I said Agatha had gone, she got a lot redder, and said she couldn't bear to think of me here alone, and Ferdinand couldn't bear to think of it, and she didn't think it was right. I wasn't sure whether it was ghosts or Mrs. Grundy. But she's a kind soul, and when she offered to come and stay for a day or two, I'm afraid I jumped at it."

"She offered to come and stay!" Julian's face was as expressive as Julian's voice.

Amabel's amusement deepened. That portentous frown, that furious voice. "Julian, my dear, I'm not going to be trampled on," was her thought.

Julian got up, paced a step or two, and came back.

"You don't seriously mean that you're going to have Miss Miller to stay?"

"Yes, I do. I nearly fell on her neck and wept, I was so grateful."

"Is Ferdinand coming too?" There was no doubt that Julian Forsham had a quick temper.

"I haven't asked him—yet." She looked up at him, suddenly, teasingly, sweetly. "Don't be cross, Julian, and I'll ask you."

He frowned, and melted.

"I'm a brute. But I don't want Miller butting in."

"I gathered that."

"Will you come, then?"

"Yes, of course I will."

Amabel laughed.

"You're just like Ellen," she said. "Ellen doesn't hold with the Millers either. She was dreadfully sniffy about them when I told her to get Miss Miller's room ready. She says, pushingness is what she can't abide. You'll have to be careful, or she'll think you're pushing too."

"She seems to give her opinions rather freely."

"Oh, well, after nineteen years one does, you know."

They talked a little longer. Julian harked back to what had happened the evening before.

"I want to make a very careful search of the house and cellars; and I'd like to do it before your visitor arrives."

His search of the house revealed nothing. The unused rooms that looked upon the terrace were dusty, close, and empty. Julian's footsteps made such marks on the boards as to leave no doubt that no other foot had trodden there lately. He spent some time in the hall, paced it, tested it for echo, and walked several times up and down the stairs, listening carefully to see if his step made a double sound. Everything was as normal and ordinary as could be; there was no echo, and the stairs did not even creak.

After examining the kitchen and offices, he tried the door that led down to the cellars, and found it locked. Jenny had the key, and Jenny seemed reluctant to produce it.

"There's water standing in those old cellars, Master Julian. They want seeing to dreadful bad. We keep the coal in the wash-house."

"Well, I just want to have a look round. If they're as bad as that, Mr. George will have to do something about it. Give me the key."

Jenny gave it to him, and he went down the dozen steps into darkness and a very mouldy smell. His torch showed a large cellar, empty except for a few lumps of coal in one corner. He swung his torch up, and found the grating that should have ventilated it choked.

An open archway led into another empty cellar. In this there was a low wooden door, bolted on the near side. Julian examined the bolt. It had evidently not been opened for a very long time, for it had rusted into the socket, and it was only after several attempts that he managed to push it back and get the door open.

The cellar beyond was the one he remembered—the one in which he and George had played at explorers. The torch showed a broken bench, and some odds and ends of chair-legs, together with part of a bed and the skeleton of a bureau with all the drawers missing. It also showed a heap of rubble and broken brick in the far corner, rising to about five feet from the ground. Julian looked over the top of this, and saw that it had been piled against a door, obviously with the intention of blocking it. This confirmed his recollection of extensive cellars which had been pronounced unsafe. The rubble very effectually prevented this door from being opened. He swung his torch all round, and found only the unbroken walls.

The cellars were not as damp as he had expected. This one was, in fact, quite dry. The other two had moisture on the walls, but none upon the floor. Jenny had been romancing, or else she had not wished him to go down into the cellars. Odd creature, Jenny.

He retraced his steps, locked the door, and, after some hesitation, pocketed the key himself. To Jenny, hovering in the passage, he observed that he was keeping it as the gratings required seeing to.

Chapter Twenty-Four

"AND, WHERE DOES that door lead to?" asked Anne Miller.

Julian had dined with them, and they had just bidden him goodnight. Amabel had accompanied her guest into the room that had been Miss Georgina's, and was lingering a moment before going to her own.

"That door? It goes through into my room."

"Oh, that's nice," said Miss Miller with obvious sincerity.

"And Mr. Forsham is just across the passage—the door opposite yours."

A look of gratitude overspread the large, plain face.

"I don't know how you stayed here by yourself," said Miss Miller. "I've often been quite alone in the Bungalow, and never minded a bit. Ferdinand's away such a lot, you know; it wouldn't do for me to mind. But I couldn't stay *here* by myself. I can't think how you do it."

"Well, it's very nice to have you to-night," said Amabel. "You're sure you've got everything you want? Good night, then."

She opened the connecting door, and was about to close it again behind her, when Miss Miller's voice called a little breathlessly:

"Mrs. Grey!" She turned and met an anxious, pleading gaze. "Would you mind—would you think it strange if I asked—I mean would you mind leaving the door open when you're ready for bed?"

"No, of course I don't mind. I'm so glad you asked. If you want anything you've only to call out; I'm a very light sleeper."

When she was ready Amabel went to the window for a moment, and looked out. There was a light wind and scudding clouds. As she stood, she could see, first the shrubbery—a dense shadow, formless as water,—and above it, the waving blackness of trees. Higher still those dark scudding clouds. There was no peace in the night; but

Amabel's thoughts were at peace. Kind, solid Miss Miller next door; and Julian just across the way. She drew a long breath of relief from strain. She would sleep to-night.

She turned back into the room, opened the connecting door a couple of feet, and called out "Good night." As a sleepy voice answered her, she got into bed and switched off the light. Her oil lamp burned in the corner by the bureau; the light, turned low and screened from her eyes by the towel-horse, made a yellow ring on the ceiling. Amabel lay down, and went to sleep.

It seemed to her afterwards that she passed at once into a dream. In her dream she was climbing a long stair that went up, and up, and up endlessly. She could not see where it began, and she could not see where it ended; but it went on through black, tossing tree-tops—always more and more of them. They waved, and bent, and strained in a wind that she could neither feel nor hear. They were pomegranate trees, thick with fruit. As she climbed she could hear someone climbing behind her, and the dreadful panic of nightmare shook her with its invisible wind, just as that other wind was shaking the trees. At the height of her terror she turned and looked back, and it was Julian who was climbing after her—Julian with a cleft pomegranate in his hand. He came to where she stood, and smiled at her. In her dream terror was gone, but there was a happiness too great to be borne. She called out, "No! No!! No!!!" and woke up.

For a moment she was bewildered. It was as if she were a musical instrument which had been played upon. Her whole consciousness still throbbed with the tune that had been played. Then it came to her, not all at once but slowly, that the room was different, the room was dark. The subdued glow of the lamplight was gone. The yellow ring on the ceiling was no longer there. The room was quite dark. She put out her hand and pressed the switch of the reading lamp. Nothing happened. The room was dark.

Amabel sat up in bed, her heart beating faster than she liked. There were some matches on the bureau; she had used them to light the lamp that afternoon. She was just about to get out of bed, when she heard the sound for the first time. It was a new sound. With a sort of rush she remembered Nita King's words—wings in the passages. Yes, that was what the sound was like—the beat of wings.

She sat listening, holding her breath to listen. The wings seemed to beat down the passage. She heard them faintly now; and now she could not hear them at all. She began to breathe again. Whatever happened, *whatever* happened, she would not leave the room. Nothing should tempt her from its shelter. As long as she stayed here she was safe. And Miss Miller was in the next room, with an open door between them; she could call to her at any moment if she wanted to; she could call to her now.

Amabel rose on her knees, and felt her way to the end of the bed. Here, leaning over the foot, she could touch the jamb of the door, she could assure herself that the door was open. She held on to the foot of the bed with her right hand, and reached out with her left hand along the wall as far as it would go. Her fingers slid over the patterned paper. The pattern was raised a little; she could feel the shape of the roses. Then she touched the jamb, the sharp edge, the curved moulding. Her hand went on, feeling for the empty space beyond. The empty space was filled. The door was shut.

A hot spurt of rage flared up in Amabel. She wasn't frightened any more; she was very angry. Her anger was against the door; a quite primitive desire to smash it into splinters made her very finger-tips tingle. She half sprang, half scrambled out over the bed-foot, and wrenched it open. The room beyond lay dark and silent. She could hear her own heart beating, and nothing more. Panting a little, she turned and groped her way to the bureau. The matches ought to be just here, on the pentray; but she couldn't find them. Her fingers searched the whole of the flap. The matches were not there. She might have left them on the top of the bureau where the tall Sheffield candlesticks stood. Yes, they were there, on the very edge. She got the box open, lit a match, and looked for the lamp. It was there on the floor, where she had left it with the towel-horse in front of it as a screen. She picked it up, set it on the bureau, and had to light a second match.

There was plenty of oil. Why had the lamp gone out? She took off the chimney, turned up the wick a little, and tried it with a lighted match. Instead of lighting at once, it sputtered and behaved rather oddly; but after using three more matches she got the flame to burn steadily, and put the chimney on again. After a little hesitation she left the lamp on the bureau where she could see it, and put the towel-horse back by the washstand. Then she stood for a moment in the open door-way between the two rooms and listened. The further room was very still indeed. Miss Miller must be a very quiet sleeper. One would have expected so large a person to sleep a little more audibly.

Amabel crossed the threshold, and went a little way into the room. She couldn't hear anything at all. Suddenly the stillness irked her; she stepped back into her own room, and was glad of the lamp-light. She was in two minds whether she would shut the door on Miss Miller or not; she even put her hand on the handle. It was that curious, unreasoning anger against the door which made her take her hand away again. If she chose to leave it open, it should stay open—yes, if she had to get up a dozen times in the night to open it.

She got into bed, and tried the switch of the electric light again; but there was still no contact. That was vexing, because she did not intend to go to sleep, and she would have liked to read. Of course, she could get the oil lamp and have it by her; but she did not want to get out of bed. Now that her anger had died away she was cold. She reached out for her dressing-gown, slipped her arms into it, and wrapped it about her closely. It was half-past one by her watch, a long time till morning. She propped herself up with pillows, and began to think about Daphne, about Agatha, about her dream. It was going to be rather hard to keep awake. As drowsiness crept over her she began to wonder whether the sound that she had heard had not been part of her dream. That was the way with the things that happened in this house; they frightened you at the time, and afterwards there seemed to be so little to take hold of, so little that could not be explained away. The drowsiness receded. So little that could not be explained away—but always something—always something. The wings—she might have dreamt about the wings. That rushing, beating sound was just such a sound as one might hear in a dream. But she hadn't dreamt about the door. It was open when she went to bed; and just now it had been shut. Of course, doors do shut of themselves sometimes. There was very little to take hold of, after all.

Her eyelids drooped, her hands, which had been clasped rather tightly, relaxed. She was on the edge of sleep, when something brought her back. Through her closed lids she was aware of light and darkness rapidly succeeding one another. With an effort she opened her eyes, and saw all the shadows in the room rush upwards and then fall again. For a moment what she saw seemed just pure nightmare, causeless and impossible. Then she understood.

What she had seen was the flicker of the expiring lamp. The light flared for a moment and fell, leapt again with a quick, erratic flame that burned high and burned blue, and then went out. As she sat there between sleeping and waking, her eyes fixed on the darkness where the last spark had showed, she felt a faint breath of moving air and heard an indefinable sound. She knew what it was. She knew it as well as if the room were flooded with light, as well as if she could see the door slowly closing. With her breath held and a coldness stealing over her, she listened for what she knew must come. It came. Quite softly but distinctly, she heard the click of the latch.

Chapter Twenty-Five

JULIAN FORSHAM had not gone to bed. After saying good-night to Amabel and Miss Miller he made up the sitting-room fire, set the door ajar, and established himself in an easy chair with a book. He had no intention of going to bed. Miss Miller's presence in the house filled him with suspicion. Why was she here? It was an unheard-of thing for her to come up at ten in the morning and thrust herself on Amabel as a guest. They were the barest acquaintances. Coming on the top of Ferdinand Miller's very inadequate explanation of his presence outside the house the night before, it aroused very strange suspicions indeed. He had an idea that something was meant to happen to-night; and he intended to be in a position to investigate anything that did happen. It was, of course, possible that his presence in the house would be a check—that had to be taken into consideration. But he had no intention of leaving Amabel alone with Anne Miller.

He meant to stay awake, but did not succeed in doing so. He read the same page three times without knowing it, after which the book slid gently to the floor, and he slept comfortably, dreamlessly.

He woke with the sound of a laugh in his ears. Some one had laughed—just as he woke up some one had laughed. That was the first thought. The second brought him to his feet with a start. The room was pitch dark. He had gone to sleep with the fire glowing and a reading lamp alight on the table behind him. Now the fire was out. But the lamp was out too, and the room was in total darkness.

He made for the door, found the switch on the wall beside it, pressed it down. A little click, but no light. He felt for the switch that controlled the passage light, with the same result. And then, just as his hand went to the electric torch which he had pocketed before settling down for the night, he heard the laugh again. It was a horrible sound, very harsh and inhuman, more like the sound some animal might make—not quite the hyæna cry, but as horrible. It seemed to come from one of the rooms opposite, and, as he got the torch out and switched it on, the door of Amabel's room opened and he heard quick, panting breath and the sound of bare feet running. He heard before he saw anything. The light from the torch was focussed on the stairs. He swung it round, and saw Amabel in her blue dressing-gown standing still in the dark passage, her hands stretched out in front of her, her fair hair loose about her shoulders. The light flashed into her eyes, showing them set with terror. As the beam touched her she gave a quick cry, not loud, but piteous in the extreme, and swung round as if to run from some new terror.

A great anger and a great warmth of tenderness rose together in Julian. He said, "Amabel—my dear!" made a stride forward, and caught her in his arms. "It's Julian. My dear, what is it? You're safe, you're quite safe."

For a moment she was rigid in his arms. Then quite suddenly he felt her relax. The soft hair swept his cheek, her head was pressed against his shoulder, and she was clinging to him desperately and weeping. Her sobs shook them both. He held her close, and the wave of tenderness went on rising until every other feeling was submerged. It was like a river of light flowing through the darkness and shutting them in together. The darkness was too far away to touch them. The creatures of the darkness were forgotten. They stood in the light, and held one another close, without words or any need for words.

Amabel drew away with a quick breath that was still half a sob.

"Julian," she whispered.

With his arm still round her, he said,

"What is it?"

"I don't know. Did you hear it?"

"Yes, it woke me. I was sitting up. I didn't mean to go to sleep, but I dropped off. It woke me."

Amabel's hand gripped his arm. He felt her shudder.

"It was in my room—the light went out—it was in my room. The door—the door kept shutting." Her voice failed.

"What about Miss Miller?" asked Julian sharply.

"I don't know. She's asleep—unless—oh, Julian, I couldn't hear anything in her room. She must be all right, but I couldn't *hear* anything."

"I don't think you need worry about Miss Miller," he said dryly. "But we'll just see." He drew her towards the bedroom door, throwing the light forward upon it. The beam traversed the small table which stood between the two doors, and dazzled on the reflector of the oil lamp. "Hullo, that's gone out!" he said.

"Yes, mine did too. And the one in the hall downstairs—it must be out, or it wouldn't be so dark up here."

Julian produced a box of matches, and after a little patience induced the lamp to light.

"Now, try that door," he said in a low voice. "I want to know if she's awake."

"I think she must be," said Amabel. She smiled very faintly. "She must be the world's best sleeper if she isn't." She tried the door as she spoke and found it fast. "It's bolted on the inside."

"But you can get in through your room."

"Yes." Her distressed eyes met his, and he touched her on the arm.

"It's all right. I won't go away. Besides I've got to have a look round that room, if you don't mind."

They came to the door and looked in. The whole of the room was visible, and it contained only the objects with which both were familiar. Julian brought the lamp into the room, set it down, and flung open the doors of the big press. He flashed his torch into the dark corners. The few clothes that Amabel had hung there seemed lost in its big emptiness. The light showed brass rails and hooks, the panelling of back and sides, the grain of the wood, a few tiny cracks here and there—nothing more, nothing more at all.

He went back to the passage, and stood just outside the room.

"See if she's awake!" He pointed to the connecting door.

Amabel took the lamp in her hand, opened the door, and looked in. Julian, watching, saw her recoil a step and the lamp shake in her hand.

"What is it?" he asked quick and low; and Amabel turned bewildered eyes on him.

"The bed's empty!" she whispered. "She isn't there!"

Before Julian could speak, a sound from the farther room made Amabel turn again. She took a step forward, and held the lamp up high.

"Miss Miller, is that you?" she called.

There came the sound of a window being closed. The light chintz curtains that were drawn together across the window rustled and were parted. Miss Miller appeared from between them. She had on red felt bedroom slippers, a dressing-gown of purple ripple cloth, and a very large white woollen shawl. Her hair was done in tight plaits.

"Oh, Mrs. Grey, is that you? Did you want anything?"

"There was a noise," said Amabel. "Mr. Forsham was sitting up, and I called him. We wanted to know if you had heard anything. Mr. Forsham is just outside in the passage. We—we can't get the lights to work."

Miss Miller came forward, blinking placidly at the oil lamp.

"How dazzling that is," she said. "You are very wise to have some lamps—electric light is so tiresome when it goes wrong, isn't it?"

"Ask her if she heard anything," said Julian short and sharp; he was losing patience.

"Miss Miller, did you hear anything just now?" repeated Amabel.

"Well, do you know, I thought I did," said Anne Miller. "I thought it was a cat, and I went to the window and opened it to see what was happening. I don't sleep with my window open as a rule, you know, though it's so much the fashion. I do so hate a draught in bed."

"She thought she heard a cat," said Amabel over her shoulder to Julian.

Julian put his hand quickly on the switch that was just inside the door. The light sprang on, brilliantly, suddenly; the room was flooded with it. He laughed; but there was no sound of amusement in his laughter.

"I think the performance is over for tonight," he said.

Chapter Twenty-Six

JULIAN CAME INTO the sitting-room and shut the door.

"Where's that Miller woman?" he asked.

Amabel turned from the writing-table with a letter in her hand.

"She went out directly after breakfast. She said she must go down to the Bungalow and feed her hens."

"Look here, Amabel, that woman must go! You've got to get rid of her."

"Have I?" said Amabel. "And, please, why?"

Julian made an impatient movement.

"My dear Amabel! You ask me why, after last night?"

"But last night hadn't anything to do with Miss Miller."

"Hadn't it?"

"Why, of course not! Poor Miss Miller, what a shame!"

Julian took up a commanding position on the hearth-rug—the immemorial position of the man who is about to scold his women-folk. Doubtless in front of some primeval wood-fire Adam thus stood and lectured Eve.

"Perhaps, Amabel," he said, "you'll be able to tell me why poor Miss Miller was leaning out of her open bedroom window with simply stacks of clothes on, when, about half a minute before, you'd looked into her room and been fussed because you couldn't hear her breathing."

The corners of Amabel's mouth twitched.

"But, Julian, if her head was outside the window, she would have had to breathe like a grampus for me to hear her."

"Nonsense!" said Julian. "Nonsense! Look here, I didn't tell you, but I caught Miller prowling round the house the night before. He produced some cock-and-bull yarn about psychical research. And on the top of that his sister forces, literally forces, herself into your house! It's damned impertinence, if it's nothing else!"

Amabel was silent. The impulse to laugh at his suspicions, to resent his interference, to tease him a little, died suddenly. Her face was paler. Her hand closed on the letter it held.

"What does it all mean?" she asked slowly. And then, before he could answer, she went on, "It means something. I've just had the most extraordinary letter from Agatha. I want you to read it before you say anything more. Will you begin here, at the top of this page. The first sheet is just to tell me that she'd been to see some medium Mrs. King was frightfully keen about, and her reasons for going, and so on—"

"Anita King!" exclaimed Julian.

"Yes, Mrs. King swears by the woman, and Agatha went to see her for reasons of her own—nothing to do with me at all. I want to make that quite clear. She says she wasn't even thinking of me. Now, go on from here, and just see what she says." She put the letter into his hand, and watched his face anxiously as he read it.

Mrs. Moreland wrote one of those large, bold hands that cover a good deal of paper and tend to flourishes and under-linings:

"She didn't know my name or anything about me. And it was a *most dreadful* little room that smelt as if they'd been cooking Irish stew in it for years and years. But Mrs. Thompson herself— my dear, she was uncanny, she really was! And she said I needn't worry about Cyril a bit—as I told you at the beginning of this—; and I shan't any more, because I feel *quite certain* of him *now* after what she said. But then she began to talk about you—not by name of course, but she described you, and said your name began with an A, and that you were in *frightful* danger. She described you *absolutely.* And she described the Dower House down to the last detail, even that carved fruit thing on the post at the top of the stairs—the one I said was an apple and you thought was an orange, and then Mr. Forsham said we were both wrong, and that it was a pomegranate. Well, *she* said it was a pomegranate too. I *do* call that uncanny, don't *you*? I forgot to say she darkened the room, and turned on the electric light, and looked into a crystal. First, she saw you standing in your bedroom, simply frozen up with terror, and the door of the next room opening all of itself. She simply made my flesh creep. And then she saw you coming upstairs—that was where the pomegranate came in—, and she said *something* was coming up behind you. And then she gave the most dreadful sort of scream and fainted. My dear, she really *did*. It was simply *horrible*. And when I got her round she didn't remember anything at all—not a single thing. But all the time before she fainted she kept saying that you were in *fearful* danger, and that you ought to leave the house *at once*. Oh, Amy, *please do*! You can come to me, if you don't mind the small room without a fireplace. But do, *do*, DO come away from that dreadful house *at once*!"

There was some more in the same strain before the scrawled "Agatha" which slanted over half a page in letters about an inch high.

Julian read the last word, and handed the many sheets back to Amabel.

"Well?" she said, still watching his face—she found it very grave indeed.

He put both hands on her shoulders, and looked at her, a long, steady look.

"I want you to do what your sister says. I want you to leave this house at once."

He felt a little tremor run over her; but her lips were smiling.

"So anxious to get rid of me, Julian?"

He released her, and turned away.

"Yes," he said.

There was a long pause. At last:

"What do you think it means, Julian?"

"I don't know." He spoke slowly, consideringly. Then, with a sudden change of manner, "Of course it means that someone is prepared to go to pretty serious lengths to get you out of this. It means that, naturally. But who, or why—there we're all in the dark."

"And you want me to give in, go away?"

"You must go. I won't have you exposed to all this sort of thing. George and his house may go hang. You've got to go."

She shook her head, and said,

"No, Julian."

"My dear girl, you can't stay. It's impossible,"

"No, not impossible. I'm going to see it through." She dropped into a chair, and looked up at him rather tremulously. "Julian, I've got to see it through. I've taken the money, and I can't go back."

"If it's only the money," he began; but she stopped him:

"It's no use. I've taken the money, and I'm going to earn it. Yes, my dear, I know you'd lend it to me—or Mr. Berry would lend it—; but I couldn't take it from either of you. I *can't* borrow money when I know I should never be able to pay it back."

"You can't have spent it! Give it back, and let me get you out of this to-day."

Her eyes were full of tears. She looked and spoke with the simplicity of a child:

"It was for Daphne—I can't give it back because it was for Daphne—I had to have it for Daphne."

Julian restrained a forcible remark about the absent Daphne. Instead, he said quite gently,

"You're a very foolish woman, my dear,—but I suppose you know that."

"It's for Daphne," Amabel repeated. "I must stay because of Daphne."

Julian ceased to tower above her on the hearth. He came and sat down on the fender-stool, and leaning forward, put his hand lightly over one of hers.

"It's not because I'm obstinate, it's because I must," said Amabel. "You don't think I want to stay, do you, Julian?"

He put a very considerable force on himself.

"Would Daphne let you stay if she knew?" he asked.

"No, no, of course not," she said quickly. But because of the hurry in her voice and the flicker of fear in her eyes, Julian knew that she was not sure about Daphne. His hand closed on hers, the dark colour rushed into his face.

Amabel pulled her hand away and jumped up. She went to the writing-table and put Agatha's letter into a drawer. Her hands shook, but her voice was tolerably steady.

"No, no, I shall be quite all right. You mustn't worry about me—really." She turned, leaning on the table, and looked at him, no longer softly, but with defiance. "I'm going to stay," she said, with a certain hard finality.

Julian was sharply hurt, sharply jealous of Daphne. Twenty years ago he had seen just that look upon Amabel's face when she sent him away—just that transition from the tearful softness, which in any other woman would have meant yielding, to an iron determination against which a man might beat himself in vain—the same look and almost the same words: "I *must* do it," and behind that "must," the puritan conscience, unmoved, inflexible. Julian as a boy had stormed from her presence in a rage. Julian the man had rather more self-control; he cared rather more for her and rather less for himself than in the old days. After a short pause he spoke in an altered voice:

"Very well then, you stay. But you must let me take steps to ensure your safety. You really mustn't be here alone."

"There is Miss Miller," Amabel ventured, relaxing.

He waved Miss Miller away, some of his pent up feeling in the gesture.

"Impossible! She must go to-day. Look here, I suppose you can go away on a visit. You're not obliged to spend every moment of the six months here, are you?"

"I can be away for forty-eight hours."

"That will do. You can go to your sister or the Berkeleys, whilst I run up to town and make arrangements."

"What arrangements?"

"Detectives," said Julian briefly—then, "I'm going to get to the bottom of this for all our sakes. I'll get down a man and a woman; they can come in as butler and parlourmaid. And when I've got them, you can come back, but not before."

He saw the growing dismay in her face as he spoke.

"No, Julian, you mustn't. It was one of the conditions—no detectives or police, or I forfeit everything."

Julian's temper broke bounds. The expressions he permitted himself to use about his brother would have surprised George Forsham.

Amabel's spirits rose. It was rather nice to have Julian so angry on her account. When he had finished all that he had to say about George, she put her hand on his arm and said softly,

"That was very nice of you. I've really often felt like that myself." Her laughing look met his frowning one, and she added seriously, "Now let's stop being angry, and make a plan. I've been thinking—I really don't feel as if I could sleep in that room again—"

"You're not going to. If you stay here, I want you to get out of the old part of the house. I suppose Miss Miller will have to stay for tonight at least, or I shan't be able to stay myself. You'd better both move into the bedrooms up the passage—the two over the dining-room and drawing-room. I'll take a turn at sleeping in the room you've been in; and we'll just see what happens."

"I'd have moved out of it long ago if it hadn't been for the telephone." Her voice dropped a little. "Julian, you're not angry? We're friends?"

His look softened, kindled.

"Are we?"

Amabel stepped back just in time. The door opened, and Anne Miller came in.

Chapter Twenty-Seven

JULIAN WENT DOWN to the cottage in the afternoon, and wrote letters. One of the letters was to Sir Julian Le Mesurier, Chief of the Criminal Investigation Department. It was not a very formal document. It ran:

"DEAR PIGGY,

"Could you put one of your bright young men on to finding out as much as possible about a medium called Mrs. Thompson—address, 13, Earnshaw Villas, Halkindale Road, N.W.? I would like particularly to know whether in the last few days she asked for, or received, any trunk call from this part of the world. I'll run up to town to-morrow and look in on you. More then. Love to Isobel and the piglets.

"Yours, JULIAN.

"P.S. How's the forged note business doing? I hope you're not resigning till after to-morrow, anyhow!"

Quite impossible to leave the matter of Mrs. Thompson where Agatha Moreland had left it. He would go and see Piggy and talk to him in confidence about the whole thing. Something must be done; but it must be done with the utmost discretion, What with Amabel and her conscience, and the two hundred pounds which she might conceive herself obliged to hand back to George, and the possibility of Annie Brown being somewhere mixed up in the business, it behoved him to walk very delicately indeed. Amabel must have her two hundred pounds; and at all costs poor old Brownie must be shielded from any fresh shock or sorrow on Annie's account. So it was Anita King who had sent Agatha Moreland to this tame medium of hers. His mind misgave him a good deal about Anita King.

He wrote three or four more letters. In the middle of the last one he had to get up and turn on the lights, it was growing so dark. He glanced out of the window, and saw that half the sky was black with piled up clouds. He finished his last letter to the sound of the rising wind.

It was a little later, when he was sorting and tearing up some papers, that he heard the sound of footsteps and a hurried knocking at the door. In the dusk he did not at first recognize the woman who stood there. Then she spoke his name, "Mr. Forsham"—just like that. It was by her voice and the trilled "r" that he recognized Miss Lemoine.

"Mr. Forsham—I beg your pardon—I am disturbing you." She spoke as if she had been running, and with the last word she put one hand up to her throat.

"No, I had just finished my letters and was going to the post with them."

Miss Lemoine leaned against the half-open door.

"That makes me a little bolder," she said. "I have been down into the village, and I was delayed. And now I think there is a storm coming—and I am *so* stupid about storms."

Julian frowned. If she wanted to come in and shelter from this possible storm, she might be here for hours.

"Can I take you home?" he said. "If we hurry, I expect you'll get in ahead of the rain, and I can post my letters on the way back."

"Oh, that is kind. That is what I would have asked you; but my courage failed. When I saw your light from the road I thought that I would ask you to walk home with me; but when you came to the door I thought, 'No, he will think it so strange.'"

"Not a bit," said Julian politely. He took a cap from a peg, shut and locked the cottage door, and turned to the gate. It was very dark for the hour, and the wind came in gusts.

"For a moment," said Miss Lemoine, "yes, for one moment, I was more afraid of you than I was of the storm." Then, as a low rumbling sounded behind them, she started, and asked anxiously, "Do you think we shall get in in time? Do you really think so?"

"I don't know," said Julian. "I think we'd better hurry. This will be the quickest way." He lifted the latch of a little wicket gate as he spoke. "We always reckoned that this footpath saved at least two minutes."

They were in the woods which lay all about Forsham Old House, stark beeches for the most part, with the thick, sodden drift of old leaves burying the path. A great gust of wind swept up behind them, and then dropped dead. It was so sudden a thing that it startled even Julian: one minute, the straining rush and roar of it, the creak and grind of the branches overhead; and the next, stillness, and the air as black and heavy as water. Miss Lemoine uttered an exclamation. He felt her brush against him as if she had moved nearer, and he took her by the arm.

"We'd better run for it."

She said, "Yes, yes," and they had run perhaps a dozen yards or so when a first, brilliant lightning flash flared and was gone. For an instant every bare branch stood black against a background of pale violet. Then darkness again, and out of the dark the long, deep roll of thunder. With the flash, Miss Lemoine had come to a stand-still. Julian, holding her by the arm, was aware that she had covered her face.

"Come on," he said. But she stood rigid and did not move. "You can't stay here," he began—and then the second flash cut across his speech. It was brilliant beyond the first; the woods were white with it.

Miss Lemoine screamed aloud, a long, high, shuddering scream that was lost in cracking thunder. His grasp tightened. He tried to get her to move, and suddenly she was clinging to him, pressing against him, her hands locked on his arm, her voice choked with sobs calling his name:

"Julian! Save me, Julian!" And then again and again his name, always his name:

"Julian—Julian—Julian!"

Twice in twenty-four hours Julian Forsham had had a terrified woman clinging to him in the darkness. But, whereas Amabel had stirred the depths of sympathy and tenderness, Miss Lemoine merely roused in him a sense of helpless exasperation. What in Heaven's name did one do with a woman who went into hysterics over a clap of thunder?

"Miss Lemoine, do for the Lord's sake pull yourself together! I'll get you home in no time if you'll give me a chance. The worst of the storm is over anyhow, I think. It was travelling pretty fast."

As he spoke, her clasp relaxed a little. She fell back, lifting her head and drawing a quick, choking breath or two. And then the third flash came. It showed him her face; but not the face of Marie Anastasie Lemoine. It was a younger face that he saw by the quick flash of memory—just as white, just as terrified, with the piteous half-open mouth and straining eyes—it was the face of Mary Ann Brown. He said, "Annie!" before he knew that he was going to speak. And then the thunder and the rain came together, and she swayed blindly forward and fell against his shoulder half fainting.

His mind was bewildered in the extreme but the urgency of the situation precluded thought. He lifted her bodily, and had carried her about fifty yards, when he felt her arms round his neck and heard her sob his name:

"Julian! Julian!"

A most poignant sensation of annoyance stabbed right through the confusion of Julian's thoughts. The situation became suddenly clear, and in the strangest manner. All at once this was no longer Miss Lemoine, an hysterical lady with whom he had a slight acquaintance, and who might, or might not, imagine herself to have a tendresse for him, but little Annie Brown who was taking an astonishing liberty with his Christian name.

He set her on her feet, and began to hurry her along, his arm through hers.

"Pull yourself together!" he said sternly.

They came out upon the drive close to the house. Julian got her to the hall door, and found it unfastened. It was with feelings of unbounded relief that he bade her good-night. She was still trembling, but her self-control was coming back.

"You have been kind. I am not myself." He could just catch the words as she spoke very low and with her head turned away. Then, as he moved to go, she pushed the heavy door, and it fell to between them.

Chapter Twenty-Eight

AGATHA MORELAND'S LETTER describing her interview with Mrs. Thompson was written immediately after that interview and dated Tuesday. It reached Amabel Grey on the Wednesday morning, by which time Agatha herself was experiencing a slight reaction in the direction of everyday commonsense. She was ready to have Amabel to stay with her, but she couldn't help hoping that she would not come. It didn't look well to give one's sister a small room with no fireplace, when one's maid had a comfortable fire. Of course, Amabel knew how fussy Anderson was, and she had expressly mentioned that she could only give her the fireless room. All the same, it didn't look well; and she hoped that Amy would make other arrangements.

She lunched with Isobel Le Mesurier—a woman's lunch-party. She found herself, after lunch was over, sitting next to Mrs. Henry March, whom she met for the first time. Jane March, who had been Jane Smith, and who, as Jane Smith, had had an Astonishing Adventure, was a small person with indeterminate features and an engaging something about her. One could not describe Jane, but one liked her—everyone liked her. Agatha liked her at once, and found herself talking as she would have talked to an old friend. On an impulse of confidence she dropped her voice and said,

"I went to a medium yesterday."

"Why?" said Jane.

"Well—I just did. I was worried."

Jane's little nose wrinkled.

"Did she unworry you at all?" she asked briskly. "I suppose it was a she-medium—they generally seem to be women, I don't quite know why. Henry would say it's because we're the predatory sex."

Mrs. Moreland ignored Henry. She ignored everything except Jane's first question.

"She did—and she didn't," she said slowly. "That's to say, she set my mind at rest about the thing that was troubling me—the thing I really went to her about—; and then she nearly frightened me to death about my sister who has just taken an old house in the country. Do you believe in haunted houses, Mrs. March?"

"Not if you mean ghosts," said Jane. "Of course there are always rats, and smugglers, and things like that."

Scepticism had its usual effect. Agatha's cooling faith boiled up.

"It's all very well to laugh," she said, "but if you'd been *there*, Mrs. March. I just went to her on a sudden impulse. She didn't know my name, or my sister's name, or anything about us, and she described Amabel, and the house she's in, and—and everything. And she said Amabel was in the most frightful danger and ought to leave the house at once. And when I asked her what it was, she just screamed and fainted, and couldn't remember anything afterwards."

"How frightfully clever of her!" said Jane—"the fainting, I mean. I expect it made you creep about a hundred per cent. more than anything she could have described."

Agatha warmed to her subject, and enlarged upon the darkened room, the crystal, the medium's strange, far-away gaze, and the thrilling tones of her voice. When she had given Mrs. March every detail of the interview, she said,

"I don't mind saying that she convinced me—and I believe she would have convinced you too if you'd been there. Now, tell me, Mrs. March, what do you really think about it all? What would you say?"

"I should say she'd been got at," said Jane briefly.

Mrs. March did not go straight home. It was a fine afternoon, and she went for a walk along the Embankment. She found herself thinking a good deal about Mrs. Moreland and Mrs. Moreland's story. There were reasons why it touched certain chords in her memory.

She had been walking for about quarter of an hour, when she suddenly became aware that she was being followed. There was a man a little behind her, on her left, whose step kept pace with hers. She quickened her pace without looking round. The man quickened his; all at once he was beside her. He began to speak. She turned, prepared to freeze him off the face of the earth, and stared instead in unmitigated astonishment at one of the last persons whom she had ever expected to see again—Molloy, the Anarchist Uncle.

Those who read the "Astonishing Adventure of Jane Smith" will remember that, shortly before the close of that adventure, Mr. Geoffrey Ember had instructed two Comrades to eliminate Cornelius Molloy. Jane, his late wife's niece, had always imagined that this elimination had been effected, and that she no longer possessed an anarchist relation. She therefore exclaimed, "Good gracious!" and fell back a step.

"Ah!" said Mr. Molloy. "You've an affectionate heart, Jane. When all's said and done, one's own kith and kin are the best. 'It's overcome with joy she'll be, and you must be careful'—that was what I said to meself, and that was why I've been following you these ten minutes past."

"Good gracious!" said Jane again. "I thought you were dead." If she was overcome with joy, she appeared to be controlling her emotion with considerable success.

"Oh, I'm a hard one to kill," said Molloy easily.

Jane began to walk on.

"Look here, Mr. Molloy, what do you want?" she inquired. "I can't stand about here talking to you, and I'm certainly not going to take you for a walk. So, if you want anything—and I suppose you do—, you'd better tell me what it is."

Molloy looked down on her from his impressive height. His handsome features wore a look of melancholy reproach.

"There's the hard-hearted English for you," he said. "Isn't it likely that I should feel drawn towards me own flesh and blood, and feel the need of a kindly word from them?"

"No, it's not," said Jane. "Not in the least. And you know as well as I do that I'm not your flesh and blood—thank goodness. Now, will you please come to the point. What do you want?"

Molloy sighed heavily.

"It's a broken man I am, and only wishful to die in peace without interference from the police."

"I don't think you'll die for quite a long time," said Jane, "I don't really. You look like the green bay tree at the very height of its flourishing, if you don't mind my saying so. Now, it's no good beating about the bush. What do you *want*?"

"Shall we turn and walk back?" said Molloy. "I'll be telling you as we go, and not feel I'm taking you out of your way. Now, it's this way, me dear Jane,"—his voice took on a rich and luscious roll—"this is a wicked world, and we're all poor sinners, Heaven help us. But there's times when we can give one another a helping hand."

"That sounds beautiful," said Jane. "Who do you want to help— the police?"

A gleam of admiration showed for an instant in Mr. Molloy's fine dark-blue eyes. Jane was so remarkably quick in the uptake; it was a pleasure to do business with her.

"You have it," he said simply.

"I thought so. And what do you want in return?"

"Just the leave to die peaceably," said Molloy, with exquisite sadness.

Jane looked at him with an odd little smile.

"Come along," she said, "let's have the horrid details. I suppose, you've got something to sell, and you want me to tell Henry, so that he can go to the Chief and find out whether they'll let you off your just deserts."

"You have it again," said Mr. Molloy.

Jane made a grimace.

"All right, out with it! Tell me what it is, and I'll tell Henry. That's all I can promise to do. Whether Henry goes to the Chief or not, and what the Chief does about it isn't my affair. It'll all depend on whether they really want your information, I expect."

"They'll want it fast enough," said Mr. Molloy easily. "It's what they'd be giving the eyes out of their heads for. Do you think I'd have run the risk I'm running this very minute if I didn't know that what I'd got to tell would see me safe?"

"You do talk a lot, don't you?" said Jane. "I never knew anyone who talked so much and said so little." She glanced at her watch. "I'm going home in two minutes, so for goodness sake come to the point and tell me what it is you've got to sell."

Molloy looked pained.

"And that's an ugly word between friends," he said. "There's no man living can put it on me that I'm an informer."

Jane March stamped her foot.

"You've all the virtues. Would you mind just taking them for granted, and telling me what I'm to tell Henry."

"Well, then," said Molloy—he dropped his voice, came nearer, and breathed down the back of Jane's neck—"'tis the French forgeries."

"Don't do that!" said Jane involuntarily. Then, wheeling round so as to face him, she asked in rather breathless tones, "The forged notes? Do you mean it, do you really mean it, Mr. Molloy?"

Molloy resumed his full height and folded his arms.

"I do," he said. "But, mind you, Jane, it's a business that'll want delicate handling. I'm a gentleman meself, and I'll not deal except with gentlemen—and I'll not go to the Yard neither, not if they were all to go on their bended knees. I've me reputation to consider," he concluded in his grandest manner.

Jane's foot tapped the pavement.

"H'm, yes," she observed. "It wouldn't do for your friends to know that you'd sold them, would it? Now, for goodness sake, come down off that high horse of yours and get to business. Let me see, it's four o'clock, and I'll have to get hold of Henry—h'm—" She paused for a moment, then nodded and went on, "This'll be the best way, I think. I'll give you my telephone number, and you can ring me up from any public call-office at eight. They may want to see you to-night at the flat. Would that do?"

"I'd need a safe conduct," said Molloy—"just the Chief's word that I'm free to come and go whether we do a deal or not."

"Well, I can tell you all that when you ring up," said Jane. "Good-bye."

Molloy continued to walk beside her.

"You've not asked for me daughter Renata," he said—"your own cousin."

"How is she?" said Jane impatiently.

"She has twins," said Molloy. "Boys, six months old."

Visions of two little Arnold Todhunters arose in Jane's mind. She had characterized her cousin Renata as a white rabbit, and her two meetings with Renata's husband had roused her to a state of contemptuous fury.

"Good gracious, how perfectly dreadful!" she gasped.

"And there's a hard, unwomanly speech for you!" said Molloy.

"My good man, you never went up a fire-escape in the pitch dark behind Arnold Todhunter and had him dropping things on your head all the way, like I did."

Molloy contemplated her for a moment by the light of a street lamp.

"Well, well," he said, "there's one thing, nobody would take you for Renata now, as like as you used to be. I'd a photograph from her only last week, and she'd make two of you and a bit to spare."

"Life has its compensations, after all," said Jane.

Chapter Twenty-Nine

AT A QUARTER past eight that evening there were three people in Jane March's drawing-room.

Jane herself was standing on the hearth-rug in a boyish attitude with her hands behind her. Captain Henry March was at the little writing-table on the opposite side of the room. He had pulled his chair sideways, and sat with one elbow on the table and his legs crossed. In the largest armchair sat Sir Julian Le Mesurier; he filled it very completely. A writing-block lay on his knee; his large fingers fiddled with a fountain pen.

Henry March looked down the room towards the door.

"He ought to be here," he said.

"Henry, you're a fidget," said Jane. She turned to Sir Julian. "In about half a minute, I know, he'll ask me all over again whether I'm sure I've sent Lucy out, and whether the infant Henry can be depended upon to sleep through the proceedings and not listen at the door. Just in case he does, the answer in both cases is 'Yes.'"

Piggy had begun to draw a large black cat at the top of his sheet of paper.

"Henry and I are both in a fidget," he said. "I conceal it better than he does—that's all, my dear."

The cat was a heraldic cat, a cat rampant. It had long, fierce whiskers and a tail like a bottle-brush.

The bell of the flat rang suddenly. Jane went to the door. They heard her voice, and a deep, rolling answer, then her voice again. Henry March frowned. The door opened and Jane appeared. Behind her, the commanding figure of Mr. Molloy.

Mr. Molloy paused upon the threshold, and inclined his head in greeting.

"Good evening, gentlemen," he said. Then, advancing a step, he indicated Jane with a sweeping gesture. "I was saying to me niece"—Henry March winced—"I was saying to me niece Jane that it was me wish that she should be present at this interview."

Henry March said "Nonsense!"

Jane raised her eyebrows at him, and Mr. Molloy said in his deepest tones,

"I can retire, or I can remain—it is for you, gentlemen, to choose which I shall do. But"—he came forward into the room—"if I am to remain, I will ask you to remember that I am here at very considerable risk—that me motives may be impugned and me character defamed on account of the public service that I propose to render. It is, therefore, me wish that a member of me family should be present."

Henry March remembered that he had seen this man move a huge audience to tears and laughter in Chicago—the meeting had subsequently been dispersed by the police. In Cornelius Molloy the Stage had lost an actor to the world.

Sir Julian looked at Jane and nodded.

"You will remain," he said, "as a witness to Mr. Molloy's unblemished character—he seems to feel the need of one."

Jane shut the door, and took up her old position on the hearth-rug.

"Sit down, Molloy," said Sir Julian; and Mr. Molloy sat down very composedly in a Chippendale armchair. "Now," said Sir Julian Le Mesurier. "Now, Molloy, just come straight to the point. You told Mrs. March that you had information about the forged French notes."

"Ah, well," said Molloy, "that's going a little too quick. I'll not beat about the bush, and I'll tell you right here and now that I've had enough of politics, and politics has had enough of me. It's no game for a gentleman, when all's said and done; and I've the chance of marrying comfortably—the family hotel line—and settling down in peace and quiet."—Sir Julian began to draw a row of small heraldic kittens—"It's an old man I'm getting, and I'd be glad to feel that I'd be left to die in peace."

Sir Julian's small, light eyes rested on him for the merest fraction of time.

"All right, Molloy, go on," he said. "If your information's worth anything and you behave yourself, we shan't interfere with you. Now, these forgeries—are you in the game yourself?"

Mr. Molloy's shocked expression would have done an archbishop credit.

"I am not," he said. "Politics is what I've stuck to—and I'll not say that I've not been on the black side of the law now and again—; but there's half the width of hell between politics and this forging game."

Sir Julian spoke without looking up again:

"All right. You're not in it, but you know something about it? Now, will you just get on and tell us what you know."—He glanced over his shoulder—"Notes, Henry."

Mr. Molloy crossed one leg over the other, threw back his head, and gazed meditatively at the ceiling.

"Well now, where would I start?" he said, and appeared to plunge into thought. After a pause of some duration, during which Sir Julian put all his kittens into Toby frills, Molloy heaved a sigh and resumed, "Without prejudice then. I'd business last year in Barcelona, and I had to come away in a hurry because of a difference of opinion with some of the Comrades there. It suited me book to cut over the French frontier. Now there's a little place that I needn't name, on the Spanish side, that I stayed the night in. I'd used the inn before and knew the people, and when they gave me the third best room, it was reasonable enough I'd want to know why; and they told me that two gentlemen had come in ahead of me and booked the best of everything. Well now, that surprised me, and when I was up in my room and heard voices next door, I'd the curiosity to put my ear to the crack, just as it were to find out what these gentlemen might be."

It was at this juncture that Mr. Molloy observed a look of singular incredulity upon the face of his niece Jane March.

"I'll not say," he continued hastily, "that I hadn't some idea that I might be interested in their conversation. The door was a badly fitting door, and, as I stood there, I could hear a man talking French; but he wasn't a Frenchman. He was an Englishman, and what he said was just this, 'I'm late with them, but the risk gets greater every time.' The man that answered him, he was French right enough. He said, 'I was getting anxious. How have you managed this time? You are clever, you know, with your samples, and your pictures, and your Heaven knows what. What is it this time?' The Englishman laughed a little. He said, 'This time it is sketching-blocks. I have taken orders from a dozen art schools; they are enchanted with the quality of the paper.' They both laughed. Then the Frenchman asked, 'And how is Mademoiselle Anaïs?'"

Molloy, as he spoke the name, looked about him. Jane stood in frowning silence. Henry March was writing. Sir Julian had begun a new line of cats. The name apparently conveyed nothing to any one of the three. Molloy went on speaking in measured tones:

"The Englishman said 'She's well. I think she finds the country dull.' And then the Frenchman laughed and said 'Mademoiselle Anaïs, and your fogs, and your British Sunday, and your phlegm! Oh la, la, la—she has a temperament that one!'" Molloy hesitated, paused, looked round again. "That is all," he said.

Jane lifted her head in surprise. Henry was finishing a sentence. Sir Julian looked up.

"And why do you think that this interesting conversation referred to those forged notes?" he inquired.

"Ah, now," said Molloy, "that's where you have me. When I made inquiries I found that the gentleman with the English accent was travelling for a firm of paper manufacturers with samples of sketching-blocks, and the French gentleman was a traveller in light wines—all very innocent and ordinary, and nothing for anyone to lay hold of, as you say." He paused and then added, "It was the lady's name that gave the show away, gentlemen—and not the first time a very promising affair has come to grief through having a woman mixed up in it."

Piggy left his last kitten whiskerless.

"What date was this? Last year, you said. Can you give us the month and day?"

"I can. It was St. Patrick's Day, the seventeenth of March."

"Anaïs?" repeated Sir Julian, "Anaïs?—well, you seem to know more about the lady than I do, Molloy. Just go on being helpful, will you. Do you know her? Who is she?"

"I wouldn't say that I know her," said Molloy. "No, I wouldn't say that I know her. But it came to me by a side wind a year or two ago that she was doing some very high-grade work in the forged note line."

"Who is she?"

Molloy hesitated.

"They call her Mademoiselle Anaïs. She went to Russia before the war with a man called Karazoff—Prince Paul Karazoff—, and that's how I heard of her first, through the Russian Comrades. Karazoff was killed in '16, and she came back to Paris and took up this other line. And that's all I know, gentlemen."

"It's not very much," said Sir Julian.

"It's more than you knew before," said Molloy easily.

"What names were the two men using?"

"The Englishman was Robinson—"

"And his firm?"

"Ah, you have me there—I never thought to ask."

"And the other?"

"Lebrun—but they would not be their real names, of course."

"And that's all you know? Surely you saw the men?"

"Devil a bit. I slept like a dog; and they were off by daylight. You've all I know, and I hope it'll be of use to you." He stood up as he spoke, pushing his chair back.

Beneath the grand manner Jane perceived that he was ill at ease, impatient to be gone.

"I think he knows something more," she said quickly. "I think he knows something more about the woman."

"Yes," said Sir Julian, "I thought so too. Come now, Molloy, you've told us little enough. You can't afford to keep anything back. You said you didn't know the woman. Have you ever seen her? Come now, describe her, please."

"I've never laid eyes on her in me life," said Molloy.

Sir Julian began to tear his sheet of paper into long strips.

"Perhaps," he suggested, "you can furnish us with a description, nevertheless."

"Some Comrade may have mentioned what the lady looked like," Mr. Molloy resigned himself. "Well, then, I have heard said that she has red hair."

It was Jane who put the last question. She had been watching Molloy very closely all the time.

"Is this Anaïs French?" she asked suddenly, and got a glance in return, half protesting, half admiring.

"English she was to start with," he said reluctantly.

Sir Julian had his comment to make on that.

"English! Anaïs? That's not a very English name, Molloy. Are you sure she was English?"

"Well, they called her Flash Annie before she went to Russia," said Mr. Molloy.

Chapter Thirty

WEDNESDAY WAS a busy day for Amabel. She and Ellen lit fires in the two disused bedrooms, swept, cleaned, dusted, and by four o'clock had them in a habitable condition. Ellen throughout maintained a demeanour which indicated that she didn't hold with "they Millers." When it came to making Miss Miller's bed she burst suddenly into speech.

"I should ha' thought that Mr. Miller, being away all day yesterday and to-day, would ha' wanted his sister 'ome in the evening," she said. "Coming back to a empty 'ouse isn't what most men likes, nor wouldn't put up with neither—and, take it or leave it, that there Miller's a man like the rest of 'em."

"*Mr.* Miller, Ellen!" said Amabel gently, but firmly. "And you haven't got the blanket straight on your side. I wish you'd look at what you're doing and leave my friends alone."

Ellen jerked the blanket fiercely.

"Friends!" she muttered. "Save us and preserve us—friends!" Then, finding that Amabel took no notice, she broke with great suddenness into excited speech. "It's the crawlingness of it that I 'ates—I can't abide creepingness and crawlingness. And all I says is this, if we'd been meant to crawl, worms we should 'ave been made to start with—worms, or snakes, or such like."

"Ellen, do be quiet," said Amabel wearily. "We shall have to make this bed again. You've got *all* the blanket now. Here, strip it back and start fresh."

"'E comes into Eliza Moorshed's front shop yesterday morning," said Ellen, her voice a little louder than usual, "and 'e bought a tuppenny-'a'penny stamp and a time-table, 'I wanted to make sure they 'adn't altered the nine-thirty for Maxton. I'll catch it comfortable,' 'e says, and off 'e goes. And that very evening we was all a-'aving of our teas—lovely jam Eliza Moorshed makes, if she is my cousin—when who should come in but that young, fair-'aired Orchard that drives the carrier's cart to Ledlington and is nephew to Eliza's 'usband's sister-in-law. Well, 'e comes in, and sits down and 'as 'is tea, and 'e says, 'I done nothing but run into Forsham people in Ledlington to-day.'"

"Well, why shouldn't he?—Ellen, that sheet is *not* straight."

Ellen gave it a perfunctory pat.

"It wasn't 'e that shouldn't," she said darkly. "It's them that says they're catching trains to Maxton, and then turns up on the steps of the Queen's Hotel in Ledlington as bold as brazen serpents."

"Now, Ellen!"

"Tom Orchard seen 'im with 'is own eyes. 'I shall catch the train to Maxton nicely,' says 'e in Eliza Moorshed's front shop at a quarter past nine; and at 'alf-past twelve Tom Orchard seen 'im coming out of the Queen's Hotel in Ledlington, which is a good fifty mile away from where 'e said 'e was a-going. Oh, yes, and for all 'is brazenness 'e didn't want to be seen neither, for when Mr. Bronson drove up in 'is Rolls-Royce car—which 'e 'appened to do at that very individual minute,—that there Miller pops back into the hotel just as quick as a weazle—Tom Orchard seen 'im."

"Well, it's really not our business," said Amabel. "The counterpane is on that chair behind you."

Ellen spread out the counterpane with an air of gloom. As she smoothed it over the pillow, she said,

"Tom Orchard seen Mrs. King in Ledlington too, with 'er 'ands just as full of parcels as they could 'old—wonderful where some folk gets the money from, and she without a penny piece if all's true that's said about 'er."

"It never is," said Amabel. "I shouldn't worry about it if I were you."

Ellen tossed her head and sniffed.

"Anyhow she don't pay 'er lawful bills at Eliza Moorshed's," she announced.

As she spoke, the first rumble of thunder sounded outside. Amabel looked out of the window.

"There's a storm coming up. You'd better hurry, Ellen. We've just got through in time."

Ellen cast one glance at the sky, and hurried in good earnest.

Julian Forsham was very silent at tea. His mind recurred again and again to that moment in the wood when the lightning flash had seemed to show him the face of Annie Brown. The impression, so startlingly vivid at the time, was, in retrospect, a stark impossibility. Brownie's story of the thunderstorm, his own recollection of Annie clinging to him in terror, and the repetition of the scene that afternoon with another hysterical woman—these were the elements out of which the sudden flash of recognition had been evolved. It seemed inconceivable that in any circumstances Miss Lemoine, the black-haired Frenchwoman, should have suggested to his mind Annie Brown with her red hair, village breeding, and speech very much what Jenny's was now. He had found Mademoiselle Lemoine a cultivated person with a taste for art and literature, and a degree of social tact unusual in her position, obviously a woman of the world, travelled and cultivated. His mind could hardly have played him an odder trick. He replied absently to Miss Miller's painstaking conversation, and relapsed again into frowning silence.

Amabel did not attempt to talk. She was glad enough to sit still and rest.

They had nearly finished tea when Anita King was ushered in.

"Mr. Bronson's going to pick me up," she announced. "I meant to get here ages ago; but I had to shelter from that horrible storm. And where do you think I sheltered?"—She addressed herself to Miss Miller—"You'll never guess, I'm sure. But when I saw that inky cloud I just rushed for your bungalow. And your brother was ever so nice to me."

"I'm glad you were able to get in," said Anne Miller.

Nita King dropped into a chair, unfastening her furs and throwing them back.

"I should have *died* if I'd had to stay out in a storm," she declared. "I'm just simply terrified of storms. I'm afraid your brother found me a great nuisance, for I just sat and *shuddered*. And when those dreadful, *dreadful* claps of thunder came, I simply had to scream a little—I couldn't help it."

Julian brought her some tea. As he gave her the cup she looked up at him, and once again he was struck by her likeness to Jenny—the rather sharp features, the close set hazel eyes, the lips too thin for beauty. It was, he told himself, a likeness of type. There were hundreds of these rather foxy looking women up and down the country. It was a type he detested, though in Anita King it had every art to flatter it; the dark furs and plain black hat made a becoming background for dead white skin and flaming hair.

"Mr. Miller was *so* kind," said Nita King, sipping her tea. Of course, your not being there and all, I felt a little awkward—one can't be too careful in a village, can one? But he was *so* kind, and absolutely insisted on walking up here with me, though he wouldn't come in."

"Oh, he likes a walk," said Anne Miller composedly. "When do you get back to your lodge, Mrs. King?"

"To-morrow," said Nita—"no, no more tea, thank you—It's been so very, *very* kind of Mr. Bronson to have me while the roof was being mended. But there *is* something about one's own tiny, wee scrap of a place, isn't there? And then, quite between ourselves, of course I'm ever so grateful to Mr. Bronson—and he's a great, *great* friend of mine. But"—she spread out her hands and looked appealingly at Julian—"you know how it is when people aren't quite, *quite absolutely* one's own sort—they don't always understand that one's just being *friendly*, do they?" She continued to talk; and if her hearers were not left with the impression that nothing except her own delicate sense of breeding stood between Anita King and the worldly goods with which Mr. Bronson could her endow, all very properly and to the tune of Mendelssohn's wedding march,—well, it wasn't Mrs. King's fault.

Mr. Bronson fetched her in due course, and the rest of the evening passed without event.

When Amabel took Miss Miller to her new room and bade her good-night, that lady remarked that it was a very nice room, and of course it was a pity to let two of the best rooms in the house go to rack and ruin for want of being lived in, but, for her part, she had been very comfortable the night before, and Amabel needn't have troubled to move her. "Cats are just as liable to come and fight under this window as any other," she concluded with a laugh.

Amabel went back into the sitting-room for a word with Julian, and found him standing on the hearth, obviously deep in thought.

When she had shut the door, he said,

"You heard what Mrs. King said—Miller walked up here with her and wouldn't come in? It's my belief that he simply wanted an excuse for prowling round the house again."

"I don't care how much he prowls when you're here," said Amabel. "Really, Julian, you're as bad as Ellen. She's got the unfortunate man on the brain, I do believe. All the time we were making beds this afternoon she kept telling me an interminable story about how Mr. Miller bought a time-table yesterday at Mrs. Moorshed's, and said he was going to Maxton, and then—prepare for a sensation!—he was actually seen coming out of the Queen's Hotel at Ledlington at half-past twelve that morning. It's almost impossible to believe in such depravity, isn't it? And, worse still, when he saw Mr. Bronson, he fled. What it is to have a guilty conscience!"

"What was Bronson doing in Ledlington?"

"I daresay Ellen knows—I don't. According to her he was in his Rolls-Royce car."

"Was anyone else in Ledlington?" asked Julian laughing.

"Only Mrs. King, who had been shopping, which Ellen seemed to consider very immoral." She changed her tone suddenly, and asked, "Julian, are you really going to sleep in that room?"

"I'm going to spend the night there—I don't know about sleeping. Why?"

"Because I wish you wouldn't. I wish you'd go back to your old room and sleep there. No, Julian, don't laugh—I really, really mean it."

Julian stopped laughing.

"What was all right for you is too risky for me? Is that it?" he asked.

"No, of course not. But last night—Julian, there was something rather horrible about last night. I've never really been frightened through and through before." Her colour changed as she spoke, her eyes widened.

Julian took an impulsive step forward. That look of appeal called to him as nothing had ever called to him before.

"Amabel," he said, "Amabel, darling!" His voice was low and shaken. He put both hands on her shoulders and went on, his words hurrying, his breath coming fast, "Amy, I can't bear it when you look like that. You know very well how it is with me, and I believe you care. Cut the whole thing and come away. Let's get married and—"

"Julian—Julian," said Amabel faintly. Her eyes closed, and he could feel her tremble. The next instant his arms were close about her, and they kissed—a long kiss sweet with memory and hope.

The old house was silent. Outside the rain fell softly, softly on to wet grass, wet paths, wet trees. Within, warmth and firelight, and the sense of home. To each there came that same sense of home-coming. Long years—long, lonely years; disappointment;

heartache; the weary round of unshared days; and then, at the end, this home-coming.

Neither spoke for a long, long while. The perfect moment was enough.

Chapter Thirty-One

IT WAS LATE when Amabel went to her room. After those long moments of silence there had been so much to talk about. They had sat over the fire and talked till midnight.

Julian was urgent that she should leave the house next day, go to the Berkeleys, marry him within the week.

"And then we'll *really* go to Italy."

"No, it's too soon," she said, "I must write to Daphne first, and—it's no use your looking like that, Julian—I really do feel under an obligation to George, quite apart from the two hundred pounds."

"My dear angel," said Julian, "are you proposing a six months' engagement, or do you suggest that we should spend our honeymoon ghost hunting?"

Amabel coloured and laughed.

"No, I didn't mean that. But I can't just clear out and leave all the stories ten times worse than they were before. Yes, you can pay the two hundred pounds if you want to. I'm not really as proud and stiff-necked as you think I am; and I'll let you do that if you're set on it."

"George can give it to us for a wedding present," said Julian cheerfully.

Amabel's dimple showed.

"George must have altered very much if he gives wedding presents on that scale now."

"Five pounds' worth of electro-plate is more in George's line," said Julian with an answering twinkle. "Anyhow, hang the two hundred pounds! Look here, when will you marry me? I was going up to town to see Piggy to-morrow—Julian Le Mesurier, you know, my cousin, the C.I.D. chap—, and I think I'd better go; only, why don't you come too?—and we'll go and buy an engagement ring and a licence all in one fell bust."

"Julian, you schoolboy! No, I can't come up to-morrow. You see, there's Miss Miller."

"Hang the woman! Why can't you leave her? Considering she invited herself, I should think you could go up to town for the day and leave her easily enough."

"No, I won't really. I'll write to Daphne and to Agatha, and—and I think I want a quiet day, Julian, just to sort my mind."

"And you'll marry me when?"

"I'll tell you that to-morrow when you come home."

When Amabel had gone to her room, Julian effectually blocked the narrow passage that led to it by the simple process of piling two large chairs one upon the other. Miss Miller and Amabel were now cut off from the rest of the house, and Julian reflected with pleasure that anyone walking about the house in the dark would probably bark his shins before he realized that the chairs were there—Mr. Ferdinand Miller, for instance,—or Miss Anne Miller.

Julian then put out the passage lights, including the oil lamps, and entered the room lately occupied by Amabel. Here, also, he had some preparations to make. The door into the passage he left unbolted, but blocked the door that led into Miss Georgina's room by moving the heavy walnut bureau across it. He laid an electric torch handy on the table at the head of the bed, and pushed under his pillow the little automatic pistol which had been his constant companion during lonely months in the desert. He then took off his shoes and lay down without undressing.

The night passed as peacefully as if the Dower House were a newly built suburban villa.

Julian caught the eight-thirty to town. He had breakfasted and left the house before Miss Miller emerged from her room. Long before she did so the chair barricade had been removed, but it had provided Ellen with another grievance.

"If it 'ad been dark, anybody might 'ave broken their leg," she grumbled when she came into Amabel's room with the tea tray, which she had taken from Jenny. "Jenny and me a-pulling and a-'awling of those two 'eavy chairs! It was Mr. Forsham thought of doing that, I suppose. And when I sees them I says to myself, 'Now, if that isn't a man all over. What's the good of that?' I says to myself. 'A chair will stop a lawful housemaid, but it isn't going to stop a 'aunting ghost, not much it isn't. Such as that will go through chairs and tables just as easy as a spoon'll go through milk.'" She set down the tray with a jerk. "But there, I suppose are women 'ud all be idling and getting into mischief if there wasn't any men for 'em to wait on. It's the men that makes work in a house, and the women that does it. Of course, I'm not saying that gentleman or two don't frighten you up a bit, if it comes to that. And, please, ma'am, would you 'ave any objections to my going into Ledlington this afternoon with Eliza Moorshed? There's a sister of her 'usband's there that's married to a baker in a very good way of business, and they've sent me a invitation to come in and 'ave tea with them to-day."

"All right," said Amabel, "you can go when you've done the bedrooms."

At breakfast it appeared that Miss Miller also had business in Ledlington that afternoon. She invited Amabel to accompany her, but took her refusal in very good part.

"I shall be back about seven," she announced. "I don't go very often, and I like to make a day of it when I do."

Julian Forsham spent a busy day. He had his publishers to see, half-an-hour's business with Mr. Berry, and sundry other matters to attend to.

To Mr. Berry he announced his engagement, and extracted from him information as to the quickest way of getting married.

When he walked into Sir Julian Le Mesurier's room he found Piggy genial but busy. He got a "Hullo, Ju-Ju!"—and then had to wait whilst Piggy finished writing a letter. When it had been despatched, Julian asked:

"I suppose you got a letter from me this morning?"

"I did—rather cryptic. Why so interested in the fair Mrs. Thompson's telephone calls? I trust you're not thinking of bringing her into the family, or anything rash like that, Ju-Ju, old man."

Julian made a face of disgust.

"No! But, I say, Piggy, you've got to produce your congratulations all the same. I'm going to be married in about a week."

Piggy had drawn a row of large question marks across a blank sheet of paper. He stopped, poised his pen, and said,

"No! Good Lord! Not really?"

"Absolutely," said Julian. Piggy grunted and began placing a cat on the top of each question mark. "Do you remember, twenty years ago, my telling you all about Amabel Ferguson, and how horribly hard it hit me when she wouldn't break off her engagement to marry me?"

"Yes, I remember. You used to walk about my rooms in the small hours and talk like Manfred. Looking back, I can't imagine why I didn't murder you and have done with it."

Julian laughed.

"Well, Piggy, old man," he said, "it's still Amabel. I found her at the Dower House as George's tenant, and I'm doing my best to get her to marry me next week."

Piggy laid down his pen and stretched out a capacious hand.

"Ju-Ju, I'm most awfully glad. And as for Isobel, she'll probably embrace you. Isobel's most endearing vice is a passionate desire to see everybody else as happy as we are. Of course, I make it my business to point out to her that, as a husband, I am probably unique, and it's therefore no use her buoying other women up with false hopes—no, seriously, Julian, I'm most frightfully pleased. It's pretty good to have a home to come back to—you can take that from me."

"Now, Piggy," said Julian, after a moment, "I've told you this partly because I'm simply yearning to tell everyone, but chiefly because I want your advice."

"All right." The cats on the top of the question marks were all standing on one hind leg, clawing fiercely in the air.

"But, first," said Julian—"I suppose you haven't had time to collect anything about Mrs. Thompson?"

"Why, yes, we have. As to what you asked about the trunk calls—I told 'em to get busy with it this morning, and I got the report just before you came in. Let me see, where did I put it?—ah, here." He picked up a sheet of paper, holding it in his left hand whilst with his right he continued to shade the cats. "Mrs. Thompson. Telephone number, um—m—m—m—Tuesday, um—m—m—Ah, here we have it. Trunk from Ledlington 202 at twelve-thirty. I forget how far Ledlington is from Forsham, but it's somewhere around, isn't it? Is that what you wanted?"

"It's seven miles," said Julian. "What's Ledlington 202? Does he say?"

"Oh, yes, he's got it down all right. It's an hotel—the Queen's Hotel, Ledlington."

Julian whistled softly. The Queen's Hotel, Ledlington,— Tuesday—Ellen's story about Ferdinand Miller, and Amabel's laughing comments on it: "He was actually seen coming out of the Queen's Hotel at Ledlington at half-past twelve"—"and worse still, when he saw Mr. Bronson he fled"—"what it is to have a guilty conscience!"—Ferdinand Miller at the Queen's Hotel at half-past twelve, the hour of the medium's call—trying to escape notice too, bolting back into the hotel, by all accounts, when Mr. Bronson happened to drive up!

Piggy's small, light eyes caught the dark look, the puzzled expression. He threw down his pen and said quickly,

"What is it, old man? Don't you think you'd better tell me a little more?"

Julian nodded.

"Half a minute," he said.

Nita King had been in Ledlington too. Yes, he'd better tell Piggy the whole thing. The bother was that, if by any chance Annie Brown was mixed up in the thing,—if Anita King were Annie Brown—, he wanted time to think, to decide how much and what to say.

"Piggy," he said, "can you give me five minutes? The fact is I'm a bit bothered, and I want to sort things out. Can you give me five minutes or so to do the sorting? I expect you're horribly busy as usual."

"Busier," said Piggy briefly. "At the moment we're engaged in the interesting pastime of looking for a needle in a bundle of hay. You don't happen in your wanderings to have come across any fair damsel known alternatively as Mademoiselle Anaïs and Flash Annie, do you?—believed to have red hair and to be up to her neck in the forged note business. As she seems to be our one real clue up to date, we're rather anxious to find her. But you'll keep that to yourself, please. Take your five minutes if you want them, by all means. I've always got letters to write, worse luck."

Julian Forsham had strolled to the far end of the room. He stared at a picture which hung there; it appeared to interest him deeply. After some moments' pause he spoke over his shoulder:

"I'm afraid five minutes won't do me. I should only be wasting your time at present. My business'll keep. Thanks awfully for getting me that information about the calls. I'll tell you why I wanted it another time."

Piggy looked up in surprise.

"My good Ju-Ju," he began.

But Julian wheeled round suddenly, and, coming across the room, clapped him on the shoulder.

"Well, I've bothered you no end, and I'll be going. I'll come and unburden my soul in a day or two. Tell Isobel she's to come to my wedding. The piglets may come too if they're good. So long."

The door shut. Piggy looked at it and raised his eyebrows.

"Ju-Ju's a bit erratic to-day," he commented. "I suppose it's being in love."

Chapter Thirty-Two

JULIAN GOT BACK to Forsham by the six-twenty. He had a carriage to himself—and plenty to think about. The moment in the office when

Piggy had asked him in jest, "You don't happen to have come across a fair damsel called alternatively Mlle. Anaïs and Flash Annie?—she's up to her neck in the note forging business," had been a moment of revelation. He had been within an ace of telling Piggy everything—the mysterious happenings at the Dower House; his fears lest Annie Brown should be mixed up in them in such a way as to bring fresh shame and sorrow on poor old Brownie—when Piggy himself had stopped him with two words, a name—Flash Annie. It was under that name that he had traced Annie Brown to Paris ten years ago and lost her there. That she was found, or half found now, he had no doubt. "Up to her neck in the note forging business"—oh, Lord, poor Brownie!

The events of the last few days began to emerge from the confusion which had veiled them, began to cohere and become intelligible. If Annie Brown were really up to her neck in the note forging business, what more convenient place for the production of those notes than the lonely Dower House with its reputation for being haunted? It was easy to see the necessity for keeping tenants away—as easy as it had been to frighten those tenants into hurried flight.

Annie Brown—what was one to do about Annie? That was the question. Get her away quietly for Brownie's sake before the rest of the gang were roped in. Yes, that was all very well; but it brought him back to a problem still unsolved. Granted that Annie Brown and Flash Annie were one and the same person, he had still to find that person in the neighbourhood of Forsham. There had been an instant when he thought that he had found her in Anastasie Lemoine; and there had been other saner moments when he had traced Jenny's features in Anita King. He must see both women to-night, and resolve these doubts for good and all.

It was Anita King who had sent Agatha Moreland to the medium. Anita King had been in Ledlington when Mrs. Thompson had been called by the Queen's Hotel. And Anita King had paid Ferdinand Miller a visit yesterday afternoon.

The train arrived at Forsham punctually. Julian walked up the hill, and stopped at the cottage for five minutes to pick up some papers.

Mr. Miller, who had arrived by the same train, had the advantage of having a bicycle at the station. As Julian approached the Dower House from the garden, Mr. Miller, in a sufficiently bad temper, was leaving it by way of the drive on the other side of the house.

If Mr. Miller was in a bad temper, Julian was in a mood of happy anticipation. He pushed away into the back of his mind the whole miserable business that had been occupying it, and allowed other words of Piggy's—pleasanter words—to come to the fore. "A home's a pretty good place to come back to." For the first time since he was a schoolboy he felt that he was coming home. For all these years he had lived in a house, a tent, an hotel, a caravanserai, or under bare skies; but no one place had been home to him. Now he was coming home. Amabel would be waiting for him.

He walked in, and called to her as he took off his overcoat and hat. When there was no answer, he ran up the stairs, as eager as a boy. The sitting-room door was open. The room was empty. He went back into the passage and called again. The doors were all shut. There was no answer. With a little chill on his mood he went back into the room he had just left, and rang the bell. As Jenny came out into the hall, he called over the stairs to her:

"Where is Mrs. Grey, Jenny?"

"I don't know, Mr. Julian," said Jenny. "Isn't she upstairs?"

"No," he said. "Just come along up and see if she's in her room or Miss Miller's room—by the way, where is Miss Miller?"

"Gone to Ledlington," said Jenny, coming up the stairs—"been gone all day."

Julian frowned, but made no comment. His thought was that there was a great deal too much Miller in this business.

They went into every room without finding Amabel, and Jenny volunteered the brilliant suggestion that "Mrs. Grey must have stepped out."

"Was she in to tea?"

"Oh, yes, Mr. Julian. Mr. Bronson called, getting on for four, and he wouldn't stay to tea. And then she had hers, and I come and cleared away at five like I always do."

"And she was here then?"

"Standing in front of the fire with her back to me, warming her hands."

"And you didn't hear her go out?"

"No, Mr. Julian. The first I heard was when Mr. Miller rang the bell."

"Miller! When did he come?"

"Just before you did, Mr. Julian. He wanted to see Mrs. Grey most particular. I come upstairs and looked for her while he stood in the hall. He seemed terribly put out when I couldn't find her. And when I told him Miss Miller'd been gone all day, he went away down the drive swearing to himself—or that's what it sounded like."

There was a pause.

"All right, Jenny," said Julian, "you can go. I expect Mrs. Grey must have gone out." Jenny went downstairs, and after standing over the fire for a minute, Julian began to walk up and down the room. His sense of homecoming had gone cold. What on earth had taken Amabel out at this hour, and in this weather?

It was as he turned for the second time that he saw the sheet of paper lying on the front of the writing-table, half on, half off the blotting-pad. He stopped, picked it up, and read the simple sentence which ran unsteadily across the top of the page: "I can't stand it any longer." The words were in Amabel's writing. The sheet of paper was one taken from her block. About an inch of the bottom of the sheet had been torn off.

"I can't stand it any longer." A ghastly stab of fear went through Julian as he read the words. Anne Miller away all day in Ledlington. Amabel alone here—quite alone from four o'clock. What happening, what suggestion of terror had made her write those words, and then go—where?

With a quick reaction he thought of the Berkeleys. "She's gone down to Susan. I urged her to go, and she's gone." Yes, of course that was it. Some sound—something—anything had startled her, and she had gone to the Berkeleys to wait there for him, leaving this scrawl to explain her absence.

He was half downstairs before the thought was complete, and out of the house before there came, chill and insistent, the conviction, "Amabel wouldn't do that. It's not like her." To lose her head and run out of the house without a word to Jenny—that wasn't Amabel at all, unless—his mind refused to picture a terror which might have driven her out, blind, unthinking.

He came into the Berkeleys' smoking-room with a short "Is Amabel here?" And when Lady Susan said "No" in a tone of surprise, the shadow in his face brought them both to their feet. He did not know himself how much he had built on her being there until Susan spoke:

"No, she's not here. Julian, what is it? You look dreadful."

Julian's face was ghastly.

"I can't explain—not now. But I want the telephone. I want a trunk call. Susan!"

Susan answered his look of appeal with a steady "All right, Julian. Just let us know if we can do anything," and turned to the door.

Edward Berkeley, book in hand, touched him on the arm as he passed, and said, "Just let's know if you want anything. Might do worse than tell Susan if anything's gone wrong."

Julian, left alone, gave the Le Mesuriers' private number, and waited an interminable five minutes for the call to come through. It was Isobel who answered, Isobel who began to pour out charming felicitations on his engagement. He stopped her with a quick "Not now, my dear. We're in horrible trouble. Is Piggy there? I want him badly." He heard her call "Piggy, darling, it's Julian. There's something wrong," and then Piggy's "Hullo, Ju-Ju! What is it?"

"Piggy, I was a damned fool this afternoon. I ought to have told you the whole thing then and there. But I didn't because I'm afraid old Brownie's daughter is badly mixed up in it."

"Hullo! Steady on, what's all this?"

"I was going to tell you; and then you said 'Flash Annie.' I traced Brownie's daughter to Paris under that name ten years ago. Now I've reason to think she's back in Forsham, and I believe the people she's working with have been using the Dower House for their purpose."

"Yes—wait a minute—you're probably right. I had a report after you left this afternoon from a special man we've had working on the case. He lives in your parts, and seems to have stumbled on a clue by accident. You'd better see him and tell him everything you know, and—"

"Piggy, for the Lord's sake, listen! I got home to find Amabel gone. (Yes, another call, please. Don't cut us off!) Are you there, Piggy? Amabel's gone! I found a scrawl saying she couldn't stand it any longer—and she's gone."

"I say, Ju-Ju, pull yourself together. What's she mean? What couldn't she stand any longer?"

"You know the stories about the Dower House—it's plain enough now how they got about. These people have been frightening tenants away for years. Amabel's been too plucky for them. I can't tell you the things she's stuck out. But, whilst I was away to-day, something worse must have happened—something that sent her right off her balance. Piggy, I've got the wind up."

"So I see. You'd better get on to our man at once. He's a most reliable fellow, and quite handy to you. Don't give him away locally if you can help it. He does special jobs for us, and prefers to blush unseen."

"Who is he?"

Piggy's voice came back very clear and distinct: "F. Miller, The Bungalow, Forsham."

Chapter Thirty-Three

AMABEL SAT DOWN and wrote letters after Miss Miller had departed for Ledlington. The letter to Daphne had to be written more than once. She had just torn up what she had written, when Jenny came in with the post, and there was a fat letter with the Neapolitan postmark. She tore it open and found sheet after sheet—just a wild scrawl of delight:

"Oh, Mums, everything's too lovely, and I'm *too* happy. It only happened last night, and I didn't believe I *could* be so happy. I didn't know that anyone could care so much as Jimmy cares for me. And it makes me feel that I'm not the very, very, very least bit good enough for him. He cares so frightfully, and he thinks I'm all sorts of things that I'm not. And, oh, Mums, it does make me want to be what he thinks I am, and it makes me feel what a *beast* I was to you before I came away. Oh, darling, I promise I'll never, never be such a pig any more. And Jimmy—" There were pages and pages about Jimmy, and a letter from Jimmy's self—a very nice letter indeed over which Amabel wept.

All the nice things seemed to be happening together. Daffy and this nice Jimmy. Herself and Julian. The world seemed just full of love and happiness. It was easier to write to Daphne now— much easier. She wrote a long, happy letter, and walked down into Forsham to post it herself.

As she was coming back, the Bronsons' car passed her. She caught a glimpse of Angela and luggage. "They'll be glad to have her back," she thought.

It was after lunch that the day changed. It had been fine all the morning, with faint sunlight and a pale turquoise sky. But the afternoon darkened at three o'clock, and the rain began to fall in floods. Amabel lighted up, and drew the curtains in the sitting-room. She remembered that she had meant to darn a rent in her waterproof, and went to her bedroom to get it. It wasn't there. She looked through the things in the wardrobe a second time. No, it wasn't there—Ellen must have forgotten to bring it from her old room. It must still be hanging in the big oak press opposite the door.

She put on the light when she came to the room, and, seeing Julian's electric torch lying on the small table by the bed, she took it up and, opening the cupboard door, flashed the light into its dark corners. The waterproof was there, and she unhung it. As she turned with it over her arm, something arrested her attention. It was a very little thing; but it stopped her, turned her back.

She lifted the torch and let the light shine full on the end hook in the corner. She had stopped because the edge of the beam had glinted on something there, and she turned to see, what it could be. The light shone full on the hook and showed, caught up on it, a tiny tangle of hair—a tiny tangle of red hair.

Amabel stood and looked at it. That the hair was Jenny's she made no doubt; but how it came to be caught up on the farthest hook in this old press was a thing that surprised her beyond measure. Surprise changed suddenly into angry comprehension. After all, it had been Jenny who had been playing tricks. Jenny must have hidden in this press at night, and stolen out in the dark to open the connecting door when it was left shut, or to shut it when it was left open. The anger died in a realization that, if this were so, Jenny must surely be, if not insane, at least on the borderline of insanity.

Amabel put up her hand and pulled at the little knot of hair. It was tangled tightly about the hook, and was strong and unyielding, as red hair is wont to be. She was hampered by the weight of the rain-coat over her arm; her hand slipped, and she caught at the hook to steady herself. As her weight came on it, it moved. The beam from the electric torch had slipped aside. She swung it back. The hook hung crooked, and a piece of the panelling seemed to have started; a crack showed—it ran downward from an inch or two to the left of the hook.

Amabel dropped her rain-coat in a heap, took hold of the hook, and pulled on it. It came round, a little stiffly, but it came. As it turned, the crack widened, and the panel pivoted on itself.

Amabel stood looking through a narrow, dark door into a black space beyond. She put out her hand and steadied herself against the wall of the press. The panel that had turned had its edge towards her. The door seemed to go right through the wall behind the press. Very, very dimly there came into her mind a faint impression of Miss Georgina saying something about a passage, an old passage—something about its not being safe, and bad old times. It was something to do with a time of religious persecution. She couldn't get any nearer to it than that. So faint was the memory that nothing less startling than what had just happened could have revived it even for an instant.

Very slowly, she moved forward until she was standing in the opening. There was a sort of tiny chamber hollowed out behind it. She let the light shine into it, and saw that there were steps going down. She came as far as the top of the steps, and looked down them. The steps went down very steeply; they were narrow stone steps, a good deal worn; they were about as steep as the stairs which would lead to an attic room.

Amabel was looking down at them, when all of a sudden she heard a sound below her in the darkness. On a quick impulse she turned the torch, pressing it against the fold of her skirt. The sound came a little nearer. Someone was at the bottom of the steps. Someone was coming up.

In that moment Amabel would have given almost everything she possessed to have been on the farther side of the press. If she had gone at once when she heard the sound, if she had only gone at once, she might have been safe in the sitting-room by now with the lights turned on and Jenny within call—no, it was Jenny coming up the stairs in the dark—or was it Jenny?—who was it?

Just for a moment a paralysed sense of not being able to move or even breathe took hold of Amabel. Then the mounting footsteps came nearer, and suddenly the instinct with which one wards a blow made her start back from the top of the stair, with both hands out as if she were pushing the unseen person away. Her right hand held the electric torch—she had forgotten it—, and as her hands went out in that involuntary gesture, the beam cut the darkness and showed her a face looking up as she herself was looking down—a white face framed in red hair—Jenny's face.

Afterwards Amabel did not know whether it was she who had cried out or the other. Someone cried out, and the next instant Amabel, her heart beating wildly, was back in the cupboard, pulling the panelled door to, and twisting the hook into its place again.

She leaned there, listening, and heard no sound. As she stepped back, her foot caught in her forgotten rain-coat, and she nearly fell. She picked it up mechanically, and stepped out into the lighted bedroom. There panic came on her, and she ran blindly into the hall towards the stairs. She wanted to get as far as she could from the dark press and the passage behind it.

With her foot on the top step, she paused. *Jenny was in the hall below*—Jenny with her back to her, lighting the oil lamp.

Amabel stood quite still. She watched Jenny replace the glass chimney and regulate the wick. She stood and waited because all the while Jenny had her back to her, and until she saw her face she could neither move nor turn. Jenny seemed to take a long time over the lamp. When she had at last finished, she took a duster out of the drawer and rubbed the front of the table with it.

Amabel felt that she could not bear the slow movements, the uncertainty, any longer. She called "Jenny!" in a sharp, dry tone; and Jenny turned with the duster in her hand. It *was* Jenny—it was certainly Jenny, and no one else. She stood looking up, and asked:

"Did you want anything, ma'am?"

Amabel said the first thing that came into her head:

"If anyone calls, I'll see them." Then she went quickly into the sitting-room.

Still clasping the rain-coat and the torch, she stood for a full minute, her eyes fixed on the open door. When the minute had passed, she laid the torch carefully on a table, and went and shut the door.

It was some time before her fingers were steady enough to thread a needle and mend the jagged tear in her rain-coat. Her mind was troubled and confused, and as the confusion lessened, the trouble grew. She had seen Jenny coming up the secret stair behind the old press, and within the same minute she had seen Jenny in the hall below trimming the lamp. It wasn't possible—it really wasn't possible. The person in the hall *was* Jenny. Then who or what was the other? Her hands shook so much that she could hardly hold the needle or her work. Agatha's story came back into her mind. Agatha had seen Jenny stand in the doorway between the two rooms some time in the night. Agatha must have seen what she herself had just seen. *What* had they seen?

She thought of Julian with such a rush of longing that it frightened her. With years of self-control behind her, it was all that she could do not to leave the house now, this very minute, and await his return at the little station. It was only half-past three—three hours at the very least before he would be back. The thought of those three hours was a heavier burden than the thought of the six months had ever been before. Her heart cried out for Julian, and she could not still its fear.

The sound of a car driving up outside broke in on her thoughts. The front door bell rang, and she heard Jenny pass through the hall.

Julian wouldn't ring. And Julian wouldn't drive up—neither would Miss Miller. She listened, wondering who it might be, and feeling that she would be glad and thankful to see anyone, no matter who.

It was Mr. Bronson who came in a moment later, very smiling and genial.

"No, you mustn't order tea for me, for I can only stay a moment. No, really, Mrs. Grey, just a moment and that is all. It's a horrible afternoon, and your fire looks very cosy, very cosy indeed. I am much tempted to linger; but I have business to attend to at home, business that won't keep." He spread out his hands to the fire, and went on, "I promised Angela I'd look in—you know we've got her back again."

"Yes, I know. I saw her go past on her way from the station this morning. I expect you're glad to get her back."

"Well, yes, we are, we are. I only hope she won't find it dull after the gay time she's been having with her cousins. That's the worst of this place as far as she's concerned; there really are no young people at all, and she's bound to find it dull. However, her idea is that we're all to turn young and play with her." Mr. Bronson laughed heartily. "What do you think of that now, Mrs. Grey?"

"I think it's quite a good idea," said Amabel, smiling.

"So do I, so do I. We let ourselves get old far too easily. And that brings me to my point. Angela's having a frivolous tea-party to-morrow at which we're all to go back into our teens and play ridiculous games. She's come back full of them, simply full of them. You'll come, won't you? And of course Miss Miller and Mr. Forsham—they are staying with you, are they not?"

"Thank you," said Amabel with a little hesitation. "I'm not quite sure if I can come."

Mr. Bronson shook his head.

"Now, now, Mrs. Grey, I can't take a refusal, I really can't. We're relying specially on you because you've a daughter of your own, I hear. So you're probably up in some of the latest games that these young people play. Now, there's one very amusing one. Angela was trying to explain it to us after lunch, but I'm not quite sure that I've got the hang of it yet—perhaps you can help me—one of those writing games." He went across to the little writing-table as he spoke. "May I take a sheet of paper and use this pen? Now, let me see if I can remember how it goes."

He sat down, pulling his chair forward until it was close to Amabel, and balanced on his knee the large block on which she had been writing to Daphne.

"Now first I write a sentence; and then you write one."

He turned round, dipped the pen, and wrote at the top of the paper, "I can't stand it any longer." He showed her the sentence, laughing.

"That's what we said to Angela this afternoon. 'My dear,' I said, 'not another game unless you want me to run away before tomorrow.' Now,"—he turned the block, and handed it to Amabel—"now, Mrs. Grey, you write the same sentence at this end of the paper."

He gave her the pen, and she wrote as he had written, "I can't stand it any longer." Curious that he should have chosen just that sentence—it fitted so well into her thought. Her hand shook a little as she wrote it.

"And now?" she said, looking up.

"Well, that's where I was hoping you could help me," said Mr. Bronson. "That's where I must confess to being just a little bit fogged. I know that I write something more, and then you write something more, and then we fold the paper up, but—no, it's vexing, I really can't remember how it goes. I'm afraid I've wasted your paper for nothing."

"I can't help you," said Amabel, as he took the block away from her and put it back on the writing-table.

"Well, well, Angela must explain it properly to us to-morrow." He tore off the used sheet and went back to the fire. "You'll come then, Mrs. Grey?"

"If I can," said Amabel. "But I'm not absolutely sure, because I may have to go up to town."

Mr. Bronson creased the paper that he held, tore off a strip, and watched it burn—all, it seemed, a little absently. He appeared to be about to take his leave, and yet to be unwilling to go.

"Well, well," he said at last, "I must be going, I really must be going. Would you mind my ringing the bell to let your maid know? I believe my man went round to the kitchen to ask for some water for the radiator; and he may be as reluctant to leave as I am." He laughed as he spoke, and held out his hand.

Amabel took it, and found it rather cold to the touch. She bade him good-bye, and rang for Jenny.

Mr. Bronson's heavy tread sounded on the stairs and in the hall below. The front door opened and shut again. She heard the whirr and thrum of the departing car.

Amabel looked at her watch. It was a little after four o'clock. Two hours and a half before Julian would be here. The time stretched before her, interminably flat and lonely. Jenny would have cleared tea away by five, and there would still be an hour and a half to wait—an hour and a half during which the evening would be getting steadily darker and colder, the house more still, the thought of the dark press and of what lay behind it more insistent. She sat down close to the lamp, took a book, and tried very hard to read.

Chapter Thirty-Four

AMABEL FOUND IT impossible to fix her attention upon the book which she had taken up. She saw black letters that formed words, and groups of words that formed sentences. They were words and sentences that had no meaning—so many words to a sentence, so many sentences to a paragraph, so many paragraphs to a page. None of it had any meaning at all. Yet she turned the page—and then another—and another.

Presently she looked at her watch again. It was five and twenty minutes past four. With a sigh of relief she threw down her book. Jenny was always very punctual; in five minutes she would be here with the tea. No need to force herself to go on reading just for five minutes.

When the tea came in, she wanted to speak to Jenny, but she could think of nothing to say. Her mind seemed dull to everything except the two vivid pictures which filled it: the face looking up at her out of the dark—the white face framed in red hair—Jenny's face; and Jenny in the hall trimming the lamp. She could think of nothing to say, either when Jenny brought the tea or when she cleared it away.

The door closed; the footsteps retreated. No one would come upstairs now until Julian came home. It was just five o'clock, pitch dark outside of course, and still raining. She went across to the window, drew back the curtain, and looked out. At first she could see nothing. She let the curtain fall behind her, and made out the black swaying of wet trees, the steady falling of the rain. Julian would come in very wet. She turned back and made up the fire.

It was about ten minutes later that she heard the telephone bell. As she started up it rang again. Amabel felt an unbelievable relief and joy. The telephone bell meant that Julian was back. He must have caught an earlier train and have turned in at the cottage on his way to the house. How dear of him to ring her up from there!

She was across the passage and at the open bedroom door before she felt a momentary recoil. She had left the light on in the room. The door of the press was a little ajar. If only the telephone had been in any other room but this.

It was with a little, cold shiver that she went across and took down the receiver. There was no current running; the line felt dead. Surely Julian couldn't have gone away. Her hesitation had really only lasted for a moment; he couldn't have thought that she had not heard the bell, and just gone away. She shook the receiver slightly, and rang through. Still no sound, no sound on the line—but quite suddenly a sound behind her.

With the most sickening throb of fear which she had ever experienced, Amabel realized that the cupboard door behind her was opening, and that someone was coming through it. She tried to call out, to turn; but before she could draw breath enough for a cry, something heavy and soft fell over her head and shoulders, and she felt herself in a grip so strong that she was utterly powerless to move. She tried to struggle; but she tried in vain. She felt herself lifted—and knew no more.

Amabel's faintness lasted only a very short time, but her first sensations were confused. Darkness; something pressing down on her; a difficulty in breathing; something soft and thick all over her face; jerky movements; and a man's voice speaking. She tried again to get her breath, to cry out, but could not do so. All at once she was set down, and the covering thrown back. She felt the arms of a chair beneath her arms. She drew a long, long, sobbing breath and opened her eyes.

She was in a cellar lit by electric light. That was the extraordinary thing—she was in a large cellar with whitewashed walls and a stone floor, but the whole place was most brilliantly illumined. Three pendant lights showed every object with great distinctness. Amabel looked at these objects, but had no idea what they were. As her mind cleared, she heard a man's voice say, "Put it on the writing-table, right in front, where he can't miss it—and for Heaven's sake take care you're not seen." There was a laugh, a rustle of skirts, the sound of a closing door. The sounds, the voice came from behind

Amabel. She tried to rise, and found that a band of something held her to the chair.

"Better take things quietly." It was the same voice speaking, the man's voice. It was most, most unbelievably, Mr. Bronson's voice. "Better take things quietly," it said; and with the last words Mr. Bronson himself came into view and stood a couple of yards away, looking at her gravely.

"Mr. Bronson!" said Amabel.

Mr. Bronson put up a deprecating hand.

"I regret the necessity very much, very much indeed, Mrs. Grey," he said. "I hope you will believe me when I say this."

"Mr. Bronson, are you mad?" said Amabel. She spoke faintly. The shock, the surprise were overwhelming. Her mind refused to work. She could only look at Mr. Bronson and wonder whether the whole scene was part of an unquiet dream.

"We are all mad; but some of us have a method in our madness," said Mr. Bronson quietly. "It was in the highest degree unfortunate for all of us that you should have discovered the passage in the wall this afternoon. You will realize how very unfortunate it was when I tell you that we were on the point of abandoning our attempts to make you leave the house."

"Your attempts?"

"Yes, it was getting too dangerous. We hadn't anticipated so much difficulty. Other tenants were more easily frightened away. And after Mr. Forsham began to mix himself up in the business we decided not to go on with it. You might have finished your six months' tenancy in peace if you hadn't stumbled on that passage by a most unfortunate accident—I suppose it was an accident?"

"Yes, it was an accident."

Mr. Bronson heaved a sigh of relief.

"Mr. Forsham, then, knows nothing about it?"

Amabel shook her head.

"Mr. Bronson, I don't understand—" she began.

"My dear Mrs. Grey, I wish you didn't have to understand," said Mr. Bronson. "The fact is that it doesn't suit me to have the Dower House occupied, because I use the cellars for business purposes."

"Mr. Forsham went through the cellars," said Amabel. (What was it that Julian had said about a bricked-up door?)

"He didn't go through these cellars, my dear lady. They were bricked up a good many years ago, as they were not considered safe. I made it my business to have them repaired, and also to put in thorough order the extremely useful passage which runs underground from this house to Forsham Old House. It only wanted a little shoring up, and it has been most useful. I may say, in fact, that we couldn't possibly have managed without it."

As he spoke, the door behind her opened; someone came in. Mr. Bronson looked past Amabel and asked sharply: "Well, did you manage it?" The answer came in a voice which Amabel knew, and did not know:

"Perfectly. Why not? There was nothing difficult."

It was not Jenny's voice: it was a deeper, more cultivated voice than Jenny's.

The woman who had spoken came forward, and touched Bronson on the arm.

"What next?" she asked. "What next?"

Amabel stared at her. It was Jenny—and yet not Jenny. At the first glance no one would have known the difference; but after the first glance there were a hundred differences. The likeness was in the hair, the eyes, the dead white skin. The differences were innumerable. Who was it?

Mr. Bronson was speaking.

"Go up to the Old House, and wait there. When Forsham finds her gone, and knows I was the last person to see her, he'll come up there hot-foot—bound to. Have him shown in the morning-room, and leave him there whilst you ring through to me. You'd better get along at once."

"All right, there's no hurry. I've got to get fit to be seen first anyhow."

It was the way in which they absolutely ignored her presence that brought home to as Amabel the fact of her extreme danger. They would not speak like this, ignore her like this, make their plans for deceiving Julian in her presence, unless that presence was negligible. It came home to her with fearful distinctness that, as far as these people were concerned, she had ceased to exist. She watched the woman cross the room and stand before a mirror that hung on the farther wall—the sort of cheap, common thing that one buys in a village shop. Under the mirror stood a littered table.

The woman who wasn't Jenny stood there, unconcernedly making her toilet. She was busy first with her face; then the red hair was all brushed up from brow, ears and neck, and pinned closely at the top of the head; finally a black wig was lifted, put on, carefully adjusted.

It was Mademoiselle Lemoine who turned round with all likeness to Jenny gone. The disappearance of the red hair took most of it. Black brows and lashes so darkened the eyes that they too lost their resemblance to Jenny's pale, red-rimmed eyes. The change was most astonishing.

"You would not have recognized me, Mrs. Grey, would you?" said Mademoiselle Lemoine, using the trilled "r" and the slight French accent.

She did not wait for an answer, but turned and went out through a door in the right-hand wall. Amabel had a glimpse of a passage beyond. Then the door was shut, and she and of Mr. Bronson were alone again.

Amabel Grey was a brave woman. The consciousness of danger steadied her nerves and cleared her mind as perhaps nothing else would have done. As soon as the door was shut, she spoke:

"Mr. Bronson," she said, "I don't ask you why you have done this. But you can't really imagine that I shall not be missed and searched for."

"Oh, no," said Mr. Bronson. "You will be missed, and you will be searched for—you are quite right there. Naturally, I have fore-seen all that, and have taken my precautions—my business demands a good deal of foresight and attention to detail." He spoke in quite a natural, ordinary voice. His whole manner, in fact, was just what it had been in the impressive drawing-room at Forsham Old House. It was very difficult to realize that, though the conventional manner remained, all the sanctions, the laws which civilization imposes, had ceased to operate. Here were not Mr. Bronson and Mrs. Grey, pleasant acquaintances, but a dangerous man who had broken the law, and a woman who stood in his way as an inconvenient witness.

"If Mr. Forsham has not already returned, he will be back by half-past six," said Amabel quietly.

"Oh, he's not back yet," said Mr. Bronson. "I suppose you thought he might be because of the telephone bell; but, of course you must realize that the bell was rung to get you into the bedroom—quite a simple device really. Mr. Forsham will arrive by the six-twenty, and when he gets up to the house he will find rather a shaky scrawl from you saying that you can't stand it any longer. He will draw his own conclusions."

Amabel cried out very sharply. Mr. Bronson's gay talk of Angela and the games they were to play to-morrow. His "Now, you write the same sentence at the other end of the paper." Her own thought of how appropriate that sentence was: "I can't stand it any longer." She saw herself writing the words with a hand not over-steady; and she saw Julian reading them. The thought hurt so much that her mind recoiled. She spoke with a sudden anger that sent a flush into her cheeks:

"You use Angela as a decoy then! Haven't you any shame at all?"

Mr. Branson's brow darkened; for the first time the conventional manner failed him.

"Here, none of that," he said roughly. "None of that, or you'll be sorry. Angela doesn't come into this at all, I tell you. She's as honest as they're made. My business is my business, and she don't know anything about it. Angela's as good a girl as your own."

So Angela was the vulnerable spot. Amabel looked at him with contempt, and spoke, partly of design, and partly on an impulse of real disgust;

"You say she's a good girl, and you put her with a woman like Miss Lemoine!"

The colour rushed into the man's face. For a moment Amabel thought he would have struck her. She saw him control himself with an effort, and heard him mutter:

"Mind what you're saying. I won't have it." His voice rose. "You mind what you're saying, and keep a civil tongue in your head. Miss Lemoine's my wife."

Chapter Thirty-Five

JULIAN FORSHAM turned from the telephone. The words F. Miller rang in his ears. Miller around whom his chief suspicions had clustered—Miller was one of Piggy's men! From anyone but Piggy himself he could hardly have believed it. Piggy having said it, it was true; and since it was true, he must get into touch with Miller at once. He was not on the telephone, but Edward would send down a note. He crossed to the writing-table and sat down. Miller had better go to the Dower House. He himself must see Bronson, since Bronson had been the last person to see Amabel. He would see him, and then join Miller. He took pen and paper and wrote rapidly:

"DEAR MR. MILLER,"

"I owe you an apology. Julian Le Mesurier has just given me your name and referred me to you for assistance. Mrs. Grey has disappeared, leaving the enclosed note, and I am in great anxiety. Bronson saw her last, and I am going to see him now. Please meet me at the Dower House. I will come straight on there."

He signed and addressed the note, and went in search of the Berkeleys. Two minutes later he was out in the rain on his way to Forsham Old House.

Miss Lemoine crossed the hall as the door opened to admit him. She dismissed the servant with a nod, and took Julian into the morning-room.

"Mr. Bronson is finishing some letters," she said. "Sit down, and I will tell him you are here."

He was still standing in frowning impatience when Mr. Bronson came in five or six minutes later.

"So sorry to have kept you waiting," he said in pleasant apology.

"Mr. Bronson," said Julian abruptly, "we are in distress about Mrs. Grey. She has left the Dower House suddenly, and—well, I believe you saw her this afternoon. Perhaps you can tell me whether she spoke of any such intention."

"Dear me!" said Mr. Bronson. "I'm very sorry to hear this. No, she certainly did not speak of going away." He seemed to hesitate.

"She didn't speak of going to see anyone?"

"No, she didn't. She did not, in fact, speak very much at all. I looked in with a message from my daughter. Mrs. Grey seemed depressed, I thought. She asked me to stay to tea, but I could not do so. I wish now—" he broke off and looked at Julian with concern— "Mr. Forsham, you do not think?—"

"No!" said Julian almost violently. "No no, of course not!"

When Julian had left the house, Mr. Bronson went back to his study. He found Miss Lemoine there, walking up and down with a light, uneasy step. She waited till he shut the door, and then broke out quickly with:

"What did he say? What did he want? He looked dreadful."

Mr. Bronson raised his eyebrows.

"Do control yourself," he said. "You're a great deal too fond of scenes, Annie, and I simply haven't any use for them. Mr. Forsham naturally wanted to know how I had left Mrs. Grey. I told him that she seemed very depressed."

"Was that all?"

"Pretty well."

There was a pause. Miss Lemoine came nearer, dropped her voice.

"Heavens, how glad I shall be to be out of this! When do we start?"

He looked at her coldly.

"When do we start? We don't start. What are you thinking about?"

"Charles, what do you mean? We ought to get away as soon as possible."

"I tell you we're not going."

"But we must, we must! Do you suppose they'll make no search for Mrs. Grey? I tell you Julian Forsham will pull the Dower House down to find her."

Mr. Bronson turned the key in the study door. Then he walked across to the fireplace, pressed an unseen spring, and opened a door in the panelling—all quite casually and as a matter of custom.

"I tell you he'll find her if he has to pull the place about his ears," she said.

"Oh," said Mr. Bronson, "they'll find her soon enough, my dear Annie. I've always intended that they should find her."

Anastasie Lemoine, who had been Annie Brown, came quickly over to him, and looked into his face.

"Charles," she said in a shaken voice, "what do you mean? How are they to find her? Where are they to find her?"

"In the river," said Mr. Bronson.

Annie cried out and caught his arm. He turned an expressionless face on her.

"What else did you think, you fool?" he said.

"Not that, not that—never that! You don't mean it—you don't really mean it!"

"Of course I mean it. And I won't have a scene about it either. From the moment she found the passage it was inevitable. It was her or us. What did you think?"

Annie had drawn back. She looked, not at him, but at the floor. Her hands gripped one another. Mr. Bronson shrugged his shoulders, and gave her an ugly look.

"I'm not going to have sulks any more than I'm going to have scenes."

"I won't have a hand in murder," said Annie in a strange voice.

Bronson laid a heavy hand on her shoulder.

"Here, none of that! Do you hear? You're not asked to have a hand in it. Why do you go asking questions if you're so squeamish? There won't be any question of murder, my dear Annie. Mrs. Grey found the Dower House very gloomy. The stories about it weighed on her mind. She became very much depressed." He shrugged his shoulders again. "She's found in the river, having left behind her an agitated scrawl saying that she can bear it no longer. The verdict will, I think, hardly be murder, and"—she looked up for a moment, saw his face, and shuddered—"I don't think, no, I really don't think that Mr. Forsham will ever get another tenant for the Dower House. It's an ill wind that blows nobody any good, you see," concluded Mr. Bronson.

He turned as if to go; but with a sudden movement Annie sprang between him and the open door in the panelling.

"No, no," she said in a low, desperate voice. "No, Charles, no— Don't do it—Don't!"

He took hold of her roughly. All at once her manner changed. She said in a quick, sobbing whisper,

"Charles, Angela's coming! I hear her."

His grasp relaxed. She slammed the panel to. As he half turned to listen, they could both hear Angela's clear, boyish whistle, her firm tread. Annie pushed him towards the door.

"Quick! Unlock it! What'll she think?" she whispered.

Mr. Bronson could move quickly when he liked, and quietly too. He opened the door as Angela reached it, and met her with a smile.

Angela Bronson was dressed for dinner. She had on a bright blue velvet frock. She looked very large, healthy, and cheerful.

"You'll be late for dinner, both of you," she said with her rather boisterous laugh. "No good jawing me about punctuality, and then setting such an awful example."

Miss Lemoine came across the room.

"Angela is quite right," she said. She glanced at the watch on her wrist, and then held it up for Mr. Bronson to see. "Why, look how late it is. The servants will surely think that something has happened." She passed behind Angela, and let her eyes dwell warningly on Bronson's face. "They will certainly think that something has happened; and that will never do. Will you not finish your business afterwards? Nowadays it is necessary to consider the servants all the time." An agonized meaning underlay the light tone.

Bronson met her glance, first with hesitation, and then with a curt nod.

"All right, let's get dinner over. I won't be ten minutes dressing. I suppose I must dress—eh, Angie?"

"Of course you must," said Angela, laughing. She put her arm through his, and all three went through the hall together.

At the foot of the stairs Bronson turned back.

"Now, what does he want?" said Angela impatiently. "Mam'selle, you're as white as a sheet—you want your dinner; and he'll be another age, I suppose."

But Bronson merely locked the study door on the outside, and came back with the key in his pocket.

"I've got a lot of papers lying about," he explained; and they went upstairs.

"He doesn't trust me—he doesn't trust me. He's locked the door because he doesn't trust me. Oh, what am I going to do?" The words went round and round in Annie's head. They said themselves over and over whilst she exchanged a couple of laughing sentences with Angela.

"Your father says ten minutes; but I must have fifteen at least."

When her door was shut, she leaned against it, shaken with terror, irresolute. If only he had not locked the study door, she could have made a bargain with Amabel Grey—something that would have given them a few hours' start. But now—what to do now? She sickened at the memory of Bronson's face when he said, "They'll find her in the river." Bronson's face, and Julian's—the two faces were before her eyes. Something rose up in her and ended the moment of wavering fear. She drew a long breath, and stood up straight. Charles would be ten minutes, neither more nor less. He must think that she was dressing. She went quickly to the bathroom that opened out of her bedroom, and set the water running. She locked the bathroom door and put the key in her pocket. Then she opened her own door a cautious inch, and looked out. The corridor was empty. Bronson's door opposite to hers was shut; she could hear him moving about. Without the least noise she slipped into the passage, closed the door, and ran down the great staircase. There was a footman in the hall—she thought he looked at her strangely. The front door was impossible—he would think her mad. She turned at the foot of the stairs, and walked with her usual slow grace to the morning-room.

If Angela were there, what should she do? She had no plan, really—only the impulse that had risen in her and which was driving her in spite of herself. The morning-room was empty and dark; Angela was not there. The faint glow of the fire just thinned the darkness into dusk. Upstairs she heard a door shut—voices. Next moment she had crossed the room, parted the curtains, and was slipping back the bolt of the glass door behind them. The air blew in, cold and sweet. She stepped out upon the terrace and closed the window behind her.

The rain had stopped. There was a high wind, and scudding clouds that let the moon through. Annie Brown went quickly along the terrace to the corner of the house. She turned the corner and came out into the drive. For a moment she looked back at the house with its lighted windows—one of them was hers. A sense of the irrevocable swept over her. She ran down the drive as if her terror had taken shape and was visibly in pursuit.

Chapter Thirty-Six

JULIAN LEFT Forsham Old House in the state of mind which thrusts its fears behind bolts and bars, and will not look at them because to look would be to face despair. At the foot of the drive he saw lights in the lodge, and remembered that Mrs. King had said that she was moving in to-day—Nita King whom he half suspected of being Annie Brown. All his suspicions gathered themselves together as he looked at the lighted windows of the lodge. If she were Annie, she might have some guilty knowledge of what had made Amabel Grey write those tremulous words: "I can't stand it any longer."

As the thought came, he was knocking at the lodge door and demanding Mrs. King of the elderly woman who opened it. Another moment, and he was in the tiny sitting-room with its disarray of chair covers half on and litter of ornaments not yet in their places.

Nita King jumped up to meet him.

"I'm so *untidy*, Mr. Forsham!" she exclaimed, her hands at her hair.

Julian cut her short.

"Mrs. King—" he began.

"Mr. Forsham, what is it? Has anything happened?"

"If you are Annie Brown," said Julian, "you know what's happened; and if you're not, you probably think I'm mad."

Nita King gave a little scream.

"Oh, what do you *mean*? Mr. Forsham, really!—you're not well."

Julian looked at her with a long, steady look keen with anguish.

"No, you're not Annie," he said at last, "you're not Annie—you can't be." He turned as if to go, and then swung back, voice and manner suddenly violent. "If you're not Annie, why did you send Agatha Moreland to Mrs. Thompson? Tell me that. Why did you send her to that medium?"

Nita King retreated before him. Her face was white. She put out her hands as if to ward off a blow, and said feebly,

"Don't look at me like that." Then she burst into tears.

"You've got to tell me!" said Julian. "Why did you send Agatha Moreland to that medium?"

"B-because Mr. B-Bronson said he'd give me a d-diamond brooch if I did. He said it was a b-b-bet," sobbed Mrs. King.

There is something about the unvarnished truth which carries conviction. Nita King very seldom spoke the truth; but at this moment she was too badly frightened to think of a lie.

Julian went on looking at her for a moment; then, without a word of explanation, he turned on his heel and flung out of the room, out of the house. The door banged behind him. He was in the drive again.

Bronson—Bronson had paid her; Bronson had sent Agatha Moreland to Mrs. Thompson. He stood quite still, not knowing whether to go back and tackle Bronson, or on to the Dower House.

He had just decided that he must see Miller before he did anything else, when he heard the sound of running feet. Someone was running down the drive from the Old House. He stepped forward, flashing on his torch. A woman screamed faintly. The light fell on the face of Miss Lemoine. She was bare-headed, and without any wrap. He called out sharply, "What is it?"—and she had him by the arm.

"Julian! Mr. Julian!"

"What is it?"

"Do you want to save her? Come at once if you do!"

"What do you mean? Come where?"

"The Dower House. Come quickly!"—she was still holding on to his arm.

She dragged him towards the gate. They came out on to the road, and began to run. It was very dark. The wind came in gusts. Between the gusts he could hear the woman's quick, distressed breathing.

"Where is she?" he said. "What has happened?"

"She's at the Dower House—she found the passage—Jenny and I found it long ago when we were children."

Light broke in on Julian, a light that showed confused and threatening things.

"Annie! *You* are Annie!" he said.

Her pace slackened. He felt her press nearer to him, and heard her say,

"Yes, Jenny and I found the passage when we were playing hide-and-seek—oh, it's so long ago—, and Jenny was too frightened to go down, but I went. And Mrs. Grey—Mrs. Grey found it to-day. Oh, Mr. Julian, come quickly!"

He urged her forward. They were in the Dower House garden now.

"I don't understand. Where is Mrs. Grey?"

Annie let go his arm.

"That's all you care for! Oh, yes, I know that's all you care for. She's there in the passage—I'm taking you there—I'm doing it for you, and because—because I can't stand by and see murder done."

"Murder! For God's sake—"

"No, there's time—we shall be in time—we must!"

As they came round the corner of the house, the hall door was open and the light streamed out on to the wet gravel.

Inside the hall stood a little group of people: Miss Miller, in her out-door things, her face very anxious and disturbed; Mr. Ferdinand Miller at his sharpest and sternest; and Jenny, weeping bitterly, her hands over her face. Mr. Miller was addressing her:

"You found a passage when you were children? Where does it open? Come, speak up!"

Jenny's shoulders heaved.

"Come, speak up!" he repeated. "Where did it lead to? The Old House? Forsham Old House? Come along, you've got to say!"

As Julian came in, Jenny turned and slipped away down the kitchen passage. Mr. Miller made a step forward.

Annie Brown ran right through the hall and up the stairs without looking at anyone. At the door of Miss Harriet's room she paused, and looked round to find Julian beside her, and Mr. Miller a pace behind. She put on the light, crossed the room, and pulled open the doors of the press. Neither of the two men saw quite what she did next. Her voice came to them from the dark cupboard:

"Mr. Julian, your torch!"

He passed it to her, and the beam showed them what it had shown Amabel—an open space, and the tiny chamber beyond, with steps going down from it.

Annie went on and down the steps, and the two men followed her. There were twenty steps, steep and rough; at the bottom just standing room, and then a door. Annie opened it and went through. They were in a cellar, empty except for a few packing-cases. She put her finger on her lips, and crossed to a door in the opposite wall. Here her hand dropped to her side, and she fell back against Julian, leaning on him heavily.

"In there—if we're in time," she breathed. A throb of emotion, of horror, seemed to pass from her to him.

He caught the torch from her hand, stepped forward, and flung the door open. They looked into another cellar. It had whitewashed walls and a stone-flagged floor. Three pendant lights illuminated every detail.

At the sight of what the room contained, Mr. Ferdinand Miller uttered a sharp exclamation. The room in which Mr. Bronson carried on his business spoke for itself. After twelve months' patient work Mr. Miller saw before him the evidence of his dreams—he saw the problem of the French note forgeries triumphantly solved. He exclaimed, "Got 'em!" in a tone of triumph.

Neither Julian nor Annie heard him. Annie had fallen back against the wall; her face was ghastly. There was a chair in the middle of the room, but it was empty. In the corner of the room there was something on the floor, something that was covered with a rug.

Julian went forward with the sound of the sea roaring in his ears. He knelt down, and felt Mr. Miller's hand on his shoulder.

There was a pause.

It was Julian who pulled the rug away with a desperately steady hand. Amabel's eyes met his. She was lying flat on the floor, her ankles strapped together, her arms bound to her sides, and a gag in her mouth. Her eyes looked steadily and piteously at him. He called her name, lifted her, began to unfasten the gag—all in such a hurry of relief and tenderness as to admit of no other thought.

It was Mr. Miller who saw the door in the opposite wall open a little, and the face of Mr. Bronson appear. It was Annie Brown who screamed.

The next instant the door was slammed and locked. The sound of running feet was heard for a moment. Julian looked up with his arms round Amabel.

"What was that?"

"Bronson. It doesn't matter if that passage comes out where I think it does—I've got men on the look-out for him. Here,"—he turned sharply on Annie, who was still leaning against the wall— "where does that passage come out? That scared-looking Jenny only told me half. Where does it come out?"

"Find out," said Annie, with a sob.

Mr. Miller frowned.

"We'd better get out of this. What about Mrs. Grey?"

"I can walk," said Amabel faintly, and could not trust her voice to say more. The last hour had been a very terrible one. Bronson's plan had come home to her in all its fiendish ingenuity, and the thoughts that had been with her had been dark indeed. Daphne. Julian. Their grief. The construction that would be placed on the words she had been tricked into writing. With Julian's arms round her, the cloud was lifting; but it had been very black. She was shaken, helpless, afraid of what she might say or do.

They came up the steep stair, and through Miss Harriet's room and the passage into the sitting-room beyond. A few embers of the fire which Amabel had made up three hours ago still glowed upon the hearth. She looked at them wonderingly. It seemed so long since she had stirred the logs into a blaze and thought of how wet Julian would be when he came in. He put her into a big chair, and knelt beside her.

Annie Brown went over to the fireplace, laid her arms upon the mantelpiece, and dropped her head upon them.

On the landing outside Mr. Miller blew a whistle. Men tramped up the stairs. His voice gave orders.

After a while Annie Brown lifted her head.

"Mr. Julian," she said, in a shaken voice.

Julian looked up, and saw her face grey and drawn, her eyes full of appeal.

"Mr. Julian," she said again; and then her voice broke. "I saved her—but there's nobody to save me," she gasped.

Julian got up, went over to her, and laid his hand on her arm.

"I saved her, Mr. Julian. Can't you do anything? Can't you?"

Mr. Miller came into the room with a brisk air of importance. He frowned at Julian's attitude.

"I've a warrant for Miss Lemoine's arrest," he began.

She threw up her head and faced him.

"I'd have been away by now if I could have brought myself to it," she said. "I've saved her, and done for myself."

A man came into the room and spoke to Mr. Miller, then went out again.

"Well, they've got Bronson," he said. "That's one comfort. As to Miss Lemoine—of course, what she did just now will count in her favour."

She clung to Julian's arm, and began to speak in a whisper broken by sobs.

"Charles will never forgive me—he'd have got away—we'd both have got away—but I couldn't let him do murder, could I? I've given him away—and he knows it—I'm his wife, but he'll kill me for it."

"His wife!" said Julian in a startled voice.

She put her hand to her head.

"Yes, I'm his wife. I don't owe him anything for that, though. He married me to have a hold on me, and to keep my mouth shut if it ever came to this." Her voice rose and vibrated. "And I married him to come back here, and have my marriage lines to show to Mother; only he'd never let me—he'd never let me. Not good enough to be Angela's mother, I wasn't, when it came to the point. Angela was all he cared for; and I wasn't good enough for Angela. He thought of what the County would say if he gave out that he'd married a governess. That's all he thought of—Angela and the County—not me—not me." Her voice trailed away. "Oh!" she said, and stopped, shaking all over. Her eyes were on the door. Her face had undergone an extraordinary change. Mr. Miller swung round. Julian turned. They all faced the door.

The door was open. On the threshold stood Mrs. Brown in a pink flannelette nightgown and a crimson cross-over. She was groaning and panting, and she leaned against the jamb of the door. Julian hurried to her.

"Brownie!" he said, and put his arm about her shoulders.

"I heard my Annie's voice," said old Mrs. Brown, looking vaguely about her. "I heard my Annie's voice, and I come."

The sound of Jenny's sobbing filled the passage behind her; but in the sitting-room itself everyone was very still. Amabel leaned forward in her chair, her eyes full of tears. Mr. Miller bit his lip, and stood aside. Annie Brown came forward quite quietly.

"I'm here, Mother," she said. And then, all of a sudden, she was down on her knees, with her arms round the old woman, crying bitterly.

"Hush, Annie, hush," said Mrs. Brown. "Don't 'ee cry, my girl, don't 'ee cry so. I'll not hold nothing up against you, Annie, my girl."

"I'm going to prison, Mother," said Annie like a child.

Mrs. Brown patted her shoulder in a feeble, distressed sort of way.

"I've got to go to prison, Mother."

"Prison?" said Mrs. Brown. Her lips trembled, her weight came hard on Julian. She turned and looked into his face, and found no comfort there. "Prison, Annie, my dear? What ha' you been doing?"

There was a silence. No one answered her.

"What ha' you been doing, Annie? Why don't nobody tell me? Mr. Julian, my dear, if she's done wrong and she's sorry, you'll speak for her—you'll not let them be hard on her, will you, my dear? What's she bin doing that no one'll tell me?"

"Brownie," said Julian, "I'll do all I can—you know I will. Don't take it too much to heart. It's—it's her husband's business really."

He felt her start, stand upright.

"Her husband?" she said in a new voice. "Annie, ha' you got a husband? Tell me the truth, my girl. Are you a lawful married woman? Have you got your lines?"

Annie lifted her wet face and met her mother's eyes.

"I've got to go to prison, Mother," she sobbed. "I've got to go to prison—there's no one can save me from going to prison. But I've got my marriage lines."

"The Lord be praised for all His mercies!" said Mrs. Brown.

Chapter Thirty-Seven

JULIAN TOOK Amabel down to the Berkeleys a little later. They walked down in silence, slowly, his arm about her. It was a strange contrast to the hurried run from the Lodge to the Dower House with Annie an hour before. Amabel was too shaken for speech. To come out of that atmosphere of dread and mystery, to be here with Julian, was enough.

The light and kindness of the Berkeleys' house welcomed them. All the strain and trouble slipped away like shadows left outside in the night. Within there was light, and that great kindness.

Amabel slept dreamlessly in the cheerful guest chamber, with its bright chintzes and welcoming fire. She slept, and waked to a new and happy world. The sun was actually shining. It was the sun that had waked her. She was smiling at it when Ellen came in— Ellen with a tray which she had wrested from the housemaid, and the air of one who is bursting with repressed conversation.

"Well, Ellen?" said Amabel.

Ellen set down the tray.

"Well it is, and well you may say so," she said with a sob, and caught Amabel's hand in both her own. "Oh, my dear ma'am, when I 'eard of it, which was ten o'clock last night and Eliza and me just going to our beds, I wanted to come to you right away then, but they wouldn't let me. Not that I'd 'ave taken any orders from that there Miller, detective or no detective—and 'e needn't think it, not if 'e 'ad the law on me ten times over. But when Mr. Forsham says to me, 'You let 'er be to-night. She wants 'er rest,'—well, then I up and took off me 'at again. Come to take my evidence, they did," concluded Ellen in a tone of much importance.

"Don't let's talk about it," said Amabel with a shudder. "No, Ellen, I do *not* want to hear what Eliza Moorshed said about it all. I've got something much nicer to talk about—something you just missed hearing yesterday. Miss Daphne is going to be married."

"Miss Daphne!" said Ellen. She took Amabel's hand and kissed it. "I didn't think it was Miss Daphne you was going to name. Isn't there no one else going to be married?—no one nearer at 'and, so to speak? Not but what I wish Miss Daphne joy, and a 'andsome 'usband, and a steady young gentleman into the bargain—for a steady one is what she wants, and no mistake. But oh, my dear ma'am, isn't there anyone else a-going to be married?" Her eyes swam with tears; one splashed down on to Amabel's hand. Amabel laughed, blushed, and pulled her hand away.

"Ellen, don't be damp, or you shan't come to my wedding."

"It's a pore 'eart that never cries," said Ellen—"a pore 'eart and an 'ard one." The tears ran down her nose. "And I wish you joy with all my 'eart, and Mr. Julian too. And I 'ope as it'll be soon, and no waiting about for Miss Daphne." Ellen mopped her eyes. "You could wear the blue costoom that Mrs. Moreland give you and you've never 'ad on. 'When'll I wear this, Ellen?' you says to me. 'It's only fit for a wedding,' you says. And we both thought Mrs. Moreland might ha' known better and given you something a bit more useful. Blue's my choice for a wedding, and always 'as been. None of your nasty greys for me that always 'as a sort of 'arking-back, 'arf-mourning kind of look to my mind. If you can't 'ave orange blossoms and white satin, 'ave blue and be cheerful, even if you do regret it afterwards, which I 'opes you won't, with a nice gentleman like Mr. Julian."

Amabel laughed again.

"We don't mean to regret it," she said.

"I've had Ellen's congratulations," she told Julian later on. "She's frightfully pleased, really. She cried for joy, and said she hoped we shouldn't regret it."

"Is she always as effusive as that?" asked Julian.

"That's just her way."

She came closer to him, and he put his arm round her.

"Julian, you're sure?"

He kissed her.

"There's just one thing I'm not sure about."

"What is it?"

"Amy darling, I'm not sure—"

She drew back, looked at him, saw his eyes full of tender mischief.

"Julian, you're laughing at me!"

"I am. It's good for you to be laughed at."

"Yes. But what aren't you sure about?"

"Well, this is Friday—and I'm not sure whether Monday or Tuesday will be the best day for us to get married."

"Julian!" She saw the mischief change to the old look—the boy's look of eager worship.

"Amy, I've waited twenty years already."

THE END

Lightning Source UK Ltd.
Milton Keynes UK
UKOW06f1940080816

280238UK00024B/406/P